The Sister's Secret

Published by Accent Press Ltd 2018

ISBN 9781786154200

Accent Press Ltd
Octavo House
West Bute Street
Cardiff
CF10 5LJ

For my sister Scilla

PROLOGUE

A door at the back had been forced open. Easy enough to follow the crowd. Hanging onto the wobbly stair rail, breathing in the choking dust, then out into the open where the protesters swarmed, like a pack of rats, over the tangle of steel scaffolding. Bodies on the move, hoodies pulled up over ears that buzzed with the deafening racket of rock music. Someone with a spanner was tampering with a link, twisting and turning, loosening, starting on another. The first pole lay on a plank of wood. Short but surprisingly heavy.

A short distance down the hill, but clearly visible, the two of them were approaching, one carrying bags of shopping, the other holding something to her mouth. Guzzling. As they grew closer, a street lamp lit up the purple wool of her beanie hat, and the red of her coat, like a bull fighter's cape.

Any minute now they would draw level. But on the wrong side of the road. And any minute now the police would storm the building, making arrests, clamping on handcuffs, turning the protesters into martyrs for the cause. Timing was everything. A high-pitched sound. A sudden movement. The mewing of a poor cat.

Mow! Miaow!

One of the protesters turned, grinning, raising a banner with his muscular, tattooed arms.

Mow! Miaow!

"Purple beanie" stopped. Crossed the road. Screwed up her eyes, scanning the building for a glimpse of a furry tail or a pair of yellow eyes.

Mow! Miaow!

And the steel tube fell.

Don't look. Run! Back, down the rickety stairs, and out through the half-open door. A police siren wailed, growing closer. Run. Faster. Lost in the maze of the dark city streets.

1

The date on Claudia's death certificate was not the same as the day she died. It was not even the same year. Before her sister's death, Erin had thought it so simple. Now she knew better.

In the twenty-third week of her pregnancy Claudia had suffered an intracranial haemorrhage, the pathological accumulation of blood within the cranial vault. Neurosurgery drained the haematoma, but during the operation she deteriorated and there was nothing the doctors could do. A corpse is cold, pale, and it is not pregnant. In Claudia's case none of this was true. But her brain was dead.

Throughout their vigil, Ollie barely spoke. Like Erin, he was dry-eyed, too shocked to cry, and gave no indication he was listening when the consultant, a sandy-haired man with a bow tie and a Scottish accent, introduced himself as Dr Macaulay. An ultrasound examination had been carried out, he said, and the baby appeared unharmed, but was too undeveloped to be delivered. A choice needed to be made – either Claudia's life support system would be disconnected, or they would try to maintain maternal homeostasis until greater foetal maturity had been achieved. Or meaning, until the baby had a chance of survival.

'What are the odds?' Erin asked. Odds – what an inappropriate word – but she was trying to be practical, take responsibility – for Ollie's sake, she told herself. Her first time in intensive care units, and when she spoke her breath came in shallow gasps. 'What I meant, how likely is it the baby could be born, and be all right?'

The consultant spoke slowly, gently. 'Had the pregnancy been less than twenty weeks I would have been unwilling to prolong maternal life. Twenty-three weeks is a different matter. I can make no promises but if gestation is allowed to continue for another month, or a little longer, and no serious problems arise . . . The baby would need special care but if everything went according to plan . . .' He broke off, turning to Ollie, who had lowered his eyes and was murmuring something that sounded like "die".

Erin squeezed his hand. 'What did you say?'

His lips were slightly parted and the pale, almost girl-like face, that Claudia had fallen for, was contorted with pain.

'Try to think what Claudia would have wanted,' she urged.

The curtained-off cubicle felt like a tent in a war zone. Above the bed a display of monitors flickered with constantly changing numbers – ninety-five, ninety-six, ninety-eight – and coloured lines with waves or spikes, and a flat line – not the heart rate. Another piece of equipment had a number that could be Claudia's body temperature, or was it the baby's? Hospital smells mingled with the sharp scent of floor polish and outside, in the main area, sounds of activity could be heard; footsteps, a trolley with squeaking wheels, the clink of glass, someone coughing. Apart from the tubes and wires and the dressing on the side of her head, Claudia could have been sleeping peacefully.

'If the baby could be saved . . .' Erin looked at Ollie then back at Dr Macaulay, willing him to come down on her side. But when he spoke it was to tell Ollie he realised it was a difficult decision and he would need a little time to think about it.

The following day Ollie refused all invitations to talk, or to share her unappetizing meals but, just when she was giving up hope, he tapped on the door of her flat – in the loft of Claudia's house – and told her he was going to the university.

'Now?'

'There's something I h-have to d-d-do.' The stutter he normally managed to control had come back. 'I d-don't know what t-time I'll be back.'

'I'm not going out.' If he was going to talk to another postgraduate student, that was good. Hearing the facts, anyone would think the baby should be saved. She was not the best person to discuss it with him – she was too involved – but surely his university friends would agree with her. Was he in touch with his family? She knew so little about him but Claudia was the talker. Ollie was quiet. He looked and sounded exhausted and, if anything even more agitated. Was he coming round to her way of thinking? Like her, he would have slept only fitfully, or not at all, but in the cold light of day he must have realised the baby had a right to live.

'Do you have any family, Ollie?'

'My father d-died a year ago.'

'What about your mother?' His mother would want her grandchild to survive.

'She's not well. Her nerves.'

'I'm sorry.' What could she say? He was alone in the world, or saw himself that way. Claudia had been his closest friend, his soulmate. Without her, he was lost.

'I thought the baby would be dead.'

3

'I know.' She had expected the same, but was not going to say so. As soon as she knew there was a chance, she had been determined to do everything in her power to save it.

'I'll see you later then.' She attempted a brief hug, but his body was rigid, and a moment later she heard him running down both sets of stairs, and the front door closed, not with the loud familiar noise of Claudia leaving the house, but a quiet, almost imperceptible click.

Claudia. Two days ago they had been discussing the birth of her first child. Now she was being kept alive artificially, but her baby was still growing inside her. How could she be dead? She was only twenty-seven, born when Erin was just a year old. Had she made a will? Since she and Ollie had been together such a short time, it was unlikely she had got round to those kind of decisions. While Ollie was out, she could look through her papers. It was far too soon to think about such things but being practical might help a little. It had when their parents died.

Soft, padding steps approached. The cat from down the road that made use of Claudia's cat flap. Erin's door was half open but it let out loud mews to announce its arrival, squeezing through the gap and spending a few moments sniffing her trainers before curling up on the bed. Claudia must have fed it. Which house did it live in? Not the people next door – they had gone abroad for several months – and not Claudia's friends, Jennie and Ben. Resting her cheek on its head, Erin breathed in someone else's perfume. *Whose*, she wondered, *the owner of the house where it had made its last visit?*

Unlike her sister, she had no particular liking for cats, and this was an ugly creature with colouring that made its mouth appear to turn down at the corners. But she was starved of company and it added a touch of homeliness to

4

the place. She had a bed – low to the ground and with an uncomfortably thin mattress – a built-in cupboard with three shelves and space for a dozen or so hangers, and a small table and two chairs. A couple of Indian rugs covered part of the bare boards, and Claudia had hung one of Ollie's grainy black and white photographs on the wall.

The coast was not far, but far enough that Erin had not explored it. Ollie's photo was somewhere with a long stretch of empty beach, the tide out so that grey sand gave way to a dark, distant sea. Not a cheerful scene, but typical of Ollie, who was a kind, sensitive person but with layers underneath the kindness that he was careful not to reveal, and a strong streak of obstinacy.

What was he doing now? Telling his friends what had happened and asking their advice, feeling a little comforted by their support, or alone, staring at his computer, trying to lose himself in rows of tables and figures? For her own part, work was out of the question. All she could do was pace up and down, picking up drawings and putting them down again, and making endless cups of coffee that made her head ache. She ate a ginger biscuit but it tasted of sawdust. She needed some fresh air but was reluctant to leave the house in case Ollie returned.

The loft felt alien. A plan chest was the only piece of furniture she had brought with her and, at first, getting it up the stairs and through the door had looked impossible. But the man with a van had helped her lift and turn it, then rest it on a step and try again, until eventually they were able to place it triumphantly in the position she had selected under the window.

At first the sparseness of the flat had pleased her, much as a nun must feel good about the simplicity of her surroundings. Not that there was anything nun-like about her existence, apart from the celibacy. Before it happened, she had eaten reasonably well – mostly pasta –and as long as she had a bottle of wine she got by. Things would change – they always did –that was what she told herself. But not this way, not an empty, echoing house, and Claudia . . . dead.

As she stroked the cat, a paw shot out and scratched her hand and, sucking away the pin pricks of blood, she gazed around the room, painfully aware of how inadequate it was compared to her studio in London. The flat in South Wimbledon had been too expensive, but it was only temporary. In a few months' time Declan's divorce would have come through and the two of them would have found a new place to live.

Would Declan's presence have made Claudia's death easier to bear? How would he have reacted? By helping her persuade Ollie that Claudia must be kept on life support until the baby could be born, or – and this was far more likely – by telling her the baby was not her responsibility and she should let Ollie get on with it? Before the accident she had envied Claudia so much, partly for her new found happiness with Ollie, but mainly because she was going to have a child. *You can be a glorified godmother, Erin. After all, it won't have any other relatives.*

If they had not chosen that particular day to go down to the shops and buy the baby shoes . . . If, as Claudia suggested, they had visited the coffee place and sampled the new chocolate pastries . . . If she had believed Declan's lies and stayed in London. So many ifs.

The cat jumped off the bed and started looking round for somewhere to sharpen its claws. She needed shelves where she could keep her Indian inks and brushes, masking tape and a hundred other things, but how long

6

would she be in the house and after that where would she go? When she felt up to it, she would try to discover if Claudia had a solicitor and whether there were any unpaid bills or outstanding mortgage repayments – or savings, although the latter was unlikely. Claudia had never been good with money. Neither had she been much interested in housework, although the baby was to have a newly decorated room.

How could it have happened? Tears sprang to her eyes, but she brushed them away. Don't think about it. Let the police make their investigations. What investigations? The building had been teeming with protesters, and it was dark, and any one of them could have meddled with the scaffolding poles.

Later, when she was on the point of going to bed, the front door opened and closed and she heard Ollie's footsteps on the loft stairs and hurried to let him in.

'I've decided.' He stood in the doorway. His face was blank and she saw he had not bothered to shave, his fair hair needed washing and had lost its usual sheen.

'Come and sit down.' Pointlessly, she plumped up an Indian cushion. 'How are you? Have you had anything to eat? Would you like a drink?'

He rubbed his eyes. 'I want them both to be allowed to die.'

With a supreme effort, she kept quiet.

'It's for the best.' The stutter seemed to have disappeared. 'It's what she would have wanted.'

'When you called in at the university did you see any of your friends?'

'It's the holidays.' He kept blinking, rubbing his eyes.

'But the other research students must be there. Did you tell them? Did any of them know Claudia? They must be so shocked.' She was talking too much because the tension in the room was making it difficult to breathe.

Ollie had his head turned away and she thought how painfully thin his neck was. It made her want to protect him. Or would have wanted to if circumstances had been different. She tried again. 'I do understand what a difficult decision it is.'

'*My* decision.'

'Yes.' But he and Claudia had not been married so surely she was her next of kin. What was the law? She could look it up, should have thought of it before? She glanced at her tablet, fingers itching to check online.

'I'm going to let the doctor know tomorrow' He waved aside her offer of a glass of wine, clutching the top of his crumpled T-shirt and winding it into a knot. 'Can you c-come with me?'

'Yes, of course, but it's your *baby*, Ollie, a person. I do understand how you feel but Claudia was my sister and I'm certain she would have wanted her baby to be born.'

'So you'll come.'

'I'll come.' Instinctively, Erin folded her arms in a gesture of self-protection. 'But I'm not going to let you kill the baby.'

2

When they returned to the hospital a different doctor was on duty; tall, with a flat, round face and receding hair. This threw Erin a little, but Ollie hardly seemed to notice. She had checked the legalities of the situation, but they were not clear. A decision regarding the patient's treatment was taken in consensus with their family. If the patient was not married, the biological father plays a major role. This was bad news. On the other hand, one of the determining factors was whether the mother had expressed a wish to be an organ donor and Erin remembered how Claudia had registered her wish online, as well as carrying a card in her purse. The website said that could be interpreted to mean the unborn baby had a right to benefit from what it described as "the mother's organic function".

She had discussed none of this with Ollie.

The cubicle was hot. The whole hospital felt too hot. Claudia lay on her back, with her hair spread out on the pillow. Someone had brushed it with care – it was long and blonde, unlike Erin's which was light brown and curled in the rain – and it made her look like Sleeping Beauty, except Sleeping Beauty was not attached to an array of monitors. And no prince was going to wake Claudia with a kiss. Their mother had always told Erin how pretty she was, with her small features and hazel eyes, but Claudia was the beauty, taller, more curvaceous, sexier.

One small blessing was that their parents would never know what had happened. They had died on holiday in India when their bus fell down a crevasse – she and Claudia had never discovered the exact details – and later Erin had traced their journey on a map and allowed herself to grieve while at the same time, being thankful they had both gone together. Neither of them would have been happy on their own.

The doctor cleared his throat and Erin opened her mouth to ask how Claudia was – she meant the baby, of course – then decided she ought to let Ollie speak first, although when the doctor started talking he addressed his remarks to her.

'We estimate the weight of the foetus as around nine hundred grams.'

Was that all? A quick calculation told her it was roughly two pounds. A baby that small might survive but, from everything she had read, the chances of it being handicapped in some way were quite high.

'Should gestation be allowed to progress,' the doctor continued, 'your sister would be fed intravenously and given drugs and hormones and antibiotics for infections, if necessary.'

'How long would it be?' Erin asked, 'I mean before it could be born.'

'Hard to say. It would depend on several factors.'

'But it stands a chance?'

'Yes.'

And after it was born, she thought, the life support system would be disconnected and Claudia's part in the survival of her child would come to an end. She turned to Ollie – so did the doctor – but his shoulders were hunched and his gaze fixed on the window, with its frosted glass. He had washed his hair – a good sign, Erin told herself –

and smelled faintly of lemon shampoo. His hands were clenched into fists.

'Ollie?'

He turned to look at them, his eyelids drooping from lack of sleep.

'I think you should tell the doctor how you feel.'

'It makes no d-difference.'

'On the contrary,' the doctor began, but Ollie interrupted angrily.

'If I don't agree I'll be accused of killing my own child.'

'No, Ollie, it won't be like that.' What a liar she was. What a hypocrite. 'We need to discuss it, talk about what Claudia would have wanted.'

'Claudia's dead.'

'But we still have to think about the baby. Your baby.' Emotional blackmail – but what else was left?

The doctor was looking unperturbed, as though it was a situation he dealt with daily. 'She carried a donor card,' Erin said.

'I see.'

Did he see? Had he taken the trouble to look up the legalities?

'Ollie? If she wanted to donate her organs that means . . .' But he was not prepared to hear the rest. Pushing past her, he stumbled out of the cubicle, and a moment later the swing doors of the unit creaked open and shut. She considered running after him, catching up with him in the corridor and trying to persuade him to return to Claudia's bedside. But what good would it do? They were never going to agree.

And the following day it became clear he had made the only decision he believed left to him. He had disappeared.

* * *

11

In the night her mind created the scene over and over again. Since she had been walking on ahead, with Claudia lagging behind, she had not actually seen the scaffolding pole fall, so much of what she pictured was in her imagination, but no less real. She was tormented by thoughts of what might have been. If only they had reached the shops earlier, or later. If only they had stayed longer in the baby goods shop. If only Claudia had not insisted on buying a jam doughnut to eat on the way home.

When she thought about Claudia – her lively, go-getting sister – the memories she allowed herself were always good ones. Games in the garden when they were small. Dolls' tea parties under the walnut tree, riding their bikes up and down the lane, dressing up and acting in improvised plays. But there had been fights too, savage ones that had escalated alarmingly. They were too close in age, their mother claimed, and Claudia's birth had been "a shock for poor Erin". Was it her fault if she was jealous of her baby sister? In any case, by the time she was five, Claudia had been bigger than she was, taller and broader, and with an expression on her face that challenged the world to thwart her in any way.

Later, after the two of them left home, they had tried to establish a different kind of relationship, where the tensions were skated over with plenty of laughter and plenty of alcohol. The premature death of their parents should have strengthened the bond between them, but seemed to have the opposite effect. True to character, Claudia had concentrated on their wills, which left everything to each other or, in the event of them both dying together, advised that their estate should be divided equally between their two daughters.

When the family home was sold and the money finally

came through, Erin had stayed in London to complete her course at Art college, but Claudia had chosen a different route, giving up her job as a trainee buyer in a department store and moving to Bristol, where she could take out a relatively small mortgage on a house where prices were not quite so high.

Thinking about it, reminded Erin how she ought to contact Claudia's bank. To tell them what? That her sister was going to die, but not until her baby had been born. That the baby's father had disappeared. They would advise a solicitor and they would be right. Did Ollie know the name of Claudia's solicitor? It might be better to find one of her own, but not yet, not when everything was in limbo, although perhaps it was precisely because of the present situation that she needed professional help. Where was Claudia's phone? Had Ollie got it, and if so why?

A weak sun crept in through the dormer window. She needed to finish her sketches – she had a deadline to meet – but drawing felt impossible, so today she would concentrate on research. During the time she had worked as an illustrator, it was young children's picture books she enjoyed the most. In the story she was currently illustrating called *The Littlest Guinea Pig*, several chipmunks lived together in a cage and made chirping noises that got on the guinea pigs' nerves. Ignorant of what chipmunks looked like, she checked online and discovered their coats were brown and grey, with contrasting stripes on the sides of their faces and across their backs and tails. And their eyes were set on the sides of their heads. They ate peanuts and sunflower seeds and the bugs that crawled in their cage, and they hid food under the sawdust. She wanted one, or two or three come to that, but imagine how delighted the cat would be.

There was a mynah bird in the story too but she would

find a picture of that later. Carrying on with her work, even though she was only researching online, felt wrong, disloyal to Claudia, but what was the alternative? Sitting staring into space, or going for endless, exhausting walks round the city.

Downstairs, the letterbox clicked and, pushing aside her drawings, she hurried to check the mail. Most of it was junk, addressed to the occupier, and two envelopes looked like bills she would check later. Pushing open the living room door brought back memories of the first time she had visited the house and been struck by the odd collection of furniture Claudia had acquired. A battered sofa, upholstered in brown velvet and strewn with brightly coloured cushions, two creaky cane chairs and a glass-topped coffee table with one of its wobbly legs propped up with a book about interior décor. The floor had been stripped and sealed and was partly covered by a large Persian rug with several holes in it, and the venetian blinds that had once looked so smart now made the room feel faintly sinister.

Three of the walls had been painted orange and the fourth was dark blue, half-completed. Had the paint run out or had Claudia changed her mind? She should have asked her, but could imagine how she would have reacted. *Honestly, Erin, you're so organised. I like to experiment, live for the day.*

A face appeared at the window. Claudia's friend, Jennie, from four doors down. Not now, not today, but it was no good shutting herself away like a hermit. Erin took a couple of deep breaths and went to let her in.

'How are you?' Jennie hesitated, wondering perhaps if she should give her a hug. Claudia had done a lot of hugging, but Jennie was giving the impression that calling round was something she had been putting off, a duty that had to be carried out, preferably as quickly as possible.

'Come in. I was trying to find Claudia's phone.' Absurdly, Erin felt the need to explain what she had been doing in Claudia's living room. 'I think Ollie must have it.'

'Is he here?'

'No. He wanted the life support switched off.'

'Oh.' Jennie frowned, not certain how to respond.

'When I told the doctor I wanted the baby to have a chance, he ran out of the hospital. He hasn't been back here. I don't know where he's gone.' Should she invite her up to the loft or take her into Claudia's kitchen? 'Would you like some coffee?'

'They think they can save the baby?'

'It's what Claudia would have wanted.'

Jennie forced a smile, and Erin suspected she agreed with Ollie. Either that, or she thought it was not up to Erin to make the decision. If she had known Jennie better she might have been able to tell, but until now they had only exchanged a few words.

When she arrived at Claudia's house, socialising had been the last thing on her mind, but one morning, several weeks back, Jennie had offered to help when her ancient Toyota Yaris had been blocked in by a van that had parked far too close. At the same time, subjecting her to a barrage of questions. Where had she moved from? What kind of work did she do? If she was Claudia's sister, why did the two of them look so different?

'Do the police know what happened?' Jennie was pushing back her hair, which was a dark shade of blonde, with darker lowlights. 'Who could have done such a thing?'

'One of the protesters must have unscrewed a pole.'

'So the police have decided it was an accident.'

15

What was she suggesting? That someone had deliberately dropped a heavy pole on the head of a passerby?

'Ben's shattered.' Ben was Jennie's actor partner. 'He and Claudia . . . He admired her determination, the way she forged ahead with new projects. And she liked his silly showbiz stories. 'If there's anything I can do.' Jennie wanted to leave. 'We must go for a coffee sometime. When you're not so busy. Ava's Place, do you know it?'

Erin nodded. 'I went there once with Claudia. She and Ava seemed close.'

'Yes.' Jennie's hand clutched at her throat, as though their conversation was making her feel queasy. 'Anyway, I'll see you again soon.' She licked her finger and rubbed at a mark on the dark green top that matched the colour of her nails. 'I'm sorry, I don't know what to say?'

'It's all right. No one does.' Erin showed her out. 'Thank you for coming round.'

'As I said, anything I can do . . . Claudia was quite a character. You'll miss her such a lot. We all will.'

Erin was thinking about Jennie's off the cuff remark. *Who could have done such a thing? So the police have decided it was an accident.* Had she heard something? Was that why she had come round? To warn her? To put doubts in her mind? Or had she felt the need to tell her that, while Ben might have found her sister an amusing character, not everyone did.

As soon as the front door closed, a loud mew heralded the cat's entrance and Erin scooped it up, turned her back on Claudia's part of the house, and carried it up to the loft where she hoped to persuade it to settle down on her bed for the rest of the morning. It opened its mouth to protest and its breath smelled of fish, the kind they put in tins of meaty cat food. If Claudia had liked cats so much, she

16

should have had one of her own, instead of luring in someone else's with bowls of food. Ollie had wanted to give her a kitten, but she had turned down the offer. *It wouldn't be house-trained. Can you imagine? Poo and pee all over the place and it's impossible to get rid of the smell.*

Wherever she went in the house, she heard Claudia's voice in her head. *Honestly, Erin, that Declan sounds like an arsehole. Why did you let yourself get caught up with him?* Followed by an apology. *Sorry, take no notice, I'm, just glad you had the guts to get away.*

The loft felt safer than the rest of the house, but not that safe. In the afternoon, she would return to the hospital, and talk to the nurses, and perhaps to a doctor. The whole notion of brain dead was so difficult to take in. A ventilator was keeping Claudia's heart beating and oxygen circulating through her blood, she was receiving nutrition through a tube and her body was kept at the correct temperature. And she was being given hormone replacement "to prolong gestation".

Erin tried to picture the unborn baby – the doctors referred to it as the foetus – and wondered how it would feel when it learned how it had developed in its dead mother's womb, and planned how she would tell it all about Claudia, plenty of stories that showed her in a good light. But as usual she was jumping ahead. There was no guarantee it would survive.

3

When she reached the unit and rang the buzzer a nurse appeared and asked if she minded waiting a few minutes.

'Nothing to worry about.' She gave Erin what she thought was a reassuring smile. 'There are some procedures we need to carry out. It won't take long. Later today Claudia will be moved to a different room.'

What procedures, Erin wanted to ask, and which other room? Was it good she was being moved, or did it mean the baby was not doing well? The nurse had used Claudia's name, instead of referring to her as "the patient". That could be a good sign. No, it was only to make her feel better. Or because Claudia was not a patient. Her brain was dead and only the rest of her body was being kept "alive".

Sitting on the cold, shiny vinyl seat, Erin stared at the print on the opposite wall. Tropical fish swimming through fronds of stylised underwater plants, bubbles rising, white rocks on a sandy bed. It was a dull, lifeless picture. Even so, it made her long to be by the sea, walking at the water's edge, taking off her shoes and paddling, feeling the gritty sand between her toes.

As children, they had spent summer holidays in Wales, staying near a sandy beach with rock pools and seaweed and crabs. They had caught shrimps in nets, not very many as she recalled, but enough to take back to the house and cook in boiling water while their mother buttered slices of bread. Sometimes she missed her mother so much she could barely breathe. As a teenager, she had been closer to her father – they were alike in several ways – but it was her mother she needed now.

'You can come through.' The nurse's smiling face appeared and she jumped up, guilty that for a few moments she had forgotten where she was, escaping into a time when she was happy and carefree, surrounded by her family and the Welsh friends they met up with each summer.

When they entered the cubicle, the nurse began filling in details on a chart. Were they good or bad? Did they refer only to Claudia, or was there a way of monitoring the baby's condition too? The nurse turned to smile and Erin smiled back, her gaze quickly returning to Claudia. 'She looks so serene.'

Serene? Not a word she ever used. Where had it come from? Lately words seemed to spring into her head and it was as though it was her mother talking.

'My name's Andrea.' The nurse was attractive, sexy in that slightly overweight way that makes women look like they have been around. Erin guessed she enjoyed evenings in the local clubs – she had no idea why she thought this – and liked her better for it because it made her more human.

'Erin,' she said, 'I'm Claudia's sister. Sorry, you know that already.'

'If there's anything you want to know I'll be happy to explain. Please, sit down.' She pulled out a chair with a red plastic seat and black metal legs.

'Thank you.' Soft music was playing, classical stuff that sounded familiar and could be Bach. Was it for the medical staff, to make the situation less upsetting, or was it to give the illusion Claudia could hear it?

'Her boyfriend's gone missing,' Erin said, 'and I'm the only one . . . The baby – is it all right?'

'The doctor was a little worried. Your sister developed an infection, but she's been treated with antibiotics and there's no immediate cause for alarm.'

'If it had to be delivered now would it die?'

Andrea put her notes to one side. 'It would stand a chance, but thirty weeks, or a little more, would be better.'

'The doctor explained about brain death but I'm not sure I understood properly.' Erin had checked online, read everything she could find, but she liked this nurse, wanted her to be her friend. She had large, expressive eyes, and her hair was similar to her own, the kind that was affected by the weather, good hair days and bad ones.

'Well.' She smoothed a crease in Claudia's blanket. 'The brain stem is connected to the spinal cord and it regulates most of the essential functions of the body, the automatic functions.'

'Like breathing and your heart beating?'

She nodded. 'And blood pressure.'

'It's not the same as... What do they call it? Persistent Vegetative State?'

'No, there's a slim chance someone can recover from PVS if the brain stem is unaffected.'

'Thank you.' Erin was ridiculously grateful for the information. She wanted to ask how many cases like Claudia she had nursed, if any. Instead, she said the whole thing felt unreal.

'I'm sure.'

They sat together in relatively comfortable silence. Relatively, because who could sit beside their brain dead sister and feel relaxed? Although it never ceased to amaze her what you could get used to. A little over a week ago, she and Claudia had been laughing, talking, making plans for the birth of her baby. It felt like another lifetime. Where *was* Ollie? Staying with a friend, another postgrad student? The police had checked the bedsit where he lived before he moved in with Claudia, but it had been taken by a girl who had never met him. Why would she have done, it wasn't a student let.

Erin wanted to tell Andrea about the baby shoes she and Claudia had bought and how Claudia had chosen them specially because she thought it was so funny, the way one had a steam engine on it and the other had a carriage, or was it one of those trucks – she thought they were called tenders – where the coal was kept?

'The baby,' she asked cautiously, 'it's a boy, isn't it?'

'Did no one say?'

'I think Claudia knew. I didn't ask her but I could tell.'

'It's a little girl.'

'A girl? Is it? Are you sure?'

'Quite sure.'

'The father's called Ollie.' Erin was trying to adjust to this new revelation. Not a boy. A girl. If Ollie had known, might it have made a difference? But why would it? 'He's very young. Actually, he can't be that young because he's doing research for a PhD. I think he's twenty-four. He just seems young. Young for his age. He wanted the baby to die.'

'But you wanted her to be given a chance.'

Erin nodded, looking up at Andrea for approval. 'I expect he could have overruled me, but he's disappeared and no one knows where he's gone. Or if they do,' she added, 'they're not going to tell me. Claudia and I – we weren't very close and I haven't been in Bristol very long so I don't know many of her friends. Only a neighbour, called Jennie, and there's a woman who runs a café Claudia used to go to, but . . .'

21

A doctor had appeared, a woman, nothing like the Scottish doctor. She was younger and brasher with so few social skills Erin wondered what they taught them at medical school. No smile. No introduction. She stood beside Claudia with an expression on her face that reminded Erin of the girl in the building society who had wanted her to tie up her meagre savings for the next five years. For the building society's benefit, not hers.

Erin stood up. 'Andrea told me you had to treat an infection.'

After checking the monitors, the doctor picked up the notes at the end of the bed and studied them before speaking without looking up. 'Yes.'

'But the baby won't be affected?'

'All being well.' She turned to Andrea to help her out.

'I've explained to Erin about her sister, and how we hope the baby won't need to be delivered for a few weeks yet.'

'Good.' The doctor looked relieved, as though she had been let off the hook and would not have to spend time with a troublesome relative. 'Is there anything else you wanted to ask?'

Erin shook her head, then changed her mind. 'After the baby's delivered how long will it be before the life support is switched off?'

'If her organs are to be donated we'll need the consent of next of kin.'

Anger welled up and through gritted teeth – there was no way she was going to lose control – she explained that she was her sister and staying in Claudia's house and the father of the baby had gone missing. 'Does that make me the next of kin? Nobody seems to know. And why do you have to talk in that horrible deadpan . . .' She broke off, not sorry, just running out of words.

Andrea put a hand on her shoulder. 'Perhaps Claudia's partner will come back in a week or two. If not, you're her closest relative, right?'

'Her *only* relative, apart from a distant cousin in Australia.'

Out in the street, a police siren grew closer, then faded. People's lives were carrying on as normal; at work, shopping, or looking after their children.

'In that case,' Andrea said, 'you'll be the one we consult. And try not to worry about the baby. She's a good size, isn't she?' She addressed this last to the doctor.

'Yes. Are you sure your sister got her dates right?'

'How do you mean?'

'When she was brought in we were told it was twenty-three weeks' gestation. We have her notes, of course.' The doctor was back on safe ground. Facts not feelings. 'But sometimes people make a mistake about the date of their last period. Obviously, the larger the foetus and the better developed . . .'

In the silence that followed, they thought she was absorbing the good news. Instead, she had started to shake. What an idiot. Why had she never thought of it before? Ollie could have panicked because he suspected he was not the baby's father. Supposing Claudia had been pregnant when she asked him to move in with her. Pregnant when Erin arrived in Bristol? She had boasted about her lack of morning sickness, but it could have come and gone when she was living in the house by herself. Her lover could have done a bunk, or the baby was the result of a one-night stand and, not wanting to be a single parent, she had picked poor Ollie and pretended to be madly in love with him.

And then felt compelled to tell him the truth? Or he had guessed. Or someone else had told him. Who? But

23

another possibility, a much worse one, made her catch her breath. Where had he been on the afternoon of the accident? Claudia had tried to phone him, and given a derisive snort when she was put through to voicemail. *He had a meltdown but I'll cook him something nice, or buy him a present. Soon talk him round.* Talk him round? At the time, Erin had not inquired what the row was about, partly because she doubted Claudia would tell her, but mainly because Ollie having a "meltdown" had seemed so improbable. In her experience, he was such a calm, good-natured person, settling into Claudia's house like a stray dog, glad of a home. No, that was wrong. He had been as besotted with Claudia as she was with him.

Tomorrow, she would make some cautious inquiries, starting with Jennie, although she doubted Claudia would have confided in her. Then there was Ava, at the café, although, if she and Claudia had been close, Ava was unlikely to tell tales.

Even though Claudia was dead?

4

While she was searching online for a picture of a mynah bird, her phone rang. Jon, whose daughter she was teaching how to draw, and who was heading the research project Ollie was working on. Had he been in touch? Did Jon know where he was living? But when he asked if there was any news her hopes were dashed.

'He hasn't been into the university?'

'No.' Jon's sharp intake of breath had made her throat constrict. What was he afraid of? What did he think Ollie was going to do?

'The baby,' he said. 'What have the doctors told you?'

'I think they're quite optimistic.' Were they? Online she had found a list of complications that could affect a brain dead mother. Acute respiratory distress, diabetes, and something called intravascular coagulation.

'Look, I'm sorry, Erin . . .' There was a pause and she wondered if someone had come into the room and Jon was checking to make sure no one had heard from Ollie. But when he came back on the line it was to ask if she knew how large the baby was.

'About nine hundred grams.' She had decided not to tell anyone it was a girl. It had come as a surprise, a shock, but she was glad. Baby girls were supposed to be stronger than baby boys. Something else she had checked online.

'They can tell, can they?'

'Sorry?' But he meant the weight, not the sex. 'It needs to reach thirty weeks. It's nearly twenty-four.'

'The accident . . . has anyone . . . have the police . . . ?'

'Have they what?' Did he know something? If he did, he should come straight out with it. But that was not his style.

Now he was telling her it would be best to leave Maeve's art lessons for the time being.

'No!' Her response was stronger than she had intended, but she had been looking forward to seeing her. Maeve was Jon's ten-year-old daughter and she came round twice a week, after school, and on Saturday afternoon. 'I'd like to see her. She always cheers me up.'

'Are you sure you're up to it?'

'Absolutely. Oh, don't worry, I won't talk about what's happened.'

'I'll see you later then.'

'Yes.' Why did he sound so uneasy? And not just uneasy, annoyed, as though he thought Ollie's disappearance was her fault.

The first time they met she had thought his eyes had a haunted look, and she had warmed to him, partly because he was he exact opposite of Declan. Quiet, thoughtful, an introvert, the archetypal academic, his narrow face and deep set eyes had reminded her of her father, although her father had been shorter and his hair had started to recede when he was still in his twenties. Jon's hair was thick and dark, and she had found him attractive. Until Ollie mentioned his wife. Never again would she allow herself to fall for a man with a partner.

Just now, Jon might be at home, with Maeve's mother standing by his side, mouthing her misgivings about her daughter spending time with someone who was likely to be in a traumatised state.

26

Not long after she came to live in Claudia's house, Ollie had brought Jon back with him and the four of them had shared a couple of bottles of wine. The project they were working on was about the neurobiology of how we perceive the outside world, and Claudia had asked a string of questions, designed to give the impression she was well up on such matters. She had drunk too much, clutching Ollie's hand and starting on a childhood myth about how hopeless she was at art and how unfair it was that Erin had inherited their grandfather's talent. Not true – their mother had taught her to draw, a long difficult process – but faced with Claudia's highly embellished story Erin had kept quiet.

Later, Jon had phoned to ask if she took private pupils. For his young daughter, he said, who had a few problems with physical co-ordination, but loved painting and drawing. At first, Erin had been reluctant – working on the illustrations was effort enough – but as soon as she met Maeve she knew she had made the right decision.

Seeing her today would be a welcome diversion and, when Jon returned to collect her, she would take her downstairs and sit her in front of Claudia's wide-screen TV, handing her the remote control so she could flick through the channels until she found something she liked. Maeve was no fool – she would know they wanted her out of the way – but being Maeve she would give one of her worldly-wise smiles and raise no objection.

The weather had changed. It was warmer, damper, and the loft felt airless. After pushing open the dormer window as far as it would go, she took her sketches of guinea pigs out of a drawer in the plan chest and spread them out, standing back to study them as objectively as she could. The deadline for the illustrations was seven weeks off and by then . . . But it was better not to think that far ahead, better to take one day at a time, something she had attempted to do after she told Declan she never wanted to see him again.

Someone was banging on the front door. A package that was too large to fit through the letterbox? Something Ollie had ordered. Or Claudia. If it was one of Claudia's impulse buys, she would have to send it back. A food mixer? Lights for the garden? A cashmere jumper for Ollie?

When she opened the door, a dark-haired girl was standing on the path, twisting her hands.

'Oh' She looked all about her, as though she was afraid she was being followed. 'Please, is Clowda in?'

'No. No, she's not.'

'When will she be back?'

Who was she and how much should she tell her? 'She had an accident. She's in hospital.'

'Clowda is hurt?'

'Yes.' Was she someone from the market where Claudia had sold her jewellery? 'I'm her sister. Perhaps I can help.'

'Her sister?' The way the girl was staring at her was slightly intimidating. As though she thought she was lying, as though Claudia was at home but had given instructions to say she was out. 'What kind of an accident?'

'A bad one.'

'Oh.' The girl's expression softened a little. 'I will come when she is better.'

'What was it you wanted?' She was older than Erin had thought at first, possibly in her late twenties. Thick, black hair, tied back and held in place by a brightly coloured scarf. Large dark eyes. Several moles on her face. Possibly Eastern European.

'Perhaps next week.'

'No.' Erin made a decision. 'Look, my sister is very seriously injured. If you could explain why you need to see her?'

'Tell her I am sorry. I don't know . . . Lara – tell her it is Lara.'

'Your name's Lara?'

'Goodbye.' And she hurried away, hugging herself as though it was a freezing cold day, instead of a muggy one with the threat of rain.

Erin closed the front door. With any luck, the girl, whoever she was, would find out what had happened and stay away. Would she find out? How many people knew? Only people who read the local paper or watched the local news bulletin. Had the accident been reported on the television news? It must have been, but surely there would be no bulletins from the hospital. Claudia's condition would be confidential.

Back in the loft, Erin sat on her bed with the duvet pulled up to her chin. Her head ached and she remembered reading how the bereaved feel worse if their relationship with the person who has died was stormy, unhappy. Not that it was death that had separated her from Declan, but was it true of her relationship with Claudia? She was full of regrets. She should have given her better birthday presents, taken more interest in her life, visited her stall in the market, asked about her friends.

During the past few years, the two of them had met up only rarely so it must have come as a massive surprise when Erin asked if she could stay in her house for a few months while she decided what to do next. *As long as you like* – Claudia had actually sounded as though she meant it – although, arriving in Bristol almost five months ago, Erin had been mildly put out to find her bursting with excitement. She had met "the love of her life", she said, and as soon as some silly minor arrangements had been made he would be moving in. *No, don't worry, there's plenty of room for all three of us.*

What minor arrangements? Erin had thought, but when she met Ollie she discovered he was less impetuous than her sister. The room he was renting had to be re-let and he had paid a month's rent in advance. As if it mattered, Claudia had protested, but Ollie had dug in his heels. Perhaps he was being tactful – he knew Erin had only just arrived, and was not in a good state – but if that was the reason for his hesitation he was wrong. When he finally moved in, she had been heartily relieved she could now spend more time on her own.

Throwing her duvet aside, she decided to do something she should have done before, go downstairs to Claudia's kitchen and clear away the remains of Ollie's breakfast, left there the day he went missing. It felt like ages ago, but was only a few days.

The kitchen, with its moss green units and built-in cooker with a separate hob, had been one of the reasons Claudia bought the house. When she told her, Erin had laughed – Claudia had never taken any interest in cooking – but everything would be different now Ollie had moved in, she had insisted, buying herbs and spices, and even a string of onions, together with an impressively thick chopping board and six expensive kitchen knives and, for a finishing touch, a blue metal jug, filled with artificial sunflowers.

Collecting the bowl of dried up cereal, and mug of cold coffee, she added them to the rest of the stuff in the sink and filled it with hot, soapy water. Hot water was always a comfort and, like Ollie, she preferred her surroundings to be clean and tidy, something Claudia had teased him about. *I don't know how I managed without you, Ol. Proper little housewife. No, don't look like that. It's brilliant. The place has never looked so smart.*

Erin had never seen Claudia cook anything more than an omelette or cheese on toast, but when Ollie arrived he had taken advantage of the set-up and produced several ambitious meals to which she had been invited. Shoulder of lamb with green and red peppers. Trout with cheese sauce. How could they afford such banquets? Ollie was a research student and Claudia sold handmade jewellery in the market. It was possible she had a little of her inheritance left, but not enough to splash out on the kind of clothes she wore and food she ate, let alone the plentiful supply of wine.

Opening the fridge, Erin was relieved to find it virtually empty. As she carried a rotten cucumber, slimy as a slug, to the bin, together with the remains of a tub of evil-smelling liver pâté to the bin, she felt some satisfaction that she was doing something sensible, facing facts. But a moment later the emptiness of the place bore down on her and she crossed to the window and stared out at the damp, gloomy garden.

A paved area led to a strip of muddy grass, surrounded on three sides by flowerbeds, with a few straggly shrubs. During the summer months, Claudia had crammed in whatever was easily available at the local garden centre, mostly Petunias and Nicotiana. Now, it looked bleak, deserted, a garden in mourning.

According to Claudia, when she bought the house it was in quite a run-down road, but it had come up in the world. The walls at the front needed re-pointing and the cast iron gate could have done with a coat of paint. And the burglar alarm was defunct. In contrast, the adjoining house was in a good state of repair, and Erin wondered

31

what they thought of Claudia's. A week before the accident they had left her a note, saying they would be away for three months, in Brazil, and would be grateful if she could keep an eye on their house. They must have given her a key, but Erin had no idea where it was and had no intention of venturing next door unless she heard an intruder.

The landline started ringing, reminding her how she had still failed to find Claudia's mobile. Racing to Claudia's living room, she snatched it up, hoping it would be one of her friends. 'Yes?'

Silence.

'Who is that?'

More silence. One of those maddening cold calls. They put through six and talked to the first person who replied. But just as she was about to ring off, a male voice asked if she was Claudia.

'Who are you?'

'You know who I am.'

'You're a friend of Claudia's?' But a friend would know what had happened. 'She's been in an accident. I'm afraid—'

'What kind of an *accident*?' He repeated the word in a voice that made her angry. Like Lara, he thought she was fobbing him off.

'Look, tell me who you are and—'

'Tell her to telephone – today. If I don't hear from her—'

'I've told you. An accident. She's in hospital.'

But the line had gone dead.

5

Jon dropped off Maeve just after four, apologised for being in a hurry, and said if it was all right he would be back in an hour and a half.

'Longer, if you like,' Erin called after him, watching as he loped down the road, like a big cat, and hauled his long legs into his car. Surely it would have been better to buy something roomier, but Bristol traffic being what it was, it was probably best to have a smallish one.

Ollie disliked cars, thought they polluted the atmosphere. It was something else Claudia had teased him about. *They have TV programmes about people like you, Ol. Hey, what's the scariest thing in the house? The toilet cleaner that only gets rid of ninety-nine-point-nine percent of germs.* Why had he put up with the jokes that were not really jokes? It must have been the attraction of opposites.

Maeve was bursting with things she wanted to ask, so much so that she felt obliged to take her hands from the pockets of her jeans and put them over her mouth.

'It's all right.' Erin followed her back up the two flights of stairs and settled her at a table with a large sheet of paper and a box of oil pastels. 'I'll tell you whatever you want to know.'

Another child might have gulped. Maeve was not like that. 'Is the baby alive?'

'Yes, it is.'

'How can a dead person have a baby?' She tossed back her fringe. 'I know, they could cut her open and lift it out. Erin?'

'Mm.'

'I'm very, very, very, very sorry.' She stood up noisily and ran to her, flinging her arms round her waist. She was ten and a half, but not much taller than the average eight-year-old, yet there was nothing wrong with her intelligence. In fact, Erin considered her wise beyond her years.

'I once saw a picture of a baby inside its mother.' Maeve's cheek was pressed against Erin's shirt. 'It was only sixteen centimetres long but it had fingers and toes and eyes and everything. Poor Claudia.'

It was the first time since the accident that anyone had hugged her, and tears dripped down Erin's face.

Maeve gave her a squeeze. 'Crying's good for you. That's what my mum says. Where's Ollie gone? How could he look after a baby? He wouldn't know what to do. No, it'll be all right, you can help him.' She broke off, screwing up her nose. 'Will you still live up here or will you move downstairs?'

'Too soon to think about things like that.' Erin guided her back to her chair and gave her a bowl containing an orange, an apple and a banana. 'Don't forget, before you start drawing spend time looking at the fruit carefully.'

'And the spaces between. What I can see, not what I know in my head. The orange is round but you can only see part of it. Because of the banana,' she added, 'and because you can't see the back. Apples smell nice, sort of sweet and juicy.' She leaned over to prove her point. 'But bananas go black and smell horrible. I like the smell in here. Is it your deodorant? Mum has a herbal one. Can I see your drawings of guinea pigs?'

'Later.'

'What's the story about?'

'A pet shop. Three conceited guinea pigs and a small one that's frightened of the others.'

'Poor thing.' Maeve thought about it. 'Are there any other animals?'

'Chipmunks, rabbits, and a mynah bird.'

'Does the mynah bird talk?'

'Yes, but it doesn't say very much.'

'Birds carry diseases. No, I think that's parrots. After we'd been to the zoo, I had a rash and Mum thought I must have touched something, but we didn't go to the doctor. Mum doesn't like doctors. She goes to a herbalist. Herbs are good for you. They're natural.'

'That's true.'

'If you can't go to sleep you can put bay leaves under your pillow.'

'Good idea. I might try it. There's a bay tree out at the back, although it looks as though it's on its last legs.'

'Trees don't have legs.' Maeve grinned, touching the apple with the tip of her finger. 'Dad thinks . . .'

'What? What does he think?'

Maeve put an arm into the old shirt Erin had given her, to keep her clothes clean, and in the process knocked the box of oil pastels off the table. 'Sorry.'

'It doesn't matter. They're easier to hold if they're in small pieces.'

'Are they, or did you say that so I wouldn't feel bad?'

'You know me better than that.'

Maeve laughed, narrowing her eyes to study the fruit. 'Why has Ollie disappeared?'

'I expect he's staying with a friend.'

'Dad's worried about him. Are the police looking for him? Is he in trouble?'

'No.' What had Jon been saying? 'What did your dad tell you?'

'I heard him and Mum talking. I like Ollie.'

'I know you do.' It was something she had said before, shortly after she first met him, but never that she liked Claudia. Had Claudia said something? Maeve was sensitive about her clumsiness, and her lack of height. Surely Claudia had not been so tactless as to remark on it.

'When he was a little boy, Ollie had a rabbit. It was called Ethel.'

'Really? Funny name for a rabbit. When did he tell you that?'

'His mother's a nervous wreck.'

'The two of you seem to have had a good chat.'

'My hands are sticky. No, it's all right, I'll lick them and wipe them on a tissue. And his father had a stroke and he couldn't talk properly and then he died.'

'Poor Ollie.' Erin was trying to remember when she had left Maeve alone with Ollie. The day Claudia had shouted that her laptop had crashed? And once or twice, they had spent time in the garden together and Ollie had showed Maeve how to stop her yoyo unwinding immediately. What else had he told her?

The two of them had been working so hard – with only a short break for apple juice and ginger biscuits – that when Maeve pushed back her chair with a contented sigh, Erin was surprised to discover almost an hour and a half had passed.

'Finished.' Maeve's legs jigged up and down as she waited for Erin to look at her latest drawing.

'That's good, Maeve, especially the banana.'

'The third time I drew it I looked at it properly. I like oil pastels, you can smudge them so the colour goes all blurry. It's nice and warm in here. Warmer than our house.'

'Is it?' Erin was surprised. Perhaps, as well as her liking for herbs, her mother was keen on fresh air. The family had moved to Bristol when Maeve was four, and Jon got a job at the university. That was all she knew about them, apart from the gossip Maeve passed on – her mother's herb garden and Jon's dislike of buying new clothes. And how he suffered from insomnia. Maeve loved long words and said her favourite was "soporific" and she had read it in a book by Beatrix Potter.

She was washing her hands, with plenty of soap, like a surgeon preparing to operate. Then she picked up a towel, dried each stubby finger in turn, and gave Erin one of her beaming smiles.

'Why haven't you got a husband?'

'I don't know.' She was not up to that one, not just now. 'Not everyone's married.'

'No, some people have a partner, and it said on TV that millions of people live on their own. Do you like living on your own? I wouldn't mind. I mean, when I'm grown up.'

Erin made no comment, and sensing her reluctance to talk about partners, Maeve changed the subject. 'Where's Miss Havisham?'

It was the name she had given to the cat. Rather a good one, since it had a look about it, as though it was dressed in scruffy black and white clothes. 'How do you know it's a female?'

'I don't.' She grinned. 'It wouldn't let me look.'

'You've read *Great Expectations* then?'

'Me and Mum watched the film. Miss Havisham lived in a ruined mansion with her adopted daughter. She was mad but I felt sorry for her. I don't think she could help it. Erin?'

'Now what?'

'I wish I had hair like Jennie down the road.'

'Oh, you know Jennie.'

'She's married to an actor. Actually, I don't know if they're married. He's called Ben. Mum says I have to keep my hair short in case I get nits. Your hair's nice. Hair like yours always looks all right. Claudia's hair . . .' She broke off, afraid it was wrong to mention her.

'Go on. Yes, you're right, a better colour than mine. When we were little it was so fair it was almost white.'

'Oh.'

'It's all right, Maeve, I don't mind talking about her. Now, what are you going to draw next, or are you tired?'

'I'm never tired.'

Erin handed her another sheet of paper. 'Lucky you.'

They worked on and by the time Jon rang the bell, interrupting a conversation about the relative merits of breast and bottle feeding, Maeve had been with her for two hours and it was clear Jon was in a hurry, needing to get her home in time for their evening meal.

'If there's anything I can do . . .' His half-hearted offer was to make up for the fact that he was going to leave straight away and there would be no chance to talk.

'There isn't,' she said, and he flinched at the coolness in her voice. 'Unless someone tells you they've seen Ollie.'

'Have the police . . .'

'Going missing is not a crime.'

'No.' His eyes met hers and she guessed he was thinking about the accident although, on second thoughts, he could have noticed how rough she looked. Her jeans were ragged where the hem of each leg brushed the ground and her shirt stained with Indian ink. Still, artists were allowed to look a mess. But not have tear-stained faces and unwashed hair.

'Someone phoned,' she said, 'a man.'

38

'Did he tell you his name? Could have been Hoshi I suppose.'

'Hoshi?' Maeve said. 'That's a funny name.'

Jon was studying the back of his hand. 'He used to be a student but dropped out. He and Ollie were friends.'

'Can't have been him who phoned,' Erin said. 'A friend would have known what's happened. And before that a girl knocked on the door, said her name was Lana, no Lara. Could this Hoshi know where Ollie's hiding out?'

'Is he hiding?' Maeve squealed. 'Look, Dad, I drew some fruit.' She pulled at the sleeve of Jon's dark blue sweater and Erin wondered if his wife had knitted it, and felt a twinge of something she quickly suppressed. What did Diana look like? Was her colouring dark or fair? Was she tall or short, fat or thin. She could ask Maeve but it would sound nosy, and sooner or later she was bound to meet her.

One evening, a few weeks' back, Jon had called by when Ollie and Claudia were out, to pay for Maeve's classes, and over a glass of wine, told her a little about his work. She had enjoyed talking to him. He was passionate about his research, and Maeve was probably right about his dislike of shopping, since he gave the impression he had little interest in his appearance. Unruly hair and a long face with a deep cleft above his upper lip. Heavy-lidded eyes with thick, dark lashes. Declan had spent a fortune on clothes, especially shirts, and had his hair cut in the latest style by a barber called Fernando. Jon had different priorities.

Touched that he had trusted her enough to tell her about Maeve's birth, she had been encouraged to talk about her split with Declan, although when she blamed herself for becoming involved with him, he had reacted angrily. *You thought his marriage was over. If you want my opinion, he sounds like a self-centred bastard and you're better off without him.*

'Look, Dad.' Maeve's voice was high-pitched with frustration.

'You did that?'

'Erin likes it.' Hopping on one leg, Maeve lost her balance and crashed to the ground. 'Erin, was only Claudia hurt? What about the other people in the street?'

'She'd stopped to look up at a building.'

'Why?'

'I don't know.' It was something that ran through Erin's mind repeatedly.

'Perhaps she saw someone,' Maeve suggested.

'Someone she knew you mean?'

'If she was pregnant, she should have been being careful. She should have been holding your arm.'

'That's enough, Maeve.' Jon was waiting for her to collect her drawings. Standing in the doorway, he was so tall he had to bend his head. 'Maybe we should leave the classes for a while.'

'No.' Maeve reacted fiercely. 'Erin doesn't mind, do you, Erin, it takes your mind off things.'

Erin laughed, but Jon failed to join in, and unspoken words hung in the air between them. Then Maeve caught hold of his hand and pulled him through the door.

'See you soon,' she called, falling over her own feet and grabbing the stair rail.

'Bye, Maeve.' Erin watched the two of them descend the narrow stairs, but in her mind's eye she saw Claudia, looking up at the protesters and, a moment later, sprawled across the pavement with blood seeping from her head. Maeve was right. she should never have let her walk on her own, should have stuck to her like a leech, but at that precise moment she had been thinking how lonely she felt and how painfully aware she was that Claudia had friends she had never met and a life she knew nothing about. She should have made more effort to meet her friends. But Claudia had never offered to introduce them.

Why *had* she crossed the road to look up at the protesters?

Perhaps she saw someone she knew. Maeve's words came back, but more than the words it had been the expression on her face. And on Jon's when Erin turned to him, hoping for reassurance.

6

Claudia could have been sleeping, and the baby inside her had no reality. Erin looked away, unable to believe her sister was incapable of knowing she was by her bedside. People in a coma sensed the presence of others, especially their voices, but Claudia was not in a coma: her brain had been destroyed.

Whose idea had it been that they go to the shops together that Saturday afternoon? She preferred to think it was Claudia's, but had a vague recollection she had said she wanted to buy something for the baby, a thank you for letting her escape from London for a while.

It had been cold that day and breakfast television had shown thick snow covering London and the south-east, but Bristol had missed out and elongated clouds drifted across a clear blue sky. Erin had hoped to leave straight after lunch, but as usual Claudia had things to do, things being a string of phone calls, followed by a visit from Jennie, and a long discussion about Jennie's actor partner, Ben, who, according to Claudia, had a roving eye.

Erin remembered waiting in the garden, checking the plants while trying not to think about Declan. How could she have been so stupid? Because being in love means you are more than a little crazy, and it was only when he let slip that his wife was pregnant ("but I don't suppose it's even mine") that she had begun to use her head instead of her heart. Needing to escape – fast – Claudia's house in Bristol had been the obvious choice, somewhere where there was a faint hope she might be able to re-start her shattered life.

'Erin?' Claudia had called her name, impatient, as though *she* was the one who had been waiting for nearly an hour.

'Ten past three,' Erin said, 'soon be dark. Maybe we should leave it until tomorrow.'

'What!' She had given her a good-natured shove in the back. Good-natured but so hard she almost lost her balance. 'Of course we can't leave it till tomorrow.' And the two of them had set off, heading for a special shop where Erin had promised to buy an extravagant present for the unborn baby.

Claudia knew the place well – Erin suspected she had visited it secretly before anyone knew she was pregnant, 'Is it a boy or a girl?'

Claudia laughed. 'I told them at the clinic I'd rather wait and see.'

'I'll believe you. How are you feeling?'

'Starving. There's this new coffee place and they have these amazing pastries with a chocolate and almond filling.'

'You had a late lunch.'

'God, you're such a spoilsport, Erin. Hang on, I'd better phone Ollie.' Ollie was younger than her and slightly traumatized by the news he was going to be a father. 'He had a bit of a meltdown.'

'That doesn't sound like Ollie.'

Claudia gave her a look. 'You think he's a soft touch. Ought to see what he's like when he decides to dig his heels in. Don't worry, I'll cook him something nice. Or I could buy him a present although heaven knows what. Right then.' She crammed a purple woollen hat on her

43

head. 'Honestly, Erin, you're getting so bossy, like you're my mother or something.'

'Somebody has to knock some sense into you.' At the words "like you're my mother or something" Erin had flinched. Claudia had always been the bossy one.

They had expected a post-Christmas lull but if anything the shops were even more crowded than the previous week. People fed up with sitting at home, enjoying the festivities, or shopaholics unwilling to waste a precious second of bargain hunting? The shop Claudia made a beeline for was stuffed with baby walkers, high chairs, nappy pails, and a special display of organic cotton dolls with flaxen pigtails and flowered smocks. A pram or a cot, even a first-size sleep suit was out of the question – they were both far too superstitious – but somehow the shoes were different and, when the baby was born, Erin would dash out and buy whatever else was needed.

'Look at them,' Claudia crooned, 'they're so cute.'

'Yes, they are.' Cute was not a word Erin had heard her sister use before. Ollie must have been working on her. Ollie was a softie. Claudia was as tough as old boots. 'Quite sure they're the ones you want?'

'Certain.'

Erin opened her purse, and took out her card, and an assistant wrapped the shoes in tissue paper and placed them in a shiny carrier bag, holding it out with a smile, not sure which of them was to carry the treasured gift.

Claudia gave Erin an unexpected kiss on the cheek. 'Thank you.'

'You're welcome.'

'It's a lovely present.'

'It certainly is.'

They stared at each other and burst out laughing. It was such an unfamiliar situation – devoted sisters shopping for a new arrival – and even Claudia, not known for her sensitivity, must have been aware how Erin was feeling. Not that she would have dreamed of mentioning it since she disliked tears, her own or anyone else's.

Ahead of them, a woman with a double buggy was struggling to open the shop door and Erin hurried to help, glancing into the buggy and causing one of the infants inside to let out a piercing wail.

'Driving me insane,' the woman said, and Erin imagined a time in the not too distant future when the novelty of her baby had worn off and Claudia wanted her to childmind. *Just for an hour or two, Erin, so I can get some rest.*

The woman with the double buggy had disappeared and Claudia was waiting impatiently for Erin to emerge from her daydream.

'Sorry' She snapped back into the present. 'Is that all or are there more shops you want to visit?'

'What were you thinking?' Claudia struggled with the top button on her coat.

'Nothing'

'Liar. Hang on, I need a couple of ready meals. And some bananas. See, I told you I was looking after my health.'

When they finally reached the end of the road, they had to wait several minutes before it was safe to cross. Erin was being sensible, taking care, and later the irony of this hit her, like a punch in the stomach. If, as she normally did, she had hurried Claudia across in advance of the coming traffic . . .

Having reached the other side, Claudia slowed down to a snail's pace. Still almost four months to go, but her bump stuck out like someone on the brink of giving birth. Not because of the baby, Erin thought, all those blueberry muffins, Danish pastries stuffed with dried fruit and gooey filling, and lemon drizzle cake, her favourite, devoured in a single sitting. Some people lost weight when they were expecting – Erin guessed she would be like that – but Claudia had latched on to the proverbial eating for two. *Freshly baked, Erin, smell it, who could resist?*

As far back as she could remember, Claudia had been larger than her, taller, broader, even though she was the second born and, according to their mother, quite a scrawny baby. And, since Erin had been only fifteen months old at the time, she had to take her mother's word for it. Claudia was also noisier, more gregarious, untidier and more popular. They were different in every way imaginable but, as their father liked to say, comparisons were invidious.

'Mum would have loved grandchildren,' Erin said, but a bus was passing and Claudia had to ask her to repeat what she had said, the second time she changed it. 'I said, that woman over there's got a lot of kids.'

'Rather her than me,' Claudia laughed, 'some people breed like there's no tomorrow.'

'I'm looking forward to being an aunt,' Erin said, 'but I want to be called Erin, not Auntie Erin.'

'Auntie Erin.' Claudia thought about it with a silly smile on her face.

'Don't say it.'

'You don't know what I was going to say.'

'Yes, I do, a dried up old spinster. I hate the word spinster.'

'Anyway, you can't be a spinster. Spinsters are virgins.' She pulled at Erin's sleeve. 'You never talk about Declan.'

'No point. Ancient history. And don't say there are plenty more fish.'

'I wish I'd met him. I can spot a bad one a mile off. What did he look like? When you're feeling better I'll introduce you to scores of beautiful young men. There's this Japanese guy. . .'

As they made their way home, Claudia complained that the walk to the shops had been fine but returning up the hill, was likely to finish her off for the day. 'Oh, well, never mind, soon be back and now the central heating's been fixed the house should feel like a furnace.'

The previous evening, a man Erin had never seen before had turned up at the house. She had no idea why he was there but when she came down from the loft, to empty her pedal bin, she heard Claudia say, 'No. No, I'm sorry, you'll have to find someone else.'

What were they talking about? Not the central heating. The jewellery Claudia made, and sold in the market? The man was in his late twenties or early thirties, possibly Turkish or Greek, and Claudia had not introduced him when she came out of her den and found Erin skulking in the hall, and a moment later he was shown unceremoniously through the front door.

Much of Claudia's life was a mystery, but that was fair enough and Erin had long since given up asking about it, something she now regretted profoundly. Back in August, after she split with Declan, she had been only too grateful for a temporary home in the converted loft space, and had also hoped for some moral support which, as it turned out, had failed to materialise. Claudia was so besotted with Ollie she talked of little else and when, a few weeks later, he moved into the house, Erin had felt like an intruder and stayed in her "penthouse" flat – Claudia's description, not hers – self-sufficient with her tiny shower room and table top cooker, licking her wounds like an abandoned cat. But self-pity gets you nowhere, and the dormer window let in

47

plenty of light, so it was not long before she unpacked her materials and started on the first of the illustrations.

'Wait!' Claudia yelled.

'Sorry.' She was day dreaming again, and walking too fast.

'I asked how your illustrations were progressing.'

'Not too bad. The book's about—'

'Yes, guinea pigs. You said. I always wanted one but Mum wouldn't let us have any pets.'

'She was afraid you wouldn't look after them.'

'All right, I did neglect the goldfish, but—'

'I found it floating on its side in murky water.'

'And I screamed the place down, right?'

'I expect so,' As a child, Claudia had always made her feelings abundantly clear. She was a strong character – everyone said so – and at the time Erin had been unsure if that was a compliment or a criticism. In any case she had mellowed a little as she grew older, or was it that Erin had learned how to stand up to her? Their relationship had remained tricky and she had often felt she had to tread on eggshells, whereas Claudia was free to speak her mind.

'The editor wants some line drawings,' she said, 'as well as the full colour illustrations. Line drawings are cheaper to reproduce.'

'Sorry?' Claudia was brushing crumbs off her coat.

'I said . . .' But Claudia had no interest in the illustrations, and Erin recalled how once she had remarked, in all seriousness, that it must be nice having your hobby as your work. It was getting dark and, as they passed the protesters at the building site, Erin wondered how the police had allowed them to invade the place. It was being converted into luxury apartments and the locals were angry, wanted – needed – affordable homes. Dressed in dark clothes, some wearing balaclavas, they shouted through megaphones, and one had handcuffed himself to a scaffolding pole. Erin's hands were full with the baby shoes in one bag and a collection of ready meals in the other. Claudia held a doughnut in sticky paper. Red jam ran down her chin and she wiped it away with the back of her hand, glancing at Erin and grinning.

'Got to keep my strength up.'

'Of course.'

'After the sprog's arrived I'll go on starvation rations. I mean, after I've stopped breastfeeding.'

Claudia breastfeeding? It was such an unlikely idea. But people changed when they had a baby. Hormones kicked in. Maternal feelings took over. For the first time, it occurred to Erin that Claudia might be quite a good mother. Inconsistent, strict one minute, indulgent the next, but that was no bad thing for a child to learn. Life was not constant. Neither was it fair. Exhaust fumes from the line of traffic filled the cold air and made them cough. A cyclist, clad in yellow lycra, raced by, his muscular leg jerking Erin's arm and making her mouth a silent obscenity. Claudia had crossed the road and was looking up, calling out to one of the protesters. Impossible to hear what she was saying. Words of support, Erin assumed.

What happened next would return endlessly, in slow motion like one of those nightmares when your muscles refuse to work. A crashing noise as a length of scaffolding fell to the ground and bounced away. Claudia's purple hat at her feet. Claudia herself lying on the pavement with one arm flung out and the taut skin of her abdomen exposed to the cold. No blood. The pole must have missed her. She had jumped out of the way and slipped. She was all right. Any moment now, she would scramble to her feet, laughing, and not even worried about the baby since she was so well padded, as she liked to describe herself.

But no sooner had Erin breathed a sigh of relief than to her horror she saw blood seeping from the side of Claudia's head and running across her half-closed eye. A crowd had gathered and a young man was shouting into his phone. Someone said, *Oh, my God*, and a child's high-pitched voice asked, 'Is she dead, Mummy, is she dead?'

What did she do? Crouch down or stand helplessly above her? Scream or remain silent, dry-mouthed? People gazed up at the building then down at the scaffolding pole. The protesters were silent. An Asian woman, with a long, dark coat over a blue and white sari, stepped forward, taking over, and Erin heard her authoritative voice ordering the young man, 'don't move her.' Traffic slowed and drivers strained their necks to get a better view. 'She's my sister,' she told the Asian woman, 'and she's pregnant.'

The woman had her hand on Claudia's neck, feeling for a pulse. Did she know what she was doing? Was she a doctor, or a nurse? Removing her coat, she draped it over Claudia's motionless body, leaving only her head visible. A siren grew closer. Cars pulled up to allow a screeching ambulance to jump the lights. Two paramedics knelt beside Claudia, checking if she was still breathing, fixing a collar round her neck and carefully lifting her onto a stretcher before disappearing into the back of the ambulance.

'Can I come with you?' Erin's voice came out as a croak. 'I'm her sister.'

One of the paramedics helped her inside and she felt her head swim, and sat down, hanging onto the edge of the seat. As they sped up the hill, she managed to get enough breath to ask if Claudia was alive. The paramedic hesitated then nodded, murmuring something about how it would only take a few minutes to reach the hospital.

7

Annoyed that yet again Jon had rushed off after Maeve's lesson, not prepared to spend even a few minutes talking to her, Erin decided to phone Jennie. Claudia had described her as being *up and down like a yo-yo, one day absurdly optimistic, the next, filled with gloom,* but Erin was not sure how well she had known her? According to Claudia, Jennie's actor partner, Ben, was either out of work, or worrying about the next job. Fortunately, during their time together, Jennie had managed to buy an old property she let out to students.

She might be busy. She had suggested they had coffee together sometime, but people often made vague invitations they had no intention of carrying out, so when Erin phoned, she was pleasantly surprised to hear how pleased Jennie sounded.

'Oh, Erin, how are you? Any news of Ollie?'

'Nothing.'

'The baby?' Jennie asked cautiously. 'It must be dreadful for you. If there was anything I could do, but of course there isn't. Still, I'm sure the doctors are wonderful.' She cleared her throat, as though to announce that was enough of all that. 'Come round whenever you like. Today?'

'Actually, I need to get out of this place.' Jennie was

in the open, somewhere where the traffic was heavy and they were digging up the road. 'I thought perhaps we could meet at Ava's Place?'

'Ava's Place? Is that a good idea?'

'Why not?'

'No reason. It's just . . . She's a bit of a gossip and someone said she's been spreading rumours.'

'What kind of rumours?'

'Oh, I don't suppose it's anything. Ava's Place it is.' Jennie was shouting above the racket. 'I've just pulled up outside my student house – the boiler's been playing up – so it'll be in about an hour.'

'Fine.' Erin had expected her to say ten minutes, twenty at most, and felt unreasonably put out. Jennie knew how worried she was, and would have little sympathy for Ollie since she believed people should take responsibility.

'Oh, Erin?'

'Yes?' She thought she had rung off.

'The accident. Do the police know what happened?'

'A scaffolding pole must have come loose. There'd been objections to the luxury apartments. The police seem to think one of the protesters interfered with it. Someone wearing a hoodie was seen running away.'

'So they may be able to trace who did it.'

'I doubt it. I expect they just wanted to convince me they were doing their best.'

'An hour then, Erin, certainly not more.'

Not enough time to make a start on a new illustration. Too long to spend sitting around, brooding. Ava's Place was chaotic, but Erin liked Ava, she was warm and friendly, and if you lived alone that was important. And her tendency to play up to her larger-than-life reputation was one of the reasons her café was so popular. She gave the impression she and Claudia had been close friends, so the accident must have upset her a lot.

For the first time, Erin forced herself to go into the room where Claudia had made her jewellery. The dining room, an estate agent would have called it, but she and Ollie had eaten in the kitchen, and spent the rest of their time in the room at the front that had a bay window and looked out on the houses opposite.

Claudia's den had been sacrosanct. No one, not even Ollie, ever entered it without knocking, and up to now the most Erin had done was put her head round the door. An image of Claudia, sitting hunched over her laptop, sprang into her mind, but the tears she expected failed to materialise. She felt numb, frozen in time, unable to accept Claudia would never sit there again.

The dark curtains, with their pattern of leaves and birds, had been drawn across and she pulled them back, letting in enough light to make the room less cheerless. How had Ollie felt, moving into a house that contained nothing of his, apart from some boxes of books? Still, in her experience, men were less attached to objects – nick-knacks and family photos – and before he arrived, Ollie had been renting a single room in another part of the city.

The hyacinth on the windowsill was in a bad way, dry, curled-up leaves, sticky with white fly. Erin dropped it into the bin, pausing to check what else had been thrown away. An old cinema ticket, a gardening glove, stiff with mud, a Milky Way wrapper and some nylon thread. Changing her mind, she retrieved the hyacinth from the bin, hoping she could revive it.

Ignoring the other signs of jewellery making – a few metal tools and a bowl of multi-coloured beads – she opened the mahogany desk that had once belonged to their maternal grandmother, the place where she assumed

53

Claudia had kept her papers. The first thing she noticed was the ink stain that had been there for as long as she could remember, possibly before she was born. If her mother was still alive, she could have joined her within hours of the accident, helped to decide about the baby, although they would both have felt the same, and together they would have grieved for Claudia; her youngest daughter and Erin's little sister. Instead, she had to make-do with Jennie, and Jon if he could be bothered to spare the time.

Worrying about the baby, and about Ollie, had put her feelings about Claudia on hold. Each time they threatened to rise to the surface she found a diversion, concentrated on practicalities, but sooner or later they would catch up with her. Or would they stay firmly under control until the baby was born and Claudia's life support was switched off?

Probably not a good move, but she had bought a book about pregnancy. At sixteen weeks, a baby was completely formed and had fine hair all over its body. At twenty weeks, its teeth began to form and the mother could feel it moving – Claudia had said it felt like the fluttering of a very large moth – and at twenty-four weeks it could suck its thumb and hiccup, and creases appeared on the palms of its hands.

As she was closing a desk drawer, a roll of twenty-pound notes caught her eye. Takings from Claudia's jewellery stall? Held in place by a red rubber band, they reminded her of every gangster film she had ever seen and she felt compelled to count them, licking her finger when they stuck together and keeping a tally in her head. Almost two thousand pounds.

Why had no one paid it into the bank? Next to the money, a single sheet of paper had a list of names, some of them foreign sounding, and next to each a date – all the dates had passed – and an amount of cash. A. Hassaud. L. Jenkins. D. Winterbourne. P. Chin. M. Balumba. And a Christian name on its own, at least Erin assumed it was Christian name. Shadrack. The amounts of money were relatively large. Two hundred pounds, two hundred and fifty, a hundred and twenty.

Her first thought was Ollie's photography. As far as she knew, he never exhibited his work, but she remembered Claudia telling her what a brilliant photographer he was and how a friend of hers had asked him to take pictures of her eighteen-month-old child, and he had spent the morning following the little boy round the park, waiting for the right moments. Two hundred pounds for a photoshoot was a possibility.

Miss Havisham had appeared and was writhing round Erin's ankles, hoping for food.

'Oh, all right then,' she told her, 'but you're as fat as a pig. How many dinners have you eaten this week?'

The cat let out a yowl and showed its sharp little teeth, and Erin was afraid she might be growing fond of it. Then her phone beeped. Jon? Someone had spotted Ollie? But the text was from Jennie, saying she was waiting for a plumber to fix the boiler but still hoped to reach Ava's Place within the hour.

Replacing the list of names, Erin picked up the bin and left Claudia's den, closing the door behind her with a guilty feeling she should never have been there in the first place. On the other hand, what was she supposed to do about the money, and the house, and all the bills that were bound to roll in? An unexpected feeling caught her off guard, anger with Claudia, but for what? For not being more careful, for leaving her to deal with the aftermath, for lying in a hospital bed, looking so serene and so alive.

Pushing the uncomfortable thoughts out of her head, she hurried towards the kitchen, followed by the cat.

Then she saw the corpse of a mouse.

It was headless, and what was left of it was lying on its side, bedraggled and with one tiny paw stretched out. Her first instinct was to ignore it, wait for Jon to come round with Maeve and ask him to dispose of it. But leaving it lying there would be worse so, finding a brush a pan, she took a deep breath and, averting her eyes, swept it up and carried it to the black wheelie bin at the front.

Jennie's partner, Ben, was coming up the road.

'Hi.' He waved, crossing to her side and dropping his bags of shopping on the pavement. 'How are you? Sorry, silly question.'

'I'm meeting up with Jennie quite soon. Coffee at Ava's Place.'

'Good. Actually, Erin . . . No, sorry, in the circumstances it doesn't seem right to ask, but have you noticed anything, about Jennie I mean?'

'I've only seen her once since . . .'

'Yes, of course. Sorry. Only if you're having coffee with her . . . Something's bothering her, has been for several weeks, and she won't tell me . . . I've tried but she denies it, says I'm fussing. Only she might open up to you.'

'I doubt it.' But he looked so worried she felt obliged to promise she would do her best.

'Only don't tell her I said anything,' he added.

'No, of course not.' Perhaps Jennie was worrying about money. Ben was the carefree kind, who thinks something is sure to turn up, and Erin guessed Jennie was the one who took responsibility, paid the bills.

Further up the street, a man with his hoodie pulled up was leaning against a tree, while he lit a cigarette. It was impossible to see his face properly, but Erin thought she might have seen him before. Where? Perhaps he lived locally. Perhaps he came down the street most days on his way to work, or to the shops.

'Having a clear up?' Ben jerked his head towards the brush and pan in her hand.

'Yes. The kitchen. You know,' She had no intention of admitting her fear of dead animals. It was not something she was proud of. Not fear exactly, just a horrible feeling of dread.

Ben had moved on and her thoughts returned to the money in Claudia's desk. It belonged to Ollie now – or did it? Since he had disappeared and left her looking after the house, surely she deserved at least some of it. What was going to happen when direct debits remained unpaid because Claudia's bank account had dried up? There were bills too, so far unopened, but quite soon she would have to do something about them. Best to take the roll of notes up to the loft for safe keeping, and hide it in the plan chest.

Thinking about the loft, made her change her mind about the hyacinth and, instead of carrying it upstairs, she put it on the corner table in the hallway where she would see and smell it when she went in and out of the house, although its scent reminded her of her mother and made her feel morbid. She wondered if Maeve's mother liked hyacinths. Jon had never suggested they meet. In fact, she sometimes thought he had decided it was best not to introduce them. Why? Did she have some objection to Maeve's art lessons? No, that was unlikely to be the reason or she could have stopped her coming. Perhaps the marriage was in trouble. No, no way was she going to fall for that again.

Jon was so unpredictable. One day, warm and

57

sympathetic. The next, distant, evasive. Something was preying on his mind, or was she reading too much into behaviour that was simply part of his personality? When he came to collect Maeve, had he left it fine deliberately in case she started questioning him about Ollie? Did he know where he was but been sworn to secrecy? After all, he had known Ollie far longer than he had known her.

On the point of leaving for the café, a thought occurred to her. Ollie's bike – was it still in the shed at the back? It was something she should have checked as soon as he went missing. Claudia had a bike too, but hers was an ancient, rusty thing. Ollie's was in mint condition – something else Claudia had teased him about. Not that he had taken any notice. In most areas of his life, he was happy for Claudia to take charge, but where his bike was concerned, and the food he liked to eat, he dug in his heels and refused to budge.

When she dragged open the shed door, the fetid smell made her take a step back. What was it? A dead rat or just rotting vegetation, plants Claudia had bought, with the best of intentions, but forgotten to water. Her bike, with its basket at the front, was leaning against one of the walls, next to a rake and a stepladder. But Ollie's had gone.

8

Ava's Place was packed. It was famous, or perhaps notorious was the word, mainly because of Ava herself and the ridiculous cocktails she made, the "healthy" food she served and the dreadful amateur watercolours displayed on lime green walls. The paintings had prices attached – amounts so small they undercut by a mile any work Erin might have tried to sell –and no doubt most of Ava's clientele thought the watercolours were far better than anything you could see at the Tate Modern.

Ava herself had a tendency to come out with alarmingly perceptive remarks. The first time they met, Erin had experienced a mixture of feelings when Ava looked her up and down and said, 'A man, was it, my darling. You've been through the mill but you're a survivor, have a cappuccino on me.'

Today, dressed in baggy trousers and a voluminous pink smock with a matching headband, she was slicing up homemade pizza while yelling instructions to her assistant, a girl with a shaved head and a single lock of green hair over one ear. Ava looked up, saw her, and waved a welcome before bending double – she was not much over five-foot-tall – to search for something in the fridge.

Three small children bounced up and down on the sofa near the window, and several buggies blocked the way through to the tables. Erin peered between two harassed looking mothers, hoping to see Jennie, but she was late. Aware she was working herself up into a hard done by mood for the second time that morning, she had to make a quick adjustment when she spotted Jennie, gesturing frantically from an alcove at the back, and realised she had been there all the time.

'Hi' She had kept Erin a stool next to a radiator. 'You poor thing, what a terrible time you're having. I would have called round again but Ben thought you'd prefer to be on your own. Is there anything I can do? I could do some shopping, or cook you something nice, except I'm not the world's greatest cook. Poor Claudia, she was so full of life. I mean, she . . . I was going to say she could be a bit tactless but even if she was, she always made up for it. So generous. I'm so sorry, Erin. I used to come here with Claudia, not very often, she was always busy, but when I saw her we always had a good exchange of news. Not that I ever had very much but Claudia had all these plans. I keep thinking of Ollie and how devastated he must be.'

'I just wish he would come back.' Jennie's roots needed touching up, something that surprised Erin since she remembered Claudia saying she was the kind of person who despised the way some women let themselves go. Despised? Erin was surprised Jennie had been so critical, although Claudia had a habit of exaggerating people's remarks, for the maximum effect. Had Jennie and Claudia really been such good friends? Reading between the lines, Jennie could have found her sister as difficult as she herself sometimes had.

Today, Jennie looked tired, as though she had been sleeping badly. She was attractive, with her finely chiselled features, but her skin was pale and blotchy. Another thing Claudia had said was that Jennie was terrified Ben would leave her for someone younger, but having met Ben, Erin thought it unlikely. He was friendly but not in the least flirtatious, and the first time she talked to him, he had admitted his greatest fear was going bald. Your greatest fear, she thought. You must have led a charmed life.

Jennie had turned towards the counter, where Ava was covering pastries with a plastic dome. 'What would you like? I was so glad you phoned. It doesn't do to hide yourself away.'

'Maeve came yesterday.' Erin leaned her aching back against the wall and breathed in the smell of coffee, and something less pleasant.

'For an art lesson?' Jennie stretched her eyes wide and Erin noticed she had been a little heavy-handed with the eyeliner. 'Surely you could have a break from all that.'

'Best to keep busy.'

'Yes, but you have to visit the hospital, don't you? Is it hopeless? Is there nothing they can do? I thought . . . if she's still breathing.'

'She's on a ventilator.'

'But the baby. It's amazing what they can do these days. I read in a magazine that a woman was having quintuplets and one of them died in the womb but they did something, I'm not quite sure what, and the other four were delivered safely.'

Erin put her hands over her ears in an attempt to cut out the sounds of children and coffee machines and scraping chairs, and a CD of a wailing girl, accompanied by a Spanish guitar, and Jennie interpreted it that she was talking too much.

'Sorry. Tell me about the hospital.'

'Not much to tell. Claudia's life support will remain switched on until it's safe for the baby to be born,'

'By caesarean section. Yes, of course. When will it be strong enough? Have they said?'

'I don't think they're looking that far ahead.' Erin was thinking about the money in Claudia's desk. Should she ask Jennie if she knew where it could have come from? Normally, it would have felt like breaking a confidence, but it was different now. 'I wanted to ask you, Jennie. I found an address book in Claudia's desk but I think it was an old one. There was a list of names too, and money, quite a lot. I can't believe she made that much from her jewellery.'

'You've no idea where Ollie could have gone?'

'That's why I hoped the address book might be useful.'

Ava was approaching and Erin prayed she would keep her comments about Claudia brief.

'Oh, Erin, I'm so desperately sorry. Such a tragedy. Poor Claudia, and poor Ollie. They were such a golden couple.'

Golden couple? What did she mean? That they were both good-looking, Ollie with his sweet baby face, and Claudia with her dramatic clothes and make-up and her expansive way of talking? No wonder she and Ava had got on so well – they were two of a kind – although Ava was a good deal older.

'But they may be able to save the baby.' Jennie was winding a strand of hair round her little finger. 'And that would be wonderful, wouldn't it?'

'Yes.' Then, aware she should have sounded more enthusiastic, 'Yes, of course.' One of her heavily-ringed hands came down on Erin's head. 'Claudia and I were two of a kind, up one minute, down the next, and determined to get our own way. We understood each other. Once she complained about the food here and we fell out, but only for a week, missed each other's company. Anyway, you must get some rest, my darling, and make sure you eat properly. Best way to keep up your spirits and . . .' Her voice trailed away and she pushed up the blue-rimmed spectacles that normally rested half way down her nose. 'I'm having a new exhibition, etchings and screen prints. Members of the local art society. I'd ask your advice, Erin, but in the circumstances . . . Any news of Ollie? You know my opinion of men, but Ollie's a different matter, not an ounce of venom in the boy. Now, what would you like?'

After she had taken their order, she moved away and Erin sensed Jennie had some news of her own but was not sure if she should mention it.

'What's up?'

'Me? No, nothing.' Jennie was watching the children playing on the floor. Ava's Place was a second home to her, but she disliked the fact there were so many kids, especially the toddlers who laughed and cried, and fell over. 'My student house. One of my tenants left with rent owing. Still, what can you expect with students, but it has the advantage, if they're bad tenants they're only there on a short let. Anyway.' She fluffed up her hair with both hands. 'This high-powered businesswoman turned up, needing to rent a place for a month. She'd done the rounds of the agencies and someone had put her in touch, and naturally I jumped at it. She moved in a few days ago and if she decides to stay on longer it won't be a problem. The basement's too dark for most people's taste.' She broke off, afraid she was talking too much. 'You've checked with Ollie's friends?'

'I don't know who they are.' Erin was still thinking about the list of names in Claudia's desk. 'I thought you might.'

Jennie's fingers were back, fiddling with her hair. 'To

be honest, Erin, even though Claudia and I were good friends, in some ways I didn't know her that well. She could be quite secretive. No, not secretive, mysterious. Oh, what am I saying? She was always so amusing, such good company.'

Didn't know her that well, or didn't like her? Erin remembered Claudia once saying if everyone liked you that meant you were boring. Surely not, she had said, although she knew what she meant. Someone might be so bland there was nothing to dislike. Bland – what a horrible word. Certainly, there had been nothing bland about Claudia.

'Other research students,' Jennie suggested. 'Ollie must have friends at the university. And surely Jon could help. He brings Maeve for her classes, doesn't he? Have you met her mother? Claudia knew her, I think, but whenever I see Maeve she's with Jon.' She tipped back her chair and closed her eyes. 'Ben had an audition yesterday. Telly ad for some disgusting slimming drink.'

'Slimming drink? Wouldn't they want someone fatter?' Suddenly, Erin was so tired she could hardly sit up straight. The strings of pink and mauve lights blurred and she turned her head towards a woman with a tiny baby then looked away when she realised she was breastfeeding.

'I'm older than he is.'

'Ben? Yes, you said.'

Jennie gave a hollow laugh. 'And I look it.'

'Actually, you don't.' So was that what was on her mind? Worry that Ben would run off with a young actress? Erin had an idea he depended on Jennie far too much to do such a thing, but who could tell? Stay with Jennie and have an affair on the side. She could hardly ask if that was what was worrying her, especially when it could be something entirely different. Something she knew about Claudia? No, Ben said the change in Jennie had happened several weeks ago.

'Want something to eat?' Jennie looked as though she was finding their conversation a strain. 'What about a mushroom tartlet or one of those mozzarella—'

'You have something, if you like.' On Erin's left, cards and brochures advertised a struggling theatre company, a Pilates class, a guy who would come to your house and repair your computer, and someone with little knowledge of the English language, advertising for a bed-sit. 'Did Claudia have any foreign friends? I mean, people with foreign sounding names?'

'Don't think so.' Jennie was gathering crumbs into a little pile. 'She had a hang up about not having a degree. Ridiculous, but you know Claudia. Incidentally, Ben would be the husband.' She was referring back to his audition. 'They want someone ordinary looking so I expect they thought Ben was too handsome. The wife's the one who's overweight.'

'Typical.' Erin managed a smile and Jennie thought talking about the audition had cheered her up, and was unable to hide her relief.

'You poor thing, but you shouldn't feel what's going on at the hospital is your responsibility.'

'If Ollie doesn't come back . . .'

'An orphan. I know. But apparently there are loads of people wanting to adopt.'

'To get back to Ollie's friends, Jon mentioned a student, ex-student, called Hoshi.'

'Oh, yes,' she said vaguely, but it was clear from her expression she knew perfectly well who Erin was talking about.

'You know him?'

'Don't really *know* him. Ben does, I think. Fantastic looking. Chinese. No, Japanese. Yes, Japanese, that's right.'

Ava had returned with the order and was nodding in the direction of the girl with a shaved head. 'Already smashed two cups and spilled decaffeinated all over the floor. Still, beggars can't be choosers.'

Erin took a deep breath. 'Ava?'

'Yes, my darling.'

'Do you know Hoshi?'

'Hmm, for a time, he and your sister were thick as thieves. He helped with the loft conversion, painted the walls.' Ava pulled a face. 'Nose out of joint when Ollie came on the scene. At least I imagine that's what happened. Your poor sister was a magnet for good-looking young men.'

As they watched Ava move away, Jennie returned to the subject of her new tenant. 'The thing is, she looks far too well-to-do to be renting my basement. I suppose it's because I agreed to a very short let. Ms Jones. First name Stella. Suits her. I'm not sure why. Tall, getting on for six foot I'd say, and she wasn't wearing heels. Red hair, natural looking, could be her own. Oh, and ultra-confident, piercing eyes and never smiles, you know the type. She asked the quickest route to the university and when I explained it had buildings all over the city, and inquired which department she wanted, she said, no problem, she would look it up online.'

'You're sure she's not a student?'

'Certain. Yes, I know there are plenty of mature ones but she's smartly-dressed, clothes look expensive. Main thing – she paid cash in advance, can't complain about that.' She yawned without bothering to put her hand over her mouth. 'Just the type Ben would fall for so I'm

66

keeping him well away. Come round with me sometime and take a look.'

'At the basement flat or your new tenant?'

'I tell you what, you can come with me when I take some stuff for the kitchen. Oh, Erin, I wish there was something I could do. At least Ollie's disappearance means you'll have the final say about the baby. I suppose it'll be taken into care.'

'I looked up Claudia's jewellery stall at the market, but they said she'd given it up.'

'Really? When did she do that?' Jennie was running her finger round the rim of her cup.

'Gave it up a few weeks ago which is odd because she used to leave the house as though she was on her way there.'

Jennie yawned again. 'Can't help, I'm afraid.'

She was lying or, at the very least, concealing something she knew. 'You said Ava had been spreading rumours. What about? What kind of rumours?'

Jennie smiled, but the tension between them was palpable. 'Oh, you know what she's like, loves to gossip. Once told me about a pig that fell from an upstairs window and killed a passer-by. No, it was a story. Actually, it might have been true. If someone dies unexpectedly, people always want an explanation. Sometimes it's just bad luck. No, sorry, I put that badly. What I meant . . .' She ran out of words and pushed back her chair, standing up and hitching her bag over her shoulder. 'Come on, did you walk? If so, I'll drive you home. Not far, I know, but it looks like rain.'

As they walked back to her car, she kept up a steady stream of chatter. Ben's audition, Ava's pink and mauve outfits, the flats she let to students. Anything, to avoid Claudia and the accident. Erin kept quiet, partly because she had nothing to add, but mainly because the time at the café had felt like a conspiracy of silence, an act devised by Ava and Jennie to stop her asking questions. They knew something, either about Claudia, or was it where Ollie was hiding out? Or the accident. Did the two of them suspect there was nothing accidental about Claudia's death?

The same thought had been on Erin's mind, but only when she woke in the night. In her more rational moments, she was certain one of the protesters must have unscrewed the scaffolding and it had slipped out of his hand. Almost certain.

9

The place would do for a student but it was a long time since Stella had seen such a shithole. Fitted carpet so mucky she wanted to rip it up and chuck it out with the rubbish. When she arrived, the flat had smelled of some disgusting air freshener and, in spite of the weather, she had been obliged to open every window. Thin curtains covered them with a hideous geometric pattern in black and red, and, on the wall, a faded reproduction of Van Gogh's Yellow Chair, an insult to the original. Maybe you could buy a job lot, like a yard of books, all classics of course, although the books in this place were probably the landlady's rejects: *A Murder has been Announced, Over My Dead Body, Final Curtain.* So she had a taste for crime. That figured.

Cracked lino in the bathroom, plus a dripping tap and a window that let in a howling draught. Contacting the landlady was a waste of time. Once landlords got their hands on the cash they couldn't give a fuck what state the property was in.

With a small degree of effort, she could have found somewhere better. What was it that had made her settle for a damp, dingy basement, approached by dangerous iron steps that would have needed sanding down and repainting a decade ago? She liked the place, relished it, because it was all she deserved, a self-imposed prison, a punishment cell.

The rest of the house was deserted. But not for much longer. In a week or two the students would be back and there would be loud music, shouting, people returning at all hours, vomit on the doorstep. Not that she had ever been a student, but everyone knew they were over privileged, irresponsible, and short on consideration for people who worked for a living.

Yesterday she had felt like shit and realised she must have picked up a bug, the gastric kind that tears at your guts and leaves you weak and depressed. All day she had lain on the lumpy mattress, crawling to the bathroom and back with her head splitting, not sure if she was boiling hot or freezing cold.

Today she had dragged herself out of bed, made some toast and a mug of weak tea, and by lunchtime was virtually restored to normal, and determined not to waste a minute more. She needed to catch up with her clients, but this evening would do, forwarding packages with advice on publicity and marketing. The business was thriving – she might have to hire another assistant when she returned to London – but just now she had something more important to attend to, something she had put off for far too long. Was it a mistake? Would she return home, full of regret, feeling worse than before? Too late to have such misgivings. When in doubt, don't dither, act!

Back in London, she had checked the phone book but without success. He must be ex-directory. The university website had his name, but obviously not his home address. If she could wangle her way into the building she was sure she could find it. The best way would be to say she hoped to talk to the students about job prospects. These days, the phrase "job prospects" was like gold dust. They would ask for her credentials, but her business card should do the trick. Then what? His address was unlikely to be stuck on a noticeboard and if she made inquiries it would arouse suspicion. Unless she asked the right questions.

In spite of the cloud cover, or perhaps because of it, the temperature had risen and it was unnaturally warm for January. Snatching her raincoat from the hook, she slammed the door behind her, ran up the steps, being careful not to catch her heels in the wrought iron holes, and set off, feeling a fair bit better than she had expected.

Beyond the swing doors, she could see a porter in uniform, standing by a turnstile. Now what? No use pretending she had an appointment. Either the porter would want to see something in writing or he would phone through to check she was expected. A student was approaching the building, carrying so many books he was almost bound to drop them. Stella lifted off the top three and he mumbled his thanks.

'I expect you know most of the people who work here.'

The student, a skinny guy, with a baseball cap, asked who she wanted, and when she mentioned a name it worked like magic. 'I don't think he's in today.'

'Oh, you know him, do you? No, he's working at home, asked me to go round there but I've mislaid the address.'

'Right.' It was clear he had no knowledge of a home address, or if he did he had no intention of divulging it. 'The office might be able to help.'

'Yes. Thanks.' But trying the "lost address" stunt with the office would cut no ice.

Returning to her car, she crunched up a couple of mints; they did nothing to satisfy her craving for nicotine, and closed her eyes, testing to make sure her headache had not returned. What next? Department websites were useless. Nothing personal on them, just lists of academics, boasting about how many papers they had written, and how many conferences they had attended. Think. Use your brain. But the bug had left her feeling befuddled.

Maybe a walk would do the trick, but first she had to find somewhere to leave the car. The meter had run out, so had her change, and she was obliged to drive round until she spotted a multi-storey. The soulless building depressed her even more. Sharp turns. Concrete pillars. Badly parked four-wheel drives that stuck out from their narrow spaces. The lift smelled of piss so she decided on the stairs, even though she was on the fifth floor, and when she finally emerged into the fresh air, she realised she had left her bed too soon and was still running a temperature.

Gazing all about her to try to get her bearings, she decided to walk to the main university building. She had seen it online, a grand-looking place with a great hall, where the students, dressed in black gowns, and with boards on their heads, were handed their degree certificates. She passed a seat, next to a sycamore tree, and sat down for a few minutes, staring up at the horizon that marked the edge of the city. What was the matter with her? There must be a better way to find his address. He was still working in Bristol – her online investigations had established that much – but he could be living anywhere, close to the university or several miles away.

Two of the seat's slats were missing and on one of the remaining ones someone had scored *Chaz fucks Sara*. Chaz! Stella pictured a spotty kid with about as much finesse as a rutting stag. On a seat nearby, a girl with long, straggly hair was giving a bottle to an infant, dressed in jeans and baseball boots. Poor kid, saddled with a baby that would turn into a demanding toddler and, later, a gawky teenager that would give her cheek, not gratitude. *I never asked to be born.* A middle-aged woman, with the uniform of a well-known store under her coat, hurried past. Her feet, in their black high-heeled boots, were enormous, and she had an arse to match.

Pull yourself together. Concentrate. Don't waste your energy on harmless strangers. Leaving the uncomfortable bench, she strolled on, past a Thai takeaway, a kebab house, and a shop selling sexy underwear. All her life, she had tried to put head before heart, so why was she here now? Because she had to know. Because it was becoming an obsession. And when she discovered the truth . . . ? But it was far too soon to think about that.

Ten minutes later, she reached the building she had been looking for. Heavy doors that had been fixed open and, since groups of people were going in and coming out, it seemed there was no restriction on entering the place. No porters in sight so she walked straight through and stood for a moment in the stone-tiled foyer. Where to start? Who to ask? Her whole body felt hot and shaky, a leftover from the bug or the result of her increasing frustration? Rubbing her forehead, she scanned the walls, stopping abruptly when a poster, propped up on an easel, caught her eye.

The speaker whose lecture it advertised was an American biologist, a television personality, popular among people with a smattering of scientific knowledge, who liked to scatter "clever" books on their coffee tables. At any other time, Stella would have curled her lip, but surely it was just the kind of event he would attend. An open lecture it said, in two days' time. Only an off-chance but the best one yet and, abandoning all rational thought, she stood with her eyes firmly focussed on the poster, and with all her might willed him to be there.

10

The illustrations were progressing, but far too slowly. For a short time, it took Erin's mind off Ollie and the baby, then she lost concentration and pushed aside whatever she was working on.

Since it was obvious why Ollie had disappeared, she was surprised the police had made inquiries, and even more surprised when she received a phone call to tell her they had checked with his mother in Norfolk, but she claimed not to have seen her son for over a year. They would keep her informed, they said, and Erin wondered if they shared her suspicions about the accident, but had no evidence, no witnesses. Or had they been merely going through the motions? People were allowed to go missing, but the particular circumstances of Ollie's disappearance had obliged them to make a few token inquiries – for the sake of his unborn baby.

Her life was divided between the illustrations, her visits to the hospital and Maeve's lessons. Somehow, Maeve's presence, and the questions she asked, was helping to keep her anxiety under control. *It's going to be all right, Erin, I know it is, and I've got magic powers. I think I might have because I wished for some new jeans and Mum bought me some, except they're pink and I don't like pink.*

The baby had reached twenty-five weeks gestation and, according to the book Erin had bought, it would be at its most active when its mother was trying to sleep. The irony of this was hard to bear. Two weeks since the accident and Ollie's disappearance. Where *was* he? Ever since she found the roll of notes in Claudia's desk, it had been on her mind that the police might have some other motive for wanting to trace him. Supposing he and Claudia had been involved in something illegal. Did Ava know about it? Or Jennie? If they did, it could account for the way they both avoided her eyes.

Her phone beeped. A text from a friend in London. How's things? Miss you xxx. Lindsey, someone she had seen most weeks – they had both enjoyed ice-skating – even though Declan had objected. Erin missed her too. Would they keep in touch? For a time, then less and less. When she moved into Claudia's house it was not just Declan she had left behind. When she felt up to it, she would spend a day or two in London, seeing her friends, but not yet. It would mean long explanations, followed by warm expressions of sympathy, that ought to be a comfort, but just now would be something else to deal with. Was she a coward, shutting herself away? No, that was unfair. She had Maeve, and Jon when he could spare the time, and Jennie and Ava, although why did she feel they were not being honest with her?

Her thoughts returned to Ollie. By now, he would know he had lost the right to decide what happened to the baby, and he would also know her decision, in consultation with the doctors, would be to try and save it. For a while, she had visited the unit every day but after a time it felt pointless. No, not pointless, masochistic, sitting by Claudia's bed, pretending she knew her older sister was keeping watch over her. Should a problem arise with the baby someone would let her know, but so far everything appeared to be going according to plan. She worried constantly, but there was nothing she could do, except wait.

Earlier in the day, she had attempted to tidy up Claudia's front garden, cutting back a sprawling shrub and picking up rubbish that had blown in from the pavement. Gardening was supposed to be therapeutic and, if it was her garden, and she was going to be there in the summer, she might have felt quite enthusiastic. Was the pile in the corner a compost heap or just a collection of weeds and leaves? She gave it a kick and something small and grey scuttled away, just as an elderly man she knew by sight, passed the house and slowed down.

'Good morning.' He had given her a questioning look. She suspected he had heard rumours and hoped she would supply him with some interesting information. He looked harmless enough, just bored and lonely. Dressed in a gabardine raincoat, and wearing driving gloves, there was one like him in most streets, someone with nothing better to do than check up on his neighbours.

'Colder today.' He jerked his head in the direction of the adjoining house. 'Gone abroad.'

'Yes, I know.'

'Risky, leaving your house unoccupied. People notice.'

'Yes, I expect they do.'

'Know them, do you?'

'No.' And before he could say any more, Erin had picked up Claudia's rusty secateurs and returned to the house.

Sometimes she wished she was back in London. Bristol's appeal had been because Claudia lived there. Not that the two of them had been close, but Erin had hoped for ready-made friends, Claudia's friends. A vain hope, as it had turned out. She thought about Lindsey, who had lived nearby, closer to Wimbledon Common, and was always glad to see her, and her other friend, Sonya, who worked in a bar but wanted to be an actress. What were they doing now? They knew nothing about Claudia's accident and probably thought Erin was enjoying her new life, glad to be free of Declan. If Lindsey had lived closer, she might confided in her. Not Sonya, the slightest thing made her burst into tears, and she never listened, not like Lindsey did. Perhaps she would phone Lindsey, but not today, not yet.

She had never felt so alone.

Jon was with her when she received the news. He had turned up to apologise, he said, for the way he had rushed off after he collected Maeve. 'A visiting academic. It was a question of getting her home then returning to the department in time for the weekly seminar.'

Erin kept her eyes focussed on the chipmunk's bushy tail. 'There's no need to explain.'

He ran a hand through the thick, wavy hair that made him look even taller. 'I could tell you needed to talk.'

'I talked to Jennie. And Ava.'

'Ava at Ava's Place?'

'She and Claudia were friends.' He had made the café sound like a den of thieves. 'She described her and Ollie as a golden couple.'

Jon ignored this, picking up a pot of pens and pencils. 'I wanted to talk about Maeve but it's not a good time, you're busy.'

'No more than usual.' She returned to her painting. 'Look, I'm sorry about last time but it was Maeve who brought up the subject of abortion and I don't like fobbing children off with rubbish answers.'

She expected him to say, no, of course not, but he had no interest in her conversation with his daughter. 'When

77

she was born . . . they were worried. They did tests. The doctors did tests and she was transferred to special care.'

'Yes, you told me.'

'Her breathing. We thought it was her breathing. No, not just her breathing. They take measurements. There's a normal range. They weren't sure, said it was too soon, but I knew something was wrong.'

Erin waited for the explanation that never materialised.

'I had a job that was only going to last for a few months so when I was offered a permanent post down here, I jumped at it. It meant Maeve would have some stability, a settled home. She's doing well, wouldn't you say?'

'Yes, I would. There doesn't seem much wrong with her to me.'

'Apart from the allergies.'

'Really? Not cats? If she's allergic to animal hair you should have—'

'Blueberries and plums. They bring her out in a rash. Diana's quite careful with her diet. Too careful I sometimes think, but she's fanatical about healthy food.'

'Nothing wrong with that.'

'No.' His eyes met hers and she noticed, for the first time, that his were grey, not blue like Maeve's, and he had a tiny mole over his left eyebrow. 'When Maeve started school we were afraid she wouldn't be able to keep up, but it's only Maths that's a problem.'

'Plenty of people have trouble with Maths. No, all right, not you. How's your research going? Has someone taken over whatever Ollie was working on? What will happen if he doesn't get in touch with you? Did he have a grant? I've no idea how higher degrees are funded these days.'

Ignoring her questions, he continued on the healthy

78

food theme. 'Diana works on Saturday afternoons, at a health food shop. She believes in herbal remedies.'

'Unless it's something serious. Some of them seem to help if you're getting a cold. Ginger tea. I don't like it much but—'

'There's something I need to tell you.'

'Go on then. Something about Maeve?'

'Another time. You're working.' His hand was on the half open door. 'Look, I'm sorry.'

For what? For interrupting her work or for starting to tell her something then changing his mind? Was he really worried about Maeve? Being a little clumsy was not that important, and plenty of people were hopeless at catching a ball. Part of her wanted to reassure him, but another part wanted to goad, make him lost his temper. Anything would be better than the blanket of dejection that seemed to have descended on him, and the trouble with blankets of dejection, they tend to envelop everything around them.

'Did Ava say anything?' He had moved back into the room.

'What about? Oh, she said the student – ex-student – called Hoshi helped to decorate this place. The loft had already been converted but when Claudia agreed to let me come and stay for a while—'

'I wouldn't take too much notice of what Ava says. She tends to dramatize, thinks up something that will make a good story, and embellishes it.'

'No wonder she and Claudia got on so well.' He was leaning over her shoulder and she could feel his breath on her neck, his close proximity was making her hand shake so that she had to make the chipmunk's eye a fraction larger than she had intended.

'He worked at Ava's Place for time. Washing up, serving food, I'm not sure.'

'Hoshi did? I wonder why Ava didn't say?'

He sighed and she turned round, angrily, then noticed how weary he looked and relented. Tiny lines spread from the corners of his eyes and there were deeper lines between them. How had he felt about Claudia's death? If what he had told her was true, they had not been friends – he had only met her two or three times. All the same, the accident, and Ollie's subsequent disappearance, must have been a shock.

'What were you going to tell me?'

He took a step back. 'I thought Ollie might have gone home, to his mother.'

'He hasn't. The police checked.'

He nodded, but his thoughts had moved on to something else and, by the look of his face, he was not going to tell her what it was. The first time they met, he had struck her as someone she would be able to talk to, someone she could trust. Someone who listened, without interrupting, and gave the impression he had been through some bad experiences and come out the other side with an increased understanding of people's pain. She had warmed to him, not just because he was the antithesis of Declan, or because he was good looking and reminded her of her father. There was more to attraction than that.

He was back, with his hand on the door. 'How's it going at the hospital?'

'As well as can be expected. Sorry.' She had not intended to sound so brisk and matter of fact. 'It'll be several weeks before the baby can be born. I'm hoping by then Ollie will have returned.'

Jon cleared his throat, and she held her breath. His parting remark was going to be something important. Something about Claudia. 'Feel like going down the road for a cup of tea?' he said. 'It would do you good to get out of here.'

She controlled a sigh. 'Not Ava's Place.'

'No.' He took her coat from the hook on the back of the door and, as he passed it to her, their hands brushed. No, she thought, no definitely not that. Never, ever again would she become involved with a married man. An agonising memory returned – when Declan told her his wife was pregnant. *It might not be mine, Erin, actually I don't think it is.* But it could be, she had said, and he had shrugged, and she had known the bitter truth. *She tricked me, Erin, must have.* No use pointing out how he had told her his marriage was over, dead, and he was in the process of getting divorced . . .

'I'm sorry, Erin.'

'What about?' Had Jon said something important and she had been too absorbed with the past to take it in?

'Everything. There's so much I want to tell you but . . .'

Someone was leaning on the front door bell.

'Probably the meter reader,' she said. 'It's hard to know what to do about Claudia's bills, or the rest of her mail. Check in case it's something important, or keep it for Ollie.'

Running down the two flights of stairs, she opened the front door, and the conversation between the two police officers stopped abruptly, their faces turning into expressionless masks. The middle-aged one had short bristly hair. The other was a woman.

'Can we come in, please?' The female officer reeled off their names.

'Is it Ollie?' Erin's throat constricted. 'Not Claudia?'

'No, not your sister.'

'In here.' Erin held open the door to Claudia's living room and, when Jon hovered in the doorway, snapped at him to go on ahead. 'This is Mr Easton. He and Ollie work together.' She gestured to them to sit down and they waited for her and Jon to do the same. The room felt unlived in and the mantelpiece had a layer of dust, and a spider had spun a web in the corner above the television.

'I don't wish to alarm you unnecessarily.' The policewoman appeared to be the senior of the two, or perhaps they had decided the occasion needed a woman's touch. 'But the body of a young man has been found and it matches the description of Oliver Mitchell. You gave us a photograph but it was not a very clear one so I'm afraid it's impossible to be certain.'

'Where? Where was he found?' The photo was one Claudia had taken when they were in a club. Flashing lights blurred part of his face. A man, with a mane of white hair, had his arm round him and Ollie was looking faintly embarrassed.

'In a barn, an old farm building,' the policewoman said, 'close to a golf club. It hadn't been there very long.'

11

The redbrick building was next to a patch of rough grass. A single tree had shed its leaves, but the sun was shining and the expression *glad to be alive* ran through Erin's mind and for an instant she was filled with guilt that she was alive and the rest of her family were dead. Except for the baby. She was her closest relative now and she desperately needed her to survive.

Outside the entrance to the mortuary, a couple of cars had been parked so carelessly there was no space for anyone else. The policewoman glanced in her mirror and swung round, pulling up in a "no parking" area next to a battered grey van, with whatever logo had been on its side, painted out a darker shade of grey.

'All right?' The policewoman said her name was DS Smith. 'Maria, please call me Maria'. That was the only piece of information she had provided during their short journey. That and the fact she had hoped Erin would be accompanied by a friend or relative.

'I prefer to do this on my own.'

'Fair enough.' Then, afraid she had sounded a little harsh. 'Yes, I can understand how you feel. You've been through a lot these past few weeks.'

It was Ollie, she was sure of it, and seeing him, facing the reality of his death would be unbearable but also, if she was honest with herself, almost a relief. She was worn out, speculating where he might have gone, and whether he was dead or alive. No, that was wrong. Not a relief. His death would turn Claudia's accident into a double tragedy.

She could have let Jon come with her to the mortuary. Someone to share the ordeal. When she said she wanted to go on her own, his face had fallen – perhaps he thought he had more right than she did to identify Ollie's body – but if it was Ollie, it was partly her fault. She should have gone along with what he wanted for Claudia and the baby. But how could she?

Already – she would not have admitted this to anyone – she was planning what would happen to the baby. She would keep her, love her, teach her how to draw and paint, bring her up as her own. But supposing they stopped her, *they* being social workers. She would have to be vetted and the fact that she was single would go against her. Or would it? Single women were allowed to adopt these days. But how could she afford to look after a child? If Claudia had not made a will what would happen to the house? Was it mortgaged up to the hilt? She ought to check, look in her desk again, search through her papers.

Whatever she found, she would sort it out somehow. For the sake of the baby. Her baby. Unless someone else came forward, claiming to be the father.

'Right then.' DS Smith sprang out of the car and opened the passenger door. 'I should warn you, when we go inside there'll be an unpleasant chemical smell. If you feel faint let me know. There may be a short wait but we can get some coffee from the machine.'

Don't worry about me, Erin wanted to say, I'm used to chemical smells. Much of my time is spent with the sick and dying, apart from when I retreat to the safety of my flat. Was her flat safe? Lately, Claudia's house had felt empty and inhospitable, and at night she heard sounds that could come from the street but could equally well mean someone had got in and was prowling about. Clicks and creaks. Tapping noises. A branch banging against a window? Except there was no wind. She thought about the basement flat that Jennie had let to the "smartly-dressed woman from London", and wondered if a basement would be preferable, and thought it might be.

As soon as they entered the mortuary building, questions flooded into her head. Who would show her the body? Would it be pulled out on a freezer tray? Would there be blood, injuries, or would only the head be visible?

DS Smith gave her a half-smile, appropriate to the situation. 'This way. I'll tell them who we are and then we wait to be called. There's always a short delay.'

Erin had expected to feel fear. Fear that it was Ollie or fear of death itself? Her squeamishness about dead mice and birds could be seen as a fear of death. Claudia had laughed about it. *Honestly, Erin, you're so sensitive. It's only a dead bird.* Or a mouse. Or once it had been a rat.

The waiting room was too large. Surely only one person at a time was allowed into the building. Instead of the dread she expected, she felt nothing. All her emotions had closed down as though she had been drugged. It was a task to be done. She was a character in one of those gruesome television series, walking down a tiled corridor, pausing while someone came out and ushered her into an ice cold laboratory.

Naturally, it was nothing like television. They sat in the waiting room for what felt like an age and she started to panic as she struggled to remember what Ollie looked like. Fair hair, small nose, firm chin. Did he have a firm chin? And what colour were his eyes? Brown, she thought, or grey, but they would be closed, at least she hoped they would. She had only known him for a few months, and had never studied his face closely, but even if you were unable to recall the details of how someone looked, you recognised them instantly, even from quite a distance, the shape of their body, the way they walked.

Ollie would be still, lying on his back with skin as white as dough. Why dough? Why had she thought of dough? Because no one's skin was pure white, not even when they were dead.

She wanted to ask if he had carried a donor card. He had a social conscience – it was one of the things Claudia loved about him – but he was too young to imagine his own death.

'Do you know how he died?' she asked, her voice sounding too loud in the silent room.

DS Smith hesitated. 'He was found hanged.'

'Oh.' It was not what Erin had been expecting. An overdose. She realised she had assumed he would have taken a lethal dose of painkillers. 'So it was definitely suicide.'

'It looks that way.'

Looks that way? But it was too late to ask any more. A man, wearing a white jacket had come to fetch them and, picking up her bag, she swallowed hard, trying to compose herself. She agreed to be escorted to the end of another tiled corridor, where they entered a small room with a bright light and a single bench, and where a body lay, covered by a sheet. The walls were bare. Of course they were. What kind of pictures could there be? More stupid thoughts raced through her brain. Did some poor person come in early and clean the place each morning? How many more corpses were lying in the freezer compartments?

After a few moments, to allow her to acclimatise she supposed, she was asked if she was ready and she nodded, watching as the sheet was drawn back to reveal the head and neck, and the top of pathetically bony shoulders.

His neck was marked – by a rope, or had he made an improvised noose from his clothes – but his face was smooth and unblemished and he looked so young and, like Claudia in her hospital bed, if he had not been so unnaturally still, he could have been asleep. Erin forced herself to study his face, although there was no need. His hair stood up in tufts and there were freckles on his nose.

It was not Ollie.

As she turned away, shaking her head, it occurred to her they thought she was too shocked to speak, and she felt obliged to take another heart-breaking look. 'It's not him,' she said, 'it's not Ollie.'

'Are you sure?'

'Certain.' Her voice cracked and DS Smith reached out a hand as though she feared she was going to faint.

'Thank you for your help.' She nodded to the pathologist. 'Come on, I'll drive you home.'

12

Stella had expected the lecture to be well attended but it had never occurred to her it could be sold out. With any luck, if she attached herself to a group, the ticket checker would lose count of how many people she had let through. But the gimlet-eyed woman looked like she was well up on that ploy.

Now what? If she waited there were sure to be a few empty seats. People who had failed to turn up. Even so, they might not let her in and she would have to walk about in the wind and rain until it was over, and could well be wasting her time since there was no guarantee he was there.

A voice behind her called her name and she spun round, nerves jangling, even, for one irrational moment, thinking it was him. But whoever it was had been talking to someone else whose name wasn't even Stella.

'Bella!' the girl yelled again. 'Sorry, can't make it. That guy I told you about.' She broke off, giggling. 'See you.'

Her friend looked daggers and Stella jumped in with an offer to buy the spare ticket.

'Have it.'

'How much?'

The girl called Bella shrugged. 'Forget it. I didn't pay, she did.'

'Thanks.' Stella waited in the queue and entered the

hall, eyes darting about until she spotted an empty seat in the back row where she would have a clear view of the whole audience. Would she recognise him? He could look different, but she doubted he would have changed very much. His clothes perhaps, but even those were likely to be the same. Jeans, jacket, white T-shirt or, at this time of year, it was more likely to be a dark sweater. A creature of habit. One of the things she had both liked about him, but also found a little irritating. As people grew older they tended to become more fixed in their ways. Was that how she had become? Surely not.

Once the majority of people were sitting down, she focussed her eyes on the front row, tracking from left to right, pausing at any likely candidate, making sure no one was missed out. When she reached the third row, she thought he saw him but the head turned and "he" turned out to be a middle-aged woman with an aquiline nose. The hall smelled of people who had come in from the rain and Stella wondered idly how many umbrellas would be left behind, calculating it would be at least a dozen. Most of them would never be claimed since their owners were too busy, or too rich. Her head had started to throb and when she pushed up her sleeve to check her watch she found the lecture should have started six and a half minutes ago.

In the fourth row from the front, a bunch of students were standing up, changing places. People waved to friends in other parts of the hall. An obese man immediately in front of her kept roaring with laughter and tipping his chair back until it was as much as she could do not to tell him to shut the fuck up. The guy sitting next to her smelled of sweat. He whispered an endearment to his girlfriend and she responded by squeezing his thigh through his filthy jeans. A passably attractive girl with pale hair and eyes to match. Surely she could have done better than that.

Two men rose from the front row, one slightly built and dressed in a suit, collar and tie, the other broader and taller, an archetypal professor with unkempt hair, steel-rimmed spectacles and a beard. As soon as the room was quiet, "the suit" introduced the great man, providing a glowing biography and informing the audience, how lucky they were to be in the company of a world famous authority on the subject.

For all Stella knew, the lecture was cutting edge neurobiology. As well as being delivered in a deep, gravelly voice, the words came up in power point on a giant screen at the front. Stella took in little, giving all her attention to the audience, checking each row again, this time from right to left.

The great man had a carefully perfected style of speaking, sometimes slow, ponderous, sometimes bursts of gunfire. Stella shielded her eyes from the white screen, afraid it's changing messages, picked up by her peripheral vision, would bring on a migraine. Every two months or so her vision became distorted by a semi-circle of jagged lines that prefaced a debilitating attack. Two quickly administered painkillers usually knocked it on the head before it got a hold, but now and again she was laid low for hours, even days, the last thing she needed just now.

Once she had scanned all but two of the rows, she realised she would have to start at the front all over again, and the thought that he might not be there made her face and neck grow hot with frustration. He must be. Why wouldn't he be? It was his kind of lecture, his area of expertise. How had she missed him? Maybe she needed her eyes tested. She pictured herself with gunmetal rimmed designer glasses and rather liked the image. Concentrate. Try the front rows again. Knowing him, he would have arrived early.

When the lecture finally came to an end, "the suit" announced that there was time for a few questions. Hands shot up and a woman in the front row was selected. Her question – she had a high-pitched upper class voice – was concerned with functional circuits in the brain. Searching in her pocket for a couple of painkillers – she never left home without them – Stella popped them in her mouth, swallowing hard, a technique she had acquired for times when no water was available, and experienced the familiar, mildly unpleasant after-taste.

The body odour guy on her right had started to cough and a moment later he stood up, and so did his girlfriend, and so did Stella, ostensibly to let them pass but her aim was to squeeze behind her chair and lean against the wall. It was fortunate she was so tall.

One question followed by another, until the guy in charge announced that he could only take two more. No hands went up and a ripple of conversation broke out. Any moment now, proceedings would be brought to a close, the audience would make a stampede for the exit, and it would be impossible to spot him. What did it matter? He wasn't there. She had endured and hour and a half of boredom for nothing.

Then she saw him.

Halfway up the hall, sitting between two girls. As she watched, he stood up, waiting patiently, characteristically, for the people on his left to move. How the fuck had she missed him? Because the girls had kept leaning across him to talk to one another. Wouldn't it have made more sense to change places? He was alone and that was a relief, but in a few minutes' time he would go out in the street where he would merge with the throng and she would lose him. Snatching her beanie from her coat pocket, she pulled it down over her eyebrows, wound her scarf round the lower half of her face, and pushed her way out of the main door, moving quickly to the place she had selected earlier, round the corner of the building, where she would be hidden but still have a near perfect view.

The rain had stopped but he was walking fast while looking all about him, almost as if he had anticipated being followed. Had he seen her? Plenty of people had red hair and she had been right at the back, out of sight. It was dark, and she was the last person in the world he would be expecting to see. Her car was parked on a meter, it had taken all her change and was still in danger of running out, but his could be anywhere, in a multi-storey or several blocks away where there was no need to pay. Or he might be within walking distance of where he lived, or he might jump onto a bus. With her eyes fixed on his receding figure, she climbed into her car, did a lightning U-turn, and began slowly moving up the hill, ignoring the hooting drivers behind her.

Ahead of her, he crossed the road and started down a side street, where she was in time to see him unlock a bike, attached to a lamppost. Now what? She had gone past the turning and the traffic was far too thick to risk another U-turn. Perhaps he lived on the other side of the gorge, in Leigh Woods or even in a village a few miles out of the city. If it was a village, surely he would use his car, except he had always been a fitness fanatic. Before she left the basement, she should have studied her map more carefully. Now, she had lost her sense of direction.

Because of the traffic lane she had selected, she was obliged to take an exit to the left. Did it lead to the Suspension Bridge? She crossed a mini-roundabout and carried straight on, following the car in front for want of anything better to do. Quite soon, it turned to the right and a few minutes later a large expanse of grass came into view. The edge of the Downs? Ahead of her, she thought she could see the back light of a bike, and beyond it, the bridge. The city was overflowing with cyclists, but fewer of them at this time of night.

When she reached the bridge, she discovered there was a toll and she was forced to hold up other drivers as she searched for some money. Come on, come on, if it was him, he would have reached the other side by now. Dropping a coin in the box, she crossed over, glancing down at the eerily lit up water, then drove on, taking the next turning on the left, which she calculated would take her back to the centre. A waste of time, but not quite since she now knew for certain he was in the city and rode a bike, and those two small pieces of information were enough to convince her she was going to accomplish her mission.

13

Erin had slept badly, but still woke early, and lying in bed meant her brain raced. Who was the man in the mortuary and why had no one come forward to identify him? Thousands of people went missing every year and now Ollie was one of them. Was it because he suspected the baby was not his? Perhaps he knew for certain and was afraid of being saddled with someone else's child. But if Ollie was not the father, who was? Hoshi, the ex-student who had decorated Claudia's loft? For all Erin knew, he was only one of half a dozen young men Claudia had collected.

Speculations were useless with so little information to go on. She decided to have a bath. It was silly, if understandable, that so far she had not made use of Claudia's bathroom. It needed updating but, compared with what she had in the loft, was luxurious. The bath was surrounded by sea blue tiles and, catching a glimpse of her reflection in the mirror above the basin, she was shocked at how strained she looked. A deep, hot bath would do her good. No curtain, but the glass was opaque so all anyone could see would be the vague, wobbly outline of a naked body.

Pulling open the cupboard on the wall, she was surprised to see how much medication it contained. The usual painkillers, plus tubes of antiseptic cream and sting relief, indigestion mixture, cough syrup, fast acting gel for mouth ulcers, a roll of white bandage and two thermometers. Erin's thoughts rushed forward to when the baby was born. What would she need? Cream to prevent nappy rash, special shampoo designed not to sting your eyes, and she thought there was something called baby oil. She pictured herself swaddling the baby in a warm towel and carrying her to a changing mat where she could dress her in a fresh sleep suit.

Please God, let her be all right.

Lying back in the pleasantly scented water, she attempted to clear her head of its confusion. She would have her hair cut, that always made her feel better, and buy a warmer coat. What with? In London she had supplemented her income from the illustrations with a part-time job in a local gift shop. Perhaps she could find one in Bristol. No, not yet, not until . . . She thought about the roll of notes in Claudia's desk and almost convinced herself she had a right to it, but when Ollie returned he would expect the money to be intact, and telling him she had needed it for bills would be a feeble excuse for what in fact would be theft. *If* Ollie returned,

Claudia had not stinted herself on bathroom preparations. Transparent green soap, chamomile bath oil, three different brands of shampoo and two of conditioner. There was even a yellow duck with a red beak. Too soon for the baby so Claudia must have been given it as present. By Ollie?

After washing herself with the soap, Erin relaxed for several minutes, then stepped out of the water and reached for a towel, only to jump back into the water when she saw a shadowy shape outside the window. She was on the first floor. No one could climb up that high. Unless it was window cleaner with a ladder. Would Claudia have employed a window cleaner? If she had, it was the first time he had put in an appearance. She must have imagined it. A bird had flown past. Yes, that was what it had been, a large bird, a seagull perhaps, distorted by the frosted glass.

Back in the loft, she returned to her drawing of a long-haired guinea pig. The guinea pigs were described in detail, but the text provided no description of Mrs Moffatt, the owner of the pet shop, so Erin had created a small, round figure, the grandmother she lacked and would have valued a lot just now. *What do you think, Mrs Moffatt? What would you do?* Crazy, like a child inventing an imaginary friend, but loss did strange things to you. Not just the loss of Claudia. The future she had planned with Declan, and the child she had longed for.

The long-haired guinea pig was preening itself and in the next cage, a group of rabbits looked on with supercilious expressions. Rabbits never have supercilious expressions, and it was not a cartoon, so it was taking some ingenuity to imply their expressions while maintaining their rabbitiness.

The visit to the mortuary had taken it out of her, and drawing came as a relief. Sometimes she surprised herself how immersed she became in her work, but never for very long. Putting down her pen, she stood up to stretch her legs, torn between liking the compactness of the flat and wishing she had more space. Was the baby doing well? How much were they telling her? She trusted the nurse called Andrea, but she could have been told to put a hopeful angle on things. Erin's thoughts alternated between the baby, Ollie, and the accident and whether someone had held a grudge against Claudia. Someone who was angry enough to want her dead?

In the night, it had rained heavily, pattering against the dormer window. Now it was showery, fine one moment, overcast the next. Unable to concentrate, she decided to talk to Ava. She knew something – Erin was sure of it – and, if she could convince her how worried she was, she might feel compelled to help.

Her phone rang. It was Jon.

'Just checking to make sure you're all right.'

'I'm fine.' He had phoned the previous evening and she had told him about the mortuary but played down how much it had shaken her.

'Where are you?'

'On my way out.' Better not to tell him where she was going. 'To buy food.'

'I'll be away for a couple of days at a conference in Manchester, but you can ring my mobile if you need me.'

If she needed him? And then what would he do? 'You mean, if Ollie comes back?'

'You've no idea how much good Maeve's lessons are doing. She spends most of her spare time drawing.' There was a slight pause. 'You're sure you're all right? I thought . . . Ollie's friend, Hoshi, I think they may have fallen out.'

Think they may have fallen out. What was he saying? 'You think he has something to do with Ollie's disappearance? Have you spoken to him?'

'Don't know where he lives but it's possible Ben may know.'

'Yes, well I hope the conference goes well.'

'Make sure the house is locked up securely, especially at night.'

'I always do.'

'Access would be relatively easy from that graveyard at the back. Have you met your immediate neighbours?'

97

'They're in Brazil. I thought I told you. Anyway, I've got the cat for company, when she decides to pay me a visit.'

He laughed. She did too. Not that she felt like laughing.

The wind blew rain into her face. She should have brought an umbrella but, like an idiot, she had assumed it would be easy to find a parking space. In the event, she had been forced to tour the side streets, searching for a gap, then hurry back towards the café. As she walked, she rehearsed the words in her head, but not too much or they would sound stilted. *Claudia could be rather outspoken. Might she have had enemies? Do you think she could have upset someone?*

When she left the house, a man had been standing a few doors up, lighting a cigarette. The one she had seen before? He'd had a hoodie, but that meant nothing. Perhaps he was the man who had phoned wanting to speak to Claudia, but why hang about in the rain when he could have knocked on her door? He was harmless, nothing to do with her.

Without warning, the rain began to pour down and she ran towards a shop and sheltered under its overhang, peering through the misted-up window at the bowls of beads, blue and purple and yellow, and the boxes of larger turquoise and silver ones. The bent nosed pliers looked familiar and she remembered seeing a pair in Claudia's den, and wondered if the shop was one of her haunts. None of the jewellery she made had been expensive and Erin had expressed surprise that she made enough money to live on, and Claudia had grinned. *Pile 'em high and sell 'em cheap.* Her words, and the accompanying laugh, had been unconvincing and she had not mentioned she was planning to give up her stall in the market.

After she arrived at the house, Erin had been so absorbed with her own problems, she had failed to take much interest in the jewellery making. Now there were so many things she regretted. The two of them should have spent more time together, talked, made more effort to break down the barriers that had divided them since childhood. During her last visit to the hospital, she had wanted to tell her all this. *Speak to her. She may be able to hear you.* But in Claudia's case this was not true. Her brain had ceased to function and all that remained was her beautiful face, now almost invisible behind the wires and tubes.

Farther up the road, the clocks in the window of a jeweller all gave different times and glancing at her watch, Erin made a dash through the downpour, arriving at Ava's Place just as Ava was opening up and had an expression on her face as though she wished she could have stayed in bed.

'Erin.' The way she spoke her name brought back memories of waiting outside the head teacher's office after committing some minor transgression. 'You're wet. Cappuccino and a croissant? Come in. You'll have to wait while I get things going.'

'Just the cappuccino, thanks, or a filter coffee would do,' Ava's muslin top, worn over a purple T-shirt, had a rip under one arm. The first time they met Erin had seen her as a kind of Earth Mother, caring for all her customers with their little problems, feeding them with falafels, and fruit tarts covered in fromage fraise. Perhaps she was a night owl, and opening up at ten was something she found deeply unpleasant. Another possibility was that she disliked her. Why? Because she had been so attached to Claudia, she resented the presence of a sister she barely knew?

'There's something I wanted to ask you.' Erin draped her dripping coat over a chair. 'No rush.' Since her trainers let in water, her socks were soaking wet, but as long as Ava was prepared to talk, it was something she would have to endure. Even if she ended up with a cold. No, colds were viruses, nothing to do with getting cold and wet. What was she thinking about? Anything to fill up the time, as she waited for Ava to come back. A man with a hacking cough had come through the door. He sat down, close to the counter, and Ava greeted him warmly. A regular, no doubt.

After a short delay, the coffee machine roared into action and Erin leaned back, closing her eyes and thought about Ollie. Relief, that he was not the man who had hanged himself had been followed by anger that he had still not been in touch. What had Claudia seen in him? Perhaps the fact that he was immature and with an air of wanting to be looked after, was what had appealed to her. Where was he? Staying with an old girlfriend? Walking in the country, glad to be free of all responsibility for the baby? But her anger always faded, in case he was dead.

Ava was adding a sprinkle of chocolate to two mugs. Then, weaving her way between tables, she joined Erin, sitting down with a thump and resting her chin on her hands. 'Fire away.'

'It's about Claudia.'

'Thought it might be.' There was no sarcasm in her tone but Erin could guess what she was thinking. She had told her all she knew and saw no point in going over it all again.

'Could she have had enemies?'

Ava's mouth tightened. The persona she adopted at work, the jolly, convivial host, had not yet switched on.

'Ollie must have friends,' Erin was uncomfortably

aware that the rain had penetrated her sweater and she smelled of wet wool. 'But I know so little about his life before he moved in with Claudia. Anything that might help to find him.'

'You think that's a good idea?' Ava scooped a teaspoon of froth into her wide open mouth.

'Don't you? The baby.'

'Are you all right, my love? Anyone with what you've got on your plate would be feeling fairly fraught.'

So she looked as rough as she felt. 'I didn't sleep very well.'

'Would you like me to give you something? Herbal, not addictive. Wish I could help but I'm afraid I'm as much in the dark as you are. If I hear anything obviously I'll let you know at once. What makes you think a lovely person like your sister would have enemies? People loved her, she was such good fun. I do miss her. And you do, of course you do. Oh, what am I saying? I talk too much, can't help it, it's in my nature, either that or working here has turned me into a garrulous old woman.'

Talked too much? Was Jennie right when she said she was spreading rumours?

'You're not old,' Erin said, and Ava put her tongue in her cheek and gave her a quizzical smile.

'Claudia and I were friends but she never confided in me. She wasn't the confiding kind.' She sipped her coffee, keeping her mug close to her face so her next words were barely audible. 'I don't know if he could be any help, but she was friendly with a man called Kent, an actor.'

Kent? Another beautiful young man? 'Do you know how I can contact him?'

'He's appearing in a new play, put on in a church hall.' She picked up a flyer that had fallen on the floor. 'Tonight's the first night.' She gave a throaty laugh. 'The

101

only night I expect. Modern day version of *Hamlet*. Not my kind of thing, and since Kent wrote it himself I imagine he must have paid to hire the hall and given himself the leading role. Claudia didn't introduce him to you?'

'Never mentioned his name.'

Ava raised an eyebrow. 'She liked actors, found them good company. Sometimes took part in play-readings. I used to tease her, she was a frustrated actress.'

Claudia liked actors? Jennie's partner, Ben? Unlikely, but not impossible. It would explain why Jennie was so edgy. Was that where Claudia had been when Erin assumed she was on her way to the indoor market?

'Kent's an expert on Shakespeare,' Ava was saying, 'used to do some teaching as well as acting. Concentrates on writing plays these days. Like a brolly?' She stood up, rubbing her back. 'There's one on the stand by the door. Don't know who left it but you're very welcome.'

So that was that, apart from the information about Kent. As she stepped onto the wet pavement, Erin was wondering why Claudia had never mentioned him. Because, like Hoshi, he was one of her cast-offs?

14

The play was called *Polonius*. All Erin could remember about him was that he hid behind a curtain, or was it a screen? But she had a clear picture in her mind of the pre-Raphaelite painting of Polonius's daughter, Ophelia, floating down the river, holding a yellow flower. Eyes open, lips parted, dress spread out on the dark water. What colour was her hair? Her eyes – she had made a study of the painting during her time at Art College – were a light grey-blue, like Jon's.

Perhaps she should ask Jennie to accompany her to the play, but she was unlikely to accept the invitation. Also, if she had a chance to speak to Kent, it would be better if she was on her own. What did he look like? She could have asked Ava, but by then it was clear the conversation was at an end. Good-looking, leading man material? Sure to be if Claudia had liked him.

Ben was a character actor, not Claudia's type. Or was each new conquest another notch on her bedpost? If she had slept with Ben, it would explain Jennie's dislike of her. If she *had* disliked her? Erin hated to think of Claudia like that, but she knew how single-minded she could be, bulldozing her way through people's objections in her determination to get what she wanted. She thought about her, lying on her hospital bed with no awareness of the baby inside her, and it felt surreal, almost ghoulish. Except how could an innocent baby be thought of that way?

At twenty-five weeks, a baby was still very small. At twenty-eight weeks, it was fatter and its head was more in proportion with its body, and it was covered in grease that stopped the skin from becoming soggy because of the amniotic fluid. Did reading books about pregnancy help? Probably not.

If Ollie was still missing, the baby would be her responsibility and she was determined no social worker was going to take her into care. Why would they, when she had a blood relative? But no sooner had she convinced herself she should be allowed to keep her than she started to wonder if it was what she wanted. Bringing up a child with Declan would have been one thing but, like Ollie, she had misgivings about being a single parent.

The once beautiful church, with its Gothic door, had been turned into a public hall. Erin had never visited that part of the city before and the street had a faintly menacing feel, mainly due to insufficient lighting. No one was about. Had she come to the right place? Had Ava got the date wrong? There was nothing to indicate a play was going to be performed.

She had left home in good time, but had trouble finding the place, and now she was afraid she might not be able to get a seat. Worse, she might be an audience of one. Perhaps she should give it a miss. She would find out what Kent looked like, but it was unlikely there would be an opportunity to meet him.

A young man came through the Gothic door and asked if she had come to the performance. 'Everyone else has gone in.' He hitched up the jeans that had slid down over his skinny hips. 'Follow me.'

After climbing the stone steps, they entered a dusty room where wooden chairs, with backs that had once held hymn books, had been placed in a semi-circle. Theatre in the round, but only half a round.

'I haven't got a ticket.'

The young man stared at her, and she thought he was going to let her in for free, but he was waiting for her to find her purse. 'Seven pounds,' he said.

Erin handed him a note and two coins, and chose a seat at the end of a row, next to an elderly lady with a fox fur round her neck. She smelled of mothballs, thinly disguised by a musky perfume, but when she gave her a welcoming smile Erin forgave her for the dead fox.

'I've never been here before,' she said.

'Same here.' The woman rubbed her bony hands together. 'Bit draughty so let's hope the antics on stage warm us up.'

'Yes.' Erin noticed that people were keeping their coats on. Eight o'clock. Time for the curtain to go up. Not that there was a curtain, apart from the one that partially covered a door where she assumed the actors would make their entrances and exits.

The background music was turned down and a man came "on stage", dressed in old-fashioned trousers and a velvet dinner jacket. The fox fur woman had a programme, a single sheet of paper, and glancing at it surreptitiously, Erin gave an inward groan when she saw Polonius and Ophelia were the only characters in the play, apart from someone called "the magician".

As soon as the man spoke, it was clear he was Polonius. *Behind an arras I conveyed myself.* And Polonius was played by Kent Blaney.

What had she expected? A young man, newly out of drama school and trying to keep his hand in by performing his own play. Kent looked well into his fifties with white hair, a substantial paunch and a deep theatrical voice. Ophelia, when she appeared, was young and pretty, but not a great actress. And the play bore little resemblance to the original. Telling herself to be more open minded, Erin concentrated on Kent, who had a stage presence all right, although it was difficult to believe he and Claudia had been close friends. Had the theatre been one of her interests? If so, it was something she had kept to herself. As Erin recalled, she had preferred the cinema.

Like *Hamlet*, the play was not a load of laughs, and when it came to the end Erin was relieved, only to discover that had been the first act and after a short interval there was more to come. Ava had said Kent was an expert on Shakespeare. If that was true, why not stick to the original text, but perhaps his play was so clever it had gone over her head.

The second half was more entertaining than the first. The magician did some tricks. But it could have done with being cut by a third. Gazing round the room, Erin tried to work out what each of the audience did for a living. Her neighbour was listening with rapt attention and could be a relative of Kent's. His wife?

The guy who had sold her the ticket was there too. A drama student? And next to her, a waif-like girl kept crossing one painfully thin leg over the other. Maybe she was studying *Hamlet* at school. Erin had done the same herself. Hamlet, the ditherer, unable to make up his mind. To do nothing or "to take arms against a sea of troubles?" Was she like Hamlet, whereas her sister had been assertive and decisive? Claudia had wanted Ollie, and she had wanted a baby, and, except for a tragic accident, both her wishes would have come true.

When the play finally came to an end, the small audience clapped enthusiastically and the three actors returned twice and stood, hand in hand, lapping up the applause. Erin hung back, waiting for the rest of the audience to leave. Was there a side door? It could be some time before the actors came out, and when they did they would be tired and Kent would not relish Claudia's sister confronting him with a barrage of awkward questions. If he knew anything important, surely he would have told Ava. Or would he? Was Ollie being protected by someone, and if so, why did he need protection?

When Kent came through the Gothic door, it took her a few seconds to realise who he was. The thick white hair was the same, but for the purposes of the play he had worn padding. The real Kent was slim and distinguished looking – no beard – and, with a jolt, she recognised the man in the photograph she had given to the police, the one with his arm round Ollie.

Stepping forward, her foot slid on a pile of wet leaves, and she almost fell.

'Allow me.' He came to her aid with a steadying arm and, as she turned to thank him, she thought, you know who I am, Ava forewarned you.

'I'm Erin Barnes,' she said, 'Claudia's sister.'

'My dear.' He sounded convincingly taken aback, but then he was an actor. 'Allow me to offer my condolences. Were you at the performance? How sweet of you. I do hope you enjoyed it.'

Nothing about his manner gave the impression he thought she had only come in the hope of meeting him, although that must have been fairly obvious.

'It was very interesting,' she said, and he laughed, tossing back his mane of hair.

'Would you do me the honour of allowing me to buy you a drink? There's a pub round the corner, not a particularly inviting one, but at least we'll be out of the rain. Un moment, si vous plait.' He turned to the actor who had played Ophelia, and Erin feared he was going to ask her to join them. 'Perfect, darling, I'll be in touch again soon.'

He was right about the pub. The carpet was black and green, with burn marks from the days when smoking was allowed. In a dark corner at the back, a couple of old men sat, staring into their beer. Had they been at the play? No, the audience was so small, she would have remembered them. While Kent was buying the drinks, she started to plan what she was going to say. Best to encourage him to talk about himself – his plays, his acting career – and hope he got around to Claudia, and told her more than he intended.

The girl behind the bar had been joined by a burly man with a bulbous nose, who was treating Kent as though he was a celebrity. They chatted for several minutes then the burly man said something that made Kent laugh, and when he joined her, he was still smiling. When it faded, Erin expected more condolences, but the performance was still uppermost in his mind.

'As I'm sure you were aware the piece can be appreciated on several levels. As a modern day metaphor or a comment on the state of the individual in a global community. No doubt you noticed how I combined Shakespeare's text with a Chaucerian element.'

'Have you written many plays?'

'Quite a few, quite a few. This evening's suffered from being a little under rehearsed but these days you're lucky if you can raise the cash for a couple of rehearsals and a performance or two. I'm hoping to put on a new production in May. Will you still be around?'

'I'm living in Claudia's house. In the loft. I moved there in the summer.'

'So you are, so you are. How remiss of me to forget.

I'm surprised we haven't met before.' He pretended to be counting back over the months. 'Such a tragedy. I was devastated. A wonderful person. So warm. So full of life.' He broke off, but not because his choice of words had been inappropriate. He was frowning, then one of his gnarled hands came down on the table. 'You're hoping I'll have news of Ollie. I know him, of course, but it was Claudia I knew best.'

'It was Ava who told me about your play.'

'Did she indeed? Poor Ollie, such a sweet boy, but suffers from a somewhat narrow education as far as the arts are concerned. Claudia and I were trying to make up for it. I gave him a reading list but I'm not sure it was such a good idea. Could have put him off the classics for life.'

'The photograph I gave to the police had been taken in a club, by Claudia I expect. You were in it.'

'And you gave it to the cops?' He feigned horror. 'A club? Ah, yes, I remember, we'd gone to hear a stand-up comedian but unfortunately he wasn't funny. Old jokes in the main and most of them relying on the filth factor. As I recall, Ollie became bored, wanted to go home, but good old Claudia stuck it out to the bitter end.'

The old men had started talking in loud voices and Kent flinched with distaste. 'Your sister would never have tolerated drinking in a place like this. She had standards and heaven help the rest of us if we failed to live up to them.'

'You know she was expecting a baby?'

'And they're keeping her on life support, the poor love. If you want my opinion . . . Terrible business. Anyway, if I hear anything you'll be the first to know. I have Claudia's number. Would I be able to contact—'

'Her landline. I can't find her mobile. It was in her

pocket when . . . I think Ollie may have it.'

'Poor boy. Gone away to lick his wounds. I suppose there've been ends to tie up. The scaffolding people, although there's little doubt it was one of those irresponsible protesters. Ollie's a sensitive soul. Young for his age but brilliant at Maths and statistics and all that kind of thing. I admire those people, don't you? Not my line of country but each to his own. Your sister – such a breath of fresh air. One of a kind.'

The more he talked the better. He had thought Ollie was not good enough for Claudia, that much was clear, and it had put his nose out of joint when he moved in with her.

'How are you, my dear? You were close, I expect. So sad. Such a tragedy.'

'Do you know any of her other friends?'

He turned to smile at the girl behind the bar. 'Have you tried the market?'

'She'd given up her jewellery stall.'

'Had she indeed?'

Now, what was he playing at? He knew about the jewellery, and there was plenty more he knew, but nothing he was prepared to tell her. 'She used to go out most days, as though she was on her way to the market. Now I'm wondering where she actually went.' Erin paused, but Kent failed to take the bait so she changed the subject. 'I expect you know Ben who lives down her road. Ben and Jennie.'

'We've met, of course, but Ben's more interested in television, and I believe he's done a little radio. Between you and me, I doubt he's much of a stage actor. The voice. You need a voice you can project.' He drained his glass, making it clear he wanted to leave. 'I'm sorry, my dear, I'm afraid I haven't been much help. If I hear from Ollie,

110

I'll let you know but I think it unlikely.'

'Thank you.' Erin stood up, abandoning the drink she had not wanted in the first place. 'Ava's been very helpful but—'

'Ah, dear Ava, what we do without her? Life and soul of the party and that café of hers is popular, mainly with young mothers but there's nothing wrong with that.' He touched the smooth skin that, in the play, had been hidden by a beard. 'We need more Ava's in the world. So good to meet you, my dear, and as I said before, do accept my condolences, and I'm so glad you enjoyed the play.'

Erin nodded and smiled, but she was thinking how, if he knew Ava so well, he must know more of Claudia's friends. Something had happened. Something nobody wanted to talk about. Kent had claimed Claudia was someone he loved and admired, but he had not given the impression he was devastated by her death.

111

15

January the sixteenth and the baby was twenty-six weeks old. By twenty-eight weeks, the lungs would be reaching maturity. That was important. It must be. Erin thought about her all the time. At first it had been accompanied by how Claudia would have been feeling, but recently she had started to think of the baby as her own.

So far, she had avoided going into Claudia and Ollie's bedroom, but if she searched through Claudia's things she might find another roll of bank notes. She felt guilty, as though Claudia was watching her, opening drawers and rifling through her bras and knickers and sweaters, checking the clothes hanging in the wardrobe, and a box containing a pair of tweezers and false eyelashes.

After their parents died, she and Claudia had done the same in the family home, at least Claudia had stood by as Erin worked out which clothes she could take to a charity shop. *That's too good to throw out, Erin. Perhaps we could sell Dad's suits.* Had she really been that callous? On the face of it, Claudia was the emotional one, easily losing her temper, or bursting into tears. Greeting near strangers with hugs and kisses. But nothing was that simple. Underneath, she could have suffered agonies. The effusiveness and exaggerated anecdotes could have been a way of disguising her true feelings.

Gazing round the bedroom, with its pale green walls and William Morris curtains, Erin found herself speculating how many lovers had spent the night there? And if they all been beautiful young men in their early twenties? Perhaps Claudia had needed to prove to herself how attractive she was? For the first time, it occurred to Erin that her sister might have resented her career as an artist, not that she sold many paintings or prints, but she made a living, more or less, with her illustrations. How had Claudia managed for money? Surely the jewellery making had not brought in enough.

Jon had promised to come round but he must have thought better of it. It was nearly seven and by now he would be home, eating his evening meal. Had he been planning to tell her whatever it was he kept starting to say? At first, she had thought it must be something about Maeve, some mild disability she had failed to notice, or something that might affect her when she was older. Now, she had decided it was more likely to be about Claudia. How well had he known her? Better than he was letting on?

The bed was unmade. Erin started to make it then decided she ought to wash the sheet and duvet cover. Ready for when Ollie returned? The cover had blue and yellow flowers – Claudia's choice – although Ollie was unlikely to have objected. Except, was he really the person she thought he was, gentle, compliant, happy to fit in? Lifting a pillow, to remove its case, she felt something small and hard. Claudia's phone? But it was only the remote control for the television. She pictured the two of them, sitting in the king-size bed, watching an old film. Claudia had liked romantic ones – *Sleepless in Seattle* was one of her favourites – and Ollie would have gone along with her choice. Or would he? She knew so little about him and it was possible he would have insisted on a Tarantino or a Guy Ritchie. Or perhaps they liked soft

113

porn. Claudia had been such a large person, in every sense of the word, and Ollie was so slight. But speculating about other people's sex lives was never a good idea.

No phone. Ollie must have returned to the house and taken it, or perhaps he had had it in his pocket when he ran out of the hospital.

It was while she was making sure the window was firmly closed, that she spotted him. A dark figure in the graveyard beyond the garden wall. Dropping the bundle of bedding, she raced down the stairs and out through the back door, just in time to see him disappear behind the trees. Had he been watching the house? What other reason could there be to lurk in a dark graveyard?

'Ollie? Is that you, Ollie?'

Climbing over the wall for the first time, she stood still, listening. One morning, when she was attempting to tidy up Claudia's garden, she had studied the churchyard with its grey gravestones, ancient oak trees and a holly bushes. The church itself had long narrow windows, with criss-cross panes, all except a stained glass one, depicting three figures and a crucifix. Long grass obscured any paths there once might have been, and ivy sprawled over everything, including a large stone coffin-like grave covered in dead leaves, the spot where the figure could be crouching now.

'Ollie?' But why would he have hidden in the churchyard? Because he was uncertain whether or not to return to the house? Because he felt bad about wanting Claudia and the baby to be allowed to die?

No footsteps, dragging through the brambles, or stepping on broken twigs. It could be the angry man who had phoned, demanding to speak to Claudia. Or someone planning a break-in? Something moved in the grass. A squirrel? Did squirrels come out at night? A cat? It jumped onto a moss-covered tree stump and perched there, and Erin froze. A rat, with darting eyes and a long stringy tail.

A sudden sound, close to the church, made it cock its head on one side, listening, and, with the dark figure forgotten, Erin raced back to the relative safety of Claudia's house.

The following morning, rain streamed down the dormer window, adding to her general feeling of doom and gloom that was only relieved by the thought that later on Maeve would be coming for her lesson. She could tell her about the rat and Maeve would laugh, and pretend there was nothing to be frightened of, then admit she would have been scared stiff, and tell Erin she should never have investigated the graveyard in the dark.

When the phone rang, it was Jon, telling her Maeve would not be coming.

'Only a sore throat but Diana thinks it's best if she stays at home.'

'Oh, I'm sorry about that.' Was she right, when she suspected Diana disapproved of Maeve's lessons? 'Tell her I hope she'll feel better soon.'

'Have the police been in touch?'

'I think they've lost interest. Apparently, a scaffolding tool was found, a spanner, but the company claim there was no way they could have left it there.'

'Only I wondered . . . I have a lecture in ten minutes, but I'll be free this afternoon.'

What was he trying to tell her? That Maeve would miss her lesson but he would drop by himself? 'How was your conference?'

'You're busy.'

115

'Not really.' Why was she sounding so indifferent to his proposed visit when the truth was she badly wanted to talk to him. 'I met an actor called Kent. I expect you know him. I had to sit through a play he'd written himself, a kind of parody of *Hamlet*, although that wasn't how he described it.'

'You spoke to him?'

'He's the man sitting next to Ollie in the photo I gave to the police. Ava told me about the play. I think she thought Ollie might have been in touch with him.'

'Have you got a copy of the photo?'

'I don't know. I could check in Claudia's desk.'

'I'll come round then, shall I? See if you've found one.'

Unable to concentrate on the illustrations, she decided to make an extra visit to the hospital. The previous day Andrea had been off duty but, with any luck, she would be there today.

On her way out of the house, she saw Jennie tipping the contents of a black polythene bag into her wheelie bin. She looked awful and when Erin spoke her name she jumped.

'Oh. Hi.'

'I'm on my way to the hospital.'

'How is everything? The baby? You'd let us know if there was any news?'

'Yes, of course.' By "news" she meant bad news. Normally, Jennie took pride in her appearance, but lately she had stopped bothering. Not that Erin was one to talk, but Jennie was the type who touched up her roots and never had chipped nail varnish. Was she depressed? Something to do with Ben? If she knew her better she could have asked, and it reminded her again how much she missed her London friends – Lindsey, who was such a good listener, and Sonya who never listened but always made her laugh. She had phoned them and told them the bare bones of what was going on, and reassured them that she was fine, something Sonya seemed to believe, but not Lindsey who wanted to come and see her. Later, she had said, in a week or two, and Lindsey had accepted this because she was considerate and knew Erin so well.

Today Jennie was wearing pyjamas bottoms and an oversized sweatshirt. 'Been having clear out,' she said.

'Good idea. I need to do the same, but I don't feel I can throw anything away, not yet.'

Jennie gave her a sympathetic smile. 'Claudia thought people spent too much time and money on their houses.'

'Did she? I've been meaning to ask you, Jennie, you say you didn't know her very well but—'

'I only meant... We were both quite busy, me with my tenants and Claudia with her jewellery and everything. Ben knew her better. She liked his funny stories.'

'Yes, you said.' Her feeling that Jennie had disliked Claudia was being confirmed. 'We must go out for a coffee again soon, or you could come round to the house.'

'Yes. Thanks.' But she could hardly have sounded less enthusiastic.

'Oh, by the way, Jennie, have you noticed someone hanging about in the road? He wears a hoodie and he smokes, at least I think he does. Every so often, he cups his hand and bends over to light a cigarette. And yesterday evening . . .' But it would be a mistake to tell her about the graveyard.

'Who do you think it is? Not Ollie?'

'No. Roughly the same height but broader, not so thin.'

Jennie smiled to herself. 'Have you met Harold Lord? Wears a gabardine raincoat. Has a little notebook, where he writes down all the comings and goings, who's weeded their front garden, or failed to cut their hedge, who's parked their car in a different place. Likes to find something to complain about, then add to it, embellish it.'

'Like Ava.'

'Sorry?' Jennie was halfway through her front door. 'Oh, no nothing like Ava. Whatever anyone says about her, she's not boring.'

'No, of course not.' Erin had regretted her words as soon as she spoke. Jennie was tricky. A friend, but not a friend. All the same, she had no wish to fall out with her. Or with Ava.

'Don't feel you have to come in every day.' Andrea was being kind, but Erin spun round as though her words had been a reproach.

'Last time I came you were off duty. No, I didn't mean . . . You must get worn out.'

Andrea was studying the array of monitors above Claudia's bed. Erin had checked online what they all meant but just now she had forgotten and the lights blurred in front of her eyes.

'I planned to go to a movie,' Andrea said, 'but in the end I spent most of the day in my pyjamas.'

Like Jennie, Erin thought, except Andrea was not in the least like Jennie. 'It's all so . . . Claudia . . . the baby.'

'I know. It's hard for you.'

Erin wanted to ask if they did regular scans. And was it true baby girls were stronger than baby boys and, if so, did it apply to premature ones because Claudia's baby was going to be born early, possibly dangerously early.

'Would you like to feel the baby?' Pulling back the bedding, Andrea took Erin's hand and placed it on Claudia's stomach. Her skin was soft and warm and for a split second Erin thought the doctors had got it wrong and she had come back to life.

'We rub her stomach,' Andrea explained, 'to give the baby the stimulation it would have received.'

She meant if its mother were walking about, carrying on her life as normal, laughing, talking, sleeping, waking. 'That's why you play music, isn't it?' So far, she had felt nothing and she decided to ask the question she had been putting off. 'If you were the baby how do you think you'd feel when you found out your mother had been kept on life support so you could be born?'

'It would make me sad, but grateful she'd given me life.'

'It wasn't Claudia's choice.'

'You've done what you thought she would have wanted.'

'Have I?' For the first time, Erin was unsure. 'The baby's father . . . Oh!' The baby gave a sudden kick, a foot, or it could have been an elbow. 'I had no idea. She's so strong. She is strong, do you think?'

Andrea replaced the blanket that covered the lower half of Claudia's body. 'She's a surprisingly good size for the period of gestation.'

That was not what she wanted to hear, although recently she had stopped thinking of Ollie as the father. Did it matter who it was? Yes, it did. She was trying to keep an open mind, but it was not something she was good at. 'If Ollie doesn't come back, who will she belong to? I suppose social services will take over.'

'They're not as bad as people sometimes make out.'

'Have the doctors said anything since I was here before?'

Andrea lifted the clipboard from the end of the bed and flicked through a couple of sheets. 'No change. That's good.'

119

'The infection has cleared up?'

'In these circumstances, infections are quite common. Try not to worry. No, that's a silly thing to say, of course you will.'

Erin found a chair and sat down next to the bed. She wanted to tell Andrea everything, her doubts about Claudia's life, and the men she had slept with. Her fear that people knew something they were refusing to tell her. Her loneliness. Above all, her growing suspicion that Claudia's death had not been an accident.

Andrea was busy updating her records, then she came round to Erin's side of the bed and pulled up another chair, and because she wanted to get to know her better, she asked if she had any children.

She shook her head. 'How about you?'

'No. I was living in London. I split up with my partner. That's why I came to stay with Claudia.'

'So you don't know the city very well.'

'I thought I'd only be here for a few months. I was feeling pretty low, trying to work out what to do next.'

'Men,' Andrea said, and Erin started to cry.

She expected Andrea to jump up, find her a tissue, even apologise for upsetting her. Instead, she put an arm round her shoulder and said nothing. A monitor beeped twice but it was something that happened often. Claudia lay motionless. Beneath the blanket, the baby moved, or had she imagined it? The room was pleasantly warm and part of her wanted to move in, stay until the baby was large enough to be born, but another part could hardly bear to see Claudia looking so peaceful, so smooth-skinned and, with her hair brushed and arranged on the pillow, so alive.

She asked Andrea if she had ever come across a case like Claudia's before.

'No, but I've read about them. It's awful for you, but for us . . . We all want to do our best for the baby. And for your sister.'

'I checked some other cases online. Newspaper reports and one website had medical details.'

She waited for Andrea to say it was probably best not to read stuff that might confuse or alarm her. Instead she started talking about the baby's birth. 'All being well, she will need to be delivered around thirty-two weeks. Mothers have been kept on life support for up to fourteen weeks, but that's unusual and there've been a few problems. Although that's only to be expected,' she added.

'I prefer to know the truth.'

'Nobody's going to lie to you. You must trust us to tell you what's going on.'

'I trust *you*,' she said, and Andrea gave her a quick hug she would like to have lasted longer. The comforting warmth of someone else's body.

'When the baby's born she will have to stay in the Special Care Baby Unit for several weeks, but you'll be able to visit as often as you like.'

Erin wanted to tell her how alone she felt, and how she suspected Ollie was not the baby's father. 'I'm living in Claudia's loft conversion,' she said. 'It's not very big, but I don't really mind. I'm an artist and at the moment I'm doing illustrations for a children's book.'

'Really?'

'There's a deadline. It helps to take my mind off things. I miss my London friends and the other artists I sometimes met up with. It's important to know people who do the same kind of work. One of them is having an exhibition. I'd like to see it but I don't expect I will.'

'I'd love to be able to draw and paint. Hang on.'

Andrea jumped up and began checking a piece of equipment and Erin started to panic. A short time ago, the baby had felt so strong, but things could change in minutes. Supposing she had died. What would happen? She would be removed and Claudia's life support would be switched off. She would have to organise a funeral. They would be buried together, or cremated. Would there be a headstone? Would Ollie come back in time?

'No problem.' Andrea sat down again. 'What's the book about? I have a niece who's going to be four at the end of March. Would it be suitable for a child that age?'

'Oh, yes, definitely.' Andrea was so important to her, Erin would like to have given her a sketch, a token of how much she appreciated her kindness. 'It's about a pet shop and some guinea pigs.'

'I love guinea pigs. All animals.'

'Do you?' Erin felt close to tears. 'So do I.'

16

Did dust collect if a room was uninhabited? Somewhere, Erin had read that dust was particles of skin, but no one has been in Claudia's front room for days. Then she remembered the police. And the time she had planned to switch the television on for Maeve, so she could talk to Jon.

A thin layer of dust covered the mantelpiece, where Claudia had positioned her collection of glass and china cats, and a pair of white kittens, nose to nose. She had enjoyed collecting, an excuse to go from junk shop to junk shop, searching. Before the cats, it had been horses but, for some reason, they had been abandoned. Why? But Erin had never understood how Claudia's mind worked. Even as a young child, she would announce her latest craze – shells, pressed flowers, marbles, or some game they all had to play with her – dropping each new obsession as quickly as she had taken it up. They had both longed for a pony, but only ever ridden them on holiday. Erin had been a natural, but Claudia had bumped up and down on the saddle, complaining that the pony was going too slowly, or too fast. Nothing was ever her fault.

Picking up one of the cats, a blue one that bore no relation to a real cat, Erin found it was sticky, as though the last person who touched it had been eating sweets. It was bound to be Claudia, with her love of chocolate and jelly babies, and Erin could almost hear her voice, loud, filled with laughter. *Look, Ollie, I bought this one in a second-hand shop in Newquay. Isn't he sweet? He's called Tom.*

Living in Claudia's house was making her morbid – if Ollie had hung around it might not have been so bad – and she was relieved when Jon turned up, just as she was dragging the vacuum cleaner out of the cupboard under the stairs, a cupboard full of junk, old cardboard boxes and cans of paint.

'Having a clear out?' He had such a serious expression, she tensed, afraid he had come with bad news. 'I could help if you like.'

'It's all right, I'll do it later.'

'Do your windows have locks?'

'I've no idea. Actually, I'm thinking of changing the locks on the front door, having stronger ones fitted. I don't suppose you know a locksmith, someone local?'

'Supposing Ollie comes back.'

'Yes, that's why I've put it off.' She was thinking about the money in the desk and wondering if Claudia had been keeping it to pay someone for work carried out on the house, cash in hand. Several small jobs needed doing, an upstairs window that refused to close, a patch of damp in the bathroom, tiles missing on the roof of the kitchen extension.

She could have told Jon about the man in the graveyard. Instead, she said she had been unable to find a copy of the photo of Ollie and Kent. 'If I do, I'll let you know. Kent's got thick white hair. In his late fifties, I'd say. I only went to the play so I could see what he was like and, to be honest, I thought he was going to be one of Claudia's beautiful young men.'

He laughed, and she thought, that's better, I need someone to cheer me up, not drag me down. He was wearing new clothes, at least they were new to her, grey jeans, a tartan shirt and a denim jacket, and as he climbed the stairs ahead of her, he had to dip his head to avoid the chandelier, another of Claudia's impulse buys.

Up in the loft, he pretended to be studying her drawing of the mynah bird. Playing for time? Preparing himself to tell her something he should have told her days ago?

'One of the doctors wondered if Claudia could have got her dates wrong,' she said

'What makes him think that?' He pointed at the dormer window where big drops of rain were landing.

'Yes, I know.' So they were going to talk about the weather. 'The doctor was a woman. I shouted at her.'

'Why?'

'She said the baby was larger than she would have expected. No, that's not why I shouted. It was the way she was talking, not looking at me, not really bothered—'

'That's good, isn't it? The baby.'

So he had failed to reach what, to her, was the obvious conclusion. 'It was all so sudden, Claudia and Ollie. They met in July and by the end of August he'd moved in. I thought . . . Do you think it's possible she was pregnant when they met but the father of the baby didn't want to know?'

Jon frowned. 'She'd have done that to Ollie?'

'If she didn't relish the prospect of bringing up a child on her own.'

He thought about this. Or perhaps he was thinking about something entirely different. With Jon, it was impossible to tell. 'Do the doctors think the baby's going to be all right?'

'I don't know.'

'But so far it's developing normally.' He was humming under his breath, a sure sign he was trying to summon up the courage to say something that would be unwelcome. 'I can't stay long. Diana's at the shop and Maeve's with a neighbour.'

So why choose this particular time to put in an appearance? 'Has she really got a sore throat?'

'When she was younger, colds tended to turn to chest infections. She's toughened up as she's grown older, but Diana still worries, she's the worrying kind. How's your work going?'

'My editor's been on at me, but that's nothing new. I told her about Claudia but I don't think it sunk in. Or if it did, it made no difference.' Her throat hurt. Perhaps she was developing Maeve's mythical cold. Pulling open a drawer, she took out her thickest cardigan, one her mother had knitted for her when she was in her teens. Even after all those years, it still had the oily scent of unwashed wool from a Jacob's sheep.

'I find a deadline helps,' Jon said. 'I had to finish a paper for the conference. Stayed up half the night.' Now he was studying the sketches of chipmunks, some leaping from branches, some curled up asleep. 'You and Claudia are so different.'

'I thought you said you didn't know her that well.' She was losing patience. 'Look, if there's something you've found out, something that was going on before the . . . Don't you think it's stressful enough with the baby and not knowing if it was an accident or . . . There's a man wearing a hoodie who stands in the road. And there was someone hanging about in the graveyard at the back. I saw him through the window but by the time I'd—'

'Did you call the police?'

'No, of course not. I expect he was looking for somewhere to shelter. Anyway, there was something far worse than a harmless tramp. A rat.'

126

'Where? In the house?'

'No, in the churchyard. Rats don't usually go inside houses, do they?' Her heart was thumping, but it had nothing to do with the rat. She needed someone she could trust and, until recently, she had thought Jon was that person. 'Well, do they?' Her phone rang and she snatched it up. 'Yes! I mean, sorry, yes, who is it?'

'Good morning, Madam, this is Julian. Unfortunately, there is a problem with your computer.'

'No, there isn't. Liar! Bugger off . . .'

Jon took the phone from her hand. 'Best to say nothing, just ring off.'

'D'you think I don't know that?'

He put her phone down on one of the drawings and she snatched it up, as though he had committed a mortal sin.

'I'd better go.' His hand was on the door. 'Maeve should be fine to come to her next class.'

'I hope so.'

'Erin?'

'Now what?' She could hear the cat mewing. 'I have to feed Miss Havisham.'

'I just wanted to thank you for Maeve's classes. They've been really good for her confidence. As well as learning how to draw.'

'You came here to tell me that?'

He was straightening Ollie's desolate black and white photograph of sand and sea. 'I wish I could do more to help.'

'Yes, well nobody can, apart from the doctors and nurses. One of the nurses . . .' But she had no wish to tell him about Andrea. He pretended to care, but Claudia's death meant nothing to him. Neither did the baby.

Someone was leaning on the doorbell. Erin ran down the two sets of stairs, missing her footing and almost falling, grabbing the banister rail, then wrenching open the door.

It was Lara.

'I'm sorry. Your sister. She is better?'

'No, I told you before, she's in hospital.'

'But she will be home again soon?'

Jon had joined them and was staring at Lara, as though he had seen her before but forgotten where it was. 'This is Lara,' Erin said, 'she's a friend of Claudia's.'

'Please. Clowda helped me. It is difficult. The university . . . They say I need—'

'You're a student?' Jon had taken over and Erin was happy to leave him to it. 'Which department are you in?'

Lara licked her lips. 'You are Clowda's husband?'

'No. I work at the university. If there's a problem, you should talk to your tutor. If you like I could . . .'

But she was edging away and, with once quick glance over her shoulder, she broke into a run.

'You've met her before?' Erin said.

'Don't think so but I doubt she'll bother you again.'

'How do you know?'

'I expect Claudia gave her money.'

'Why would she do that?'

He shrugged. He was lying. One mention of the university and the girl had panicked. She had been involved with Claudia in some way, and Jon knew what it was about, but was denying it. And nothing she said to him would make any difference.

After he left, she pulled out a drawing, but found it impossible to work. Her stomach churned and her head was full of unanswered questions. She was angry. Angry with Jon, and with Lara. At least Jon was right when he said she was unlikely to return. She had looked terrified, in a total panic. Stop thinking about it. Whatever Claudia had done, or not done, it made no difference now. If Lara *did* turn up again, she would tell her the truth. *You're wasting your time. Claudia's not going to get better. Her brain is dead.*

Fighting off feelings of frustration, she paced up and down, concentrating on her immediate surroundings. The loft would have made a good bedroom – she liked the way the wall sloped over her bed – but, as a living space, it was starting to feel claustrophobic. Her plan chest, easel, and art materials took up at least a third of the room, and much of the stuff she had brought with her from London was still in boxes, piled up in a corner. It was crazy that she was stuck up in the loft when the rest of the house was empty. But she had no intention of moving into any of Claudia's rooms. Not until Ollie came back, and she had convinced herself the accident really was an accident. Not until the baby had been born.

17

When she left the house, the students had been arriving in dribs and drabs, not that she expected them to take any interest in the tenant in the basement. Mainly girls, and a boy with grey flannel trousers and a tweed jacket, a misfit if ever she saw one. Stella wondered what they were all studying. She could ask them, of course, turn on the charm, and it could be that one of them was his department, could even have him as their tutor.

She knew that he cycled to work, but that was not a lot of use. No name in the phone book so there was nothing for it, she would have to hang about outside the university again. If she left her car on a meter, she would need to keep feeding it the exorbitant charges, so it might be better to walk. No, that was no good. When he came out – *if* he came out – he would cycle off at his usual pace and she would be unable to keep up.

Calling in at a local supermarket, she had bought two bananas, a bag of Satsuma's, and a steak and kidney pie. She paid the boy on the checkout a twenty-pound note and asked for the change in coins. Now, her car was parked a short distance from the entrance to the department, with its glass doors, and a turnstile beyond. How long would she have to wait? It was four in the afternoon and in all likelihood he worked until five or half past. Where were the bikes kept? She spotted them straight off. Row upon row, padlocked to shiny, metal bars.

Head down, counting coins, she caught a glimpse of a tall figure wearing a yellow jacket. No one was that lucky, but maybe three planets were in conjunction, or some such crap. Stella was a Scorpio, resourceful, suspicious, and unyielding. Scorpios had other characteristics too, but those were the ones she remembered. Not him. As the yellow jacket drew closer, she could see he was old, past retirement she would have thought, or did academics carry on until they dropped. A straggly beard and bags under his eyes. Head of department, or there something called an Emeritus Professor. Universities looked after their own.

A couple of students came through the doors, one with white blond hair, the other dark-skinned, and wearing a navy blue hoodie. If she asked them, it was possible they would know whether or not he was in the building. On second thoughts, it was important not to arouse suspicion. The student she had spoken to on her first visit could have reported back. *This woman was looking for you, wanted to know where you lived.*

Holding a map in her hand – the traditional "prop" of the tourist – she chose a spot, close to three green wheelie bins, and resigned herself to a long wait. What kind of a private eye would she make? At one time, the idea had appealed but she could see it meant hours of boredom, about as glamorous a job as an actor, waiting all day for a one-minute scene.

It was a cold, dry day and had been a relief to emerge from the musty basement flat and breathe in fresh air, or air as fresh as city air ever was. Further down the road, a man was swinging his leg over an old-fashioned bike and, as she watched, he shrugged his arms through the straps of a backpack. Where had he sprung from? So many of these university people

131

dressed the same, but she had to make sure.

Running back to where she had left her car, she was in time to see him struggling up the steep hill, slowing down to allow a woman with a dog to cross over, then setting off again, pedalling slowly, so slowly she would catch up with him in a few seconds. It *was* him – she was almost certain of it – and a moment later he turned his head to check what was coming up behind him, and this time she was able to see his face properly.

Almost before she had time to catch her breath, he had thrust out an arm and made a sharp turn to the right. Stella followed, crawling along, keeping her distance, but never letting him out of her sight, past large imposing buildings, then left between rows of shops. Now it was downhill and he was gaining speed. A van pulled out from a road and she had to brake sharply. Her view was blocked and there was no way she could overtake, but she was in time to see him turn right and slow down in a tree-lined road. Was this where he lived? Taking the next turning on the right, she made a U-turn, retracing the route, then left and left again and there he was, standing outside a large semi-detached house. He was searching in his pockets. For a padlock for his bike? Now he was wheeling it into the garden – the front door seemed to be round the side – and when, after a brief wait, it opened, she heard a woman's voice. He must have forgotten his key.

It was a resident parking area but she had no intention of leaving her car and if anyone came checking she would start the engine and move off. In a nearby house, someone was practising on a drum kit, a child by the sound of it, or an adult who could do with some lessons. Through the open window of her car, she strained her ears, listening for snatches of conversation, frustrated that it was inaudible above the beat of the drums. The drumming stopped and she heard a woman's soft voice. Then a deeper one. And the front door slammed shut.

Taking her street map from the glove compartment, she spent a few minutes checking where she was and noting the names of the roads. What next? He might not come out again until the following day. But she had seen him, and knew where he lived. Best to return to the basement and design a proper plan.

Stuffing two mints in her mouth, she studied the route from the university. She was getting to know the city, or at least a part of it. How long had he lived here? And why had he never let her know where he was? The promised letters had failed to materialise and it was not because he had forgotten. He was not the forgetting type.

She needed to know his habits, and the habits of the other occupant of the house. It would take time. Still, with so little to go on, she could have spent far longer tracing him. Fortune favoured the brave, but she had not needed courage, just the determination to stick it out in the gloomy basement flat and be patient, something that never came easily. For the first time for days, she felt starving. Her nervous system must have calmed down. Even the craving for a cigarette had abated a little.

Holding out her hand, she noted with satisfaction that it was steady as a rock. She was in charge, in control. But as she started the engine, and released the handbrake, she saw movement out of the corner of her eye. He was leaving again, wheeling his bike, his wife was with him, but had her back turned. They were arguing, the kind of argument when people want to raise their voices but are afraid someone will overhear. He had been in the house less than ten minutes. What had happened? Something that made him storm out. Nothing to do with *her* – how could it be? He had no inkling she was in the city. Nobody knew, apart from the negligent landlady.

Impossible to hear what the argument was about, but she still felt a small degree of satisfaction. Married people always argued, one of the reasons she was never going to fall into that trap. The mints that had been meant to last, had been crunched up. She found two more, and waited, holding her breath. But the two of them were back inside the house. Argument resolved, at least for the time being. Tomorrow she would return, bringing provisions, preparing herself for a long wait. It would be worth it.

18

Her current illustration was completed and, on an impulse, Erin decided to drive to Maeve's house in the hope of meeting her mother. At this time of day, both Maeve and Diana were likely to be in. Was it idle curiosity or a wish to reassure Diana she was not a bad influence? But the real reason was because it was just possible she might discover what it was that Jon was keeping from her.

She had the address and thought she knew how to find the road but she checked, just in case, and was surprised to find it was in walking distance. Jon always brought Maeve in the car but that was because he picked her up from school, dropped her off, and returned to the university. Diana could have brought her, but for some reason she never did. Perhaps she was one of those reclusive people who disliked leaving home. Except Jon had said she worked part-time in a health food shop.

As she walked past Claudia's car, it occurred to her she ought to take it out for a spin or the battery would go flat. Were the car keys in her desk? Claudia had driven badly, talking too much and not looking in the mirror, and her car had several scrapes and a dent in the passenger door. Once she had knocked a student off his bike. A shouting match had followed – Erin had been with her in the car at the time – but Claudia had apologised and the student had agreed it had been a bad plan, trying to overtake on the left. No harm done. The two of them had shaken hands.

But could there have been other incidents, ones that had not ended so amicably? She should have phoned Diana before she set out, but she wanted to surprise her. Why? Because she was afraid she would say she was busy, or about to go out, any excuse to put her off? From remarks Jon had made, it was clear she was very protective of Maeve, and fairly strict too. In fact, Erin had gained the impression she treated her like a much younger child, and there had been a battle to allow her to come to the classes. And now she thought Erin was corrupting her, allowing her to talk about unsuitable subjects, and answering questions she should have side-stepped.

Her phone beeped. The hospital? No, they would have phoned, not sent a text. Living off her nerves was bad for her, exhausting, but there was not much she could do about that. The text was an invitation to upgrade her car breakdown membership. Some hope. The standard one cost a fortune, exploiting drivers' fear of being stranded on the motorway, or miles from anywhere in a dark lane.

Was she going in the right direction? Maeve had described the house in her usual fashion. *Dad thinks it's ugly but Mum likes it because it's easy to keep clean. There's a steep hill and you can see the school I'll be going to next year. They're not old houses like yours but they're detached. That means they're not joined to another one.*

Earlier, it had been cold enough to have both heaters on in the loft. Now it had warmed up a little but she still needed her scarf and gloves. What had happened to the clothes Claudia had been wearing, her red coat and the purple beanie? The hospital had given them to her in a bag but she had forgotten what she did with them. Put them in Claudia's bedroom, or the cupboard where she had kept her coats, umbrellas and a jumble of shoes and boots?

Much of what she had done immediately after the accident had been wiped from her memory. She had acted like a zombie, too shocked to think what she was doing, too worried in case the hospital decided Ollie should be allowed to make the decision about the baby.

She ought to be thinking about what she was going to say to Diana. First, she would tell her how hard Maeve worked, and what good progress she was making. She always took her drawings home with her but did Diana look at them, or were they put in a drawer, or thrown away with the rubbish? Maeve had never mentioned any appreciative comments her mother had made.

When she checked the map, she had failed to spot a footpath that made the distance between Claudia's house and Maeve's even shorter. Small children were being pushed on swings, and dog walkers, who were not allowed in the play area, were exercising their pets, some on leads, others free to run about. A tiny terrier – so small you could almost have put it in your pocket – raced up to Erin and veered away and a small boy with a runny nose stopped to stare at her as though she was some strange species he had never come across before. One day, Claudia's baby would be that age. Would she be taking her to the park, holding her steady on the roundabout, or would she have been handed over to a couple who wanted to adopt? When she was born would she be all right? Might she have brain damage? Would she be alive?

She carried on over a railway bridge and along a path next to a strip of grass and several detached houses with large front gardens. Two joggers passed, out of breath and with patches of sweat on their vests. It was hardly the day for such light clothing, but some people made a point of showing how hardy they were. The postman that came to Claudia's house wore shorts, whatever the weather.

Up the hill, and, if she had not lost her sense of direction, one of the turnings on the right should lead to Maeve's road. Erin thought of it as Maeve's road because Maeve was her friend. Was Jon a friend? The tension between them was his fault, because he was secretive. He knew something – something about Claudia that was so bad he wanted to protect her from finding out?

Still speculating about what Claudia could possibly have done, she heard a squeal of excitement and saw Maeve running to greet her. 'I thought it was you.'

'Oh, hello. I was out for a walk and I had a feeling I might be quite close to your house.'

'I was talking to him.' She pointed to a cat, sitting on a wall. 'He's not ours, we haven't got any pets. He's called Rex and he lives at number twenty-seven. Mum was gardening but she got cold. She's in the kitchen now, tidying. Come on.' Maeve raced on ahead, calling over her shoulder. 'She wanted to know what you look like and I said you were nothing like Claudia.'

'You're feeling better then.'

'Oh that.' Maeve's hand moved up to her fringe. 'Dad fusses. I wasn't really ill. Only a sore throat and it was gone by the evening.' She shouted through her front door. 'Mum, Erin's here! Mum!'

Diana came through the front door, pulling off her rubber gloves, and Erin found it difficult to disguise her surprise. What had she expected? An adult version of Maeve? Tall, slim, with brown, shoulder-length hair and dark eyes with enviably thick, dark lashes, she could hardly have been more different, apart from her nose which was small and slightly upturned. Perhaps Maeve looked the way she did because of her syndrome. No, not syndrome, just a mildly faulty gene that was more than compensated for by her determination.

Diana was wearing jeans and a yellow cable-stitch sweater, expertly-knitted, like Maeve's always were. No make-up or jewellery, and Erin remembered Maeve complaining how her mother had refused to let her have her ears pierced.

Maeve was hopping up and down. 'It's Erin, Mum.'

'Yes, I heard you, darling. Come in, Erin, it's lovely to meet you at last.'

'I was out for a walk. I came through that park, the one with a children's playground, then a railway bridge.'

'We go there often, don't we, Maeve?'

'You're sure it's not inconvenient?'

'Quite sure. Give me your coat and scarf. I've been in the garden, getting rid of a euphorbia that made my skin come out in a rash. Maeve talks about you so much it's ridiculous we haven't met before. Come along through, we spend most of our time in the kitchen, don't we, darling?'

The kitchen was at the back of the house, a room large enough to eat in, with an antique dresser and farmhouse-style table. A double sink, split level cooker and supersize fridge took up most of one wall and, on another, six blue and white plates, with pictures of woodland animals, had been balanced on a narrow shelf. Erin remembered Maeve telling her how one of them had fallen onto the tiled floor and broken and her mum had been upset but her dad had found a replacement.

'Nice clock.' Erin pointed at the mantelpiece. 'I like it when they have a loud tick.'

Diana smiled. She had a small gap between her front teeth. 'It belonged to my mother. Maeve think it's too noisy, and Jonathan says the horse brasses make the place look like a pub.'

'Typical.' Erin laughed, regretting her choice of the

word since it made it sound as though she knew Jon far better than she actually did. 'Typical of a man, I mean. Where did you find the Welsh dresser?'

'We were swindled. By the man who sold it to us. After we bought it, I discovered it had been repaired and the doors are not the original ones.'

'Oh, well, you'd never know.'

'Do sit down.' Diana pulled out two chairs, giving Maeve a playful punch when she tried to sit on one of them.

'I was hoping I'd meet you,' Erin said, 'so I could tell you what good progress Maeve is making. Drawing's the difficult part and she works really hard. I expect you've noticed how much she's improved.'

Diana was silent and Erin was afraid she had overdone her praise, but the next time she spoke her words surprised her.

'Jonathan worries in case the after-school lessons are too much for her, but I think she's more than up to it. After all, she's not interested in sport or ballet dancing. Personally, I'm just pleased she's learning a new skill. It will help her in all kinds of ways.'

Jon worries? Why had he never mentioned it? Why did he always make out Diana was the worrier? Erin turned to Maeve. 'I expect you are quite tired after school.'

'No, I'm not,' she said fiercely. 'When did Dad say that? Now Erin will think I don't want to go to her house.'

'Shh.' Diana stretched out an arm but Maeve dodged out of reach.

'Dad thinks I'm delicate, like the boy in *The Secret Garden*. It's not fair. Just 'cos I used to get bad chests and I'm no good at games.'

'Oh, come on, Maeve.' Erin had never seen her look so cross. 'I'm sure your dad only meant it was quite a long

140

day for you.'

Her drawing of fruit had been pinned up, next to a leaflet with the health centre times, and the number to call if you smelled gas. 'Your picture of a banana and an apple.' Erin turned to Diana. 'It's good, isn't it?'

'And an orange.' Maeve still sounded grumpy. 'The apple's not right. She was standing by the French doors that led to the garden. Then, all of a sudden, she stood on one leg, spinning round until she lost her balance and collapsed on the floor in a fit of giggles.

'Maeve,' Diana warned, 'just because Erin paid you a compliment.'

On a shelf, next to the pin board, a large number of recipe books had been propped up between bookends in the shape of West Highland terriers. Clearly, Diana was a keen cook as well as good at knitting. She followed Erin's gaze and began explaining how she liked to try out new recipes and she used plenty of herbs and spices. 'I expect you do too. Maeve won't eat fish, silly girl, but apart from that she's not a faddy eater, are you, darling?'

'I don't like beetroot. Or aubergines. Do you like aubergines, Erin? I think they smell like cat's—'

'Yes, I do actually.' Erin came in quickly, afraid Diana would think Maeve had been picking up four-letter words. Not that Diana gave the impression she was easily shocked. It was Jon who had created the picture of a strait-laced, prudish person. 'I'm afraid my cooking arrangements are fairly primitive, but when I'm more settled . . .'

'Yes, of course.' She looked away, embarrassed. A brain dead, pregnant sister. No one knew what to say.

'Mum's made a special herb garden.' Maeve was hopping about again. 'She knows everything about herbs and we've got a greenhouse, shall I show you, Erin?'

'If that's all right with your mum.'

'Yes, of course.' Diana's face lit up. 'We won't get cold if we have a quick look.' She opened the French doors and led Erin onto a patio with pots of winter-flowering pansies, and down some steps to an immaculate lawn. Even in winter, the wide herbaceous border looked attractive, with its tall grasses and seed heads, and a sprinkling of creamy coloured flowers. It put Claudia's scruffy garden to shame, and Erin was thinking how one day she might ask Diana's advice about easy-to-grow plants. One day . . .

Under a tall tree – Erin thought it was a beech – the grass was interspersed with yellow and purple crocuses. Two rustic seats, made of logs, had been placed, side by side, and Erin pictured Jon and Diana, when the weather was warmer, sitting together, unwinding after a busy day and drinking glasses of wine, while Maeve played on the grass. An idyllic family scene that contrasted with her own solitary life.

Smoke drifted across from next door's garden, and Maeve frowned. 'I don't think people are supposed to have bonfires, are they, Mum?'

'It's only wood smoke. Rather a nice smell I always think.'

'Me too.' Erin bent to look at a large, feathery herb.

'That's fennel.' Maeve touched the plant and held her fingers to her nose. 'I don't like the smell but it goes with fish. And that's . . . what's that one called, Mum?'

'Lemon thyme. And that's sage. And the one in the pot is a dwarf basil. Coriander's good for indigestion and fennel is good for nerves. This plant has rather outgrown itself. Fennel has a habit of doing that. I could give you some if you like, Erin. Oh, I didn't mean you suffered from . . .'

'Don't worry, you're right, my nerves aren't that great.

142

I have to spend quite a lot of time at the hospital and—'

'Yes, of course. The baby. No, don't talk about it if you don't want to.'

'It's all right. The baby's doing quite well. I mean, I think it is.'

'Oh, good.' Diana's tone made it clear she was not going to ask any more questions. And Maeve's attempts to turn a cartwheel had provided a diversion. 'Honestly, darling, Erin doesn't want to see your knickers.'

'Erin doesn't mind, do you, Erin? There are more herbs in the greenhouse. One has purple flowers. Bees like purple, don't they, Mum?' She opened the greenhouse door but Diana put out a restraining arm.

'I expect Erin could do with a cup of tea. I usually have peppermint but there are plenty of other flavours.'

'Peppermint would be fine.' Erin was enjoying herself, wished she had come round sooner, but she had not forgotten the real purpose of her visit, to try to discover what Jon was keeping from her. Would Diana tell her? Did she know? And if she did, had she been sworn to secrecy? Since she was so unlike his description of her, Erin was beginning to doubt everything Jon had told her so far. Back in the kitchen, Maeve grudgingly agreed to hang out the washing, and it became clear Diana wanted an opportunity to tell her about Maeve's birth.

'You know when something's . . . when they're not telling you. They thought it was a syndrome but that only means a collection of symptoms and in any case they changed their minds. She can be a little clumsy and she suffers from one or two allergies – we both do – but we see a herbalist called Fergal. He's a wonderful person, properly trained, not one of those charlatans. It's quite a long training. You have to pass exams.'

'Yes, I'm sure.' Erin was not a great admirer of

alternative medicine, but herbalists were different, their treatments made sense.

'I do worry about the germs she picks up at school,' Diana was saying, 'but Jonathan thinks I'm irrational. He says it's important to build up immunity.'

'Plenty of things are irrational.' Erin sipped the peppermint tea, it would not have been her first choice, but was bearable. 'I have this irrational fear of dead animals. I expect Maeve's told you how a cat from down the road sometimes pays me a visit.'

'And brings in birds?'

'Mainly half-eaten mice'

'Horrible. I dislike heights, cliff tops and high bridges.'

'Oh, me too, but I think that's perfectly rational, don't you? I wanted to ask you, Diana, you've met Ollie, haven't you? Only I wondered if you could think of anywhere he might be staying. I need to talk to him, about the baby, and I've an idea Jon, sorry, Jonathan, may be protecting him.'

She had taken a risk, accused Jon of lying to her, but the question seemed to excite Diana. 'I've thought that too. He thinks it's best to leave him alone, but, as you say, what about the baby? And why should you have to cope with everything on your own. I don't know Ollie well, but he has a Japanese friend.'

'Hoshi? You mean Hoshi?'

'Oh, you've met him?'

'No, but people keep mentioning his name. Perhaps I should try and get in touch. The trouble is,' Erin made a snap decision, 'I don't want to think badly of my sister, but I've started wondering if Ollie really is the baby's father.' She expected Diana to look shocked but it was clear she and Jon had discussed this possibility already.

'The awful thing is, you may never know the truth.'

144

'I'll know if it's Hoshi's.'

Diana smiled. 'Well, yes, I suppose you will.'

'I'm sorry to keep asking you all these questions, but did you know my sister?'

'I only met her once. It was at a neighbour's house. Jennie and Ben. I expect you know them. Ben's quite a character, isn't he? All those jokes and funny stories. He and your sister . . .'

Maeve was returning with an empty basket, and Diana put a finger to her lips. 'She has a talent for overhearing other people's conversations.'

'She's such a sweet girl, so kind and appreciative. You must be very proud of her.'

'Thank you.' Diana leaned across to squeeze her hand, just as Maeve clumped in with the empty laundry basket.

'I know you're talking about me,' she said. 'Anyway, the washing won't dry. There's hardly any wind. Mum?'

'Now what?'

'You know red hair?'

'What about it?'

'Why's it called red when it's really orangey-brown? Actually, some people dye their hair a real red colour, or purple. I'd like a purple streak in mine.' Maeve was attempting to walk like a crab. 'You can buy stuff you spray—'

'Not a chance.' Diana bent to tickle her. 'Actually we were talking about Jennie and Ben.'

'Jennie's got streaks in her hair.'

'They had a barbecue the summer before last and your dad and I were invited. No, not you, you were tucked up in bed with a babysitter. Claudia wanted to know about my herb garden, Erin. I suppose Jonathan must have told her.'

'She wasn't a great gardener.' Erin had decided it was

time to leave. 'She said she was going to have it landscaped, then she lost interest. That's the trouble with gardening programmes on TV. They make it look so easy. I've been doing some cutting back, but it's not much fun in the winter.'

'If you need any help? Later on, perhaps, in the spring.'

'Thank you. I might take you up on that.' After the baby's been born. No, don't look ahead, don't make any plans. Claudia's condition could deteriorate in a matter of hours. Andrea always tried to be reassuring, but Erin was well aware of all the things that could go wrong.

Maeve was watching her mother closely and Erin hoped she was not going to tell her about their recent conversation about contraceptives. Maeve had asked why people in some countries had lots and lots of babies, even though it was difficult to get enough food.

As it turned out, she was still thinking about the barbecue. 'Was it late when you went to Jennie and Ben's house?'

'Too late for someone your age.' Diana imitated the face Maeve had pulled. 'I don't know about you, Erin, but I'm not much of a party-goer. I can never think what to say to people, but I remember how your sister put me at ease, telling me about her jewellery-making and how the beads sometimes slid off the thread and rolled all over the floor. I meant to visit her stall in the market. I do wish I had.'

Erin stood up. 'Thank you for the tea, and I'm glad we've met at last. Oh, and you're welcome to come round to the house when Maeve has one of her lessons. If you'd like to.'

'Thank you.' Diana ruffled Maeve's hair. 'Except you've grown rather fond of Erin, haven't you, darling, and I've a feeling you like keeping her to yourself.'

19

The nurse was one she had not met before and, each time Erin asked a question, she kept her head down, referring to Claudia's notes. 'Did you want to speak to a doctor?'

'Only if there's something I need to know.'

'The patient's being treated for hypotension.'

'In that case, I'd like to speak to her, or him,' she added, hoping it was the Scottish one. The last week in January and the baby had reached twenty-seven and a half weeks. Every week mattered. Every day.

The nurse lifted a phone and, from her response, Erin guessed the doctor was busy and there would be a long delay.

'I'll go to the waiting room,' she said. 'Perhaps you could let me know when he comes back.'

'Right you are.' The nurse was so casual, Erin wanted to hit her. She was overreacting, but God knows, if anyone had good reason to overreact, it was her. She had been hoping Andrea would be on duty and the contrast between Andrea and this unfeeling nurse was hard to take.

As she walked down the corridor, her trainers squeaked on the grey linoleum. An empty trolley passed, wheeled by a porter, whistling under his breath, followed by two junior doctors with stethoscopes round their necks. By now, she ought to be used to hospital smells, but they still produced a feeling of dread. For the staff, the patients,

Claudia included, were just bodies in beds, all in a day's work, or was she being unfair? Andrea seemed to care.

She wanted to tell Claudia there was no need to worry, she would look after the baby, and tell her about her real mother and how, if things had been different, she would have played with her, and taken her to the zoo, and loved her. For the first time – was it actually the first time? – she missed Claudia's loud voice and extravagant gestures. Once, alone in the loft, she had picked up her phone, thinking she would call her to tell her what was happening. Only a split second, like when you wake, thinking the dead person you were dreaming about is still alive. It had been like that when their parents were killed.

The waiting room was empty, apart from a man with the red-eyed look of someone who had cried himself dry. He offered to make her a cup of coffee, said he was making one for himself, but she declined the offer, picking up a magazine to make it clear she had no wish to talk. Perhaps he needed someone who would listen. But she was so worried about the baby and angry with the nurse.

Someone had made an effort to make the waiting room comfortable and reasonably cheerful, with the obligatory prints on the wall. There was no disguising the condensation on the windows, the collection of dog-eared magazines, or the sink with its draining board piled high with unwashed mugs and teaspoons, and the remains of a packet of stale digestive biscuits. Erin disliked digestive biscuits, but they always gave her a pang because they had been her father's favourites. When you thought about the dead, it filled you with regret. *I wish I'd eaten one of the biscuits Dad offered me. I wish I'd been more grateful when Mum knitted me a sweater that was far too big and baggy. I wish I'd asked Claudia how she made her rings*

148

and pendants and bracelets.

Prepared for a long wait, she barely had time to flick through the dispiriting pages of celebs – a feature about girls with fantastic breasts but thick ankles – when the nurse returned.

'The doctor will speak to you now.'

Hurrying along the corridor, she caught up with the nurse in the small space she had come to know so well, where they both rubbed antiseptic gel on their hands, and dried them on paper towels. This nurse was not so bad. Erin told herself not to be so critical, and not to compare everyone with Andrea. She had turned Andrea into someone who could do no wrong. Just as she had done with Declan. And look where that had got her.

When she reached Claudia's bed, the doctor – it was her bête noir – was waiting impatiently, but when she saw Erin she smiled, a kind smile that almost brought tears to Erin's eyes. The first time they met she could have been on duty for twelve hours, or more. Today, she was different, more relaxed.

'My sister,' Erin began.

'Have a seat, Erin. It is Erin, isn't it?'

'Yes. Look, I'm sorry about last time but—'

The doctor waved aside her apology. 'It's a very stressful time for you, but there's nothing to worry about at present.'

At present. The kind of throw-away remark that returns to haunt you when you lie awake, sleepless with anxiety. 'The nurse said something about hypotension.'

'Low blood pressure, but Claudia is responding well.'

She was talking as though Claudia was going to recover. But what else could she do? It was better than describing her, like a case study Erin had read online, as "the maternal organism".

'It's possible delivery may have to take place a little sooner than we would have liked. A decision will be made in a day or two. As I said before, the foetus is a surprisingly good size for the number of weeks of gestation.'

'I wonder if you could explain a few terms,' Erin said. 'There's something called olig . . .' She took a slip of paper from her jeans. 'Oligohydramnios.'

'You *have* been doing your homework. It means a deficiency in the amount of amniotic fluid. That's certainly something we monitor carefully. It can be a problem but as of now . . . Any more questions?'

'I don't suppose you can say how likely it is the baby will be all right?'

The doctor had her back turned, checking one of the electrodes attached to Claudia's upper chest. 'With premature babies, it's a question of monitoring their condition from hour to hour. Your sister's baby will have immature lungs and may have to be kept on a ventilator at first.'

Erin opened her mouth to ask the question had been putting off, but the doctor got in first.

'Let's take it one day at a time, shall we?'

When she left the hospital, she decided to stroll down to the shopping centre. She needed some more Indian ink, and while she was there she would look out for the health food shop where Diana worked part-time. Now that she had met her, she would not be taken in by Jon's complaints that she was neurotically over-protective of Maeve. Jon was the neurotic one, tossing out enigmatic remarks then closing up like a clam.

An alleyway, littered with junk food containers, led through to the shops. Deep in thought, she jumped when a

150

man, wearing a zipped-up hoodie, stepped out of a doorway and hurried past her, hands stuffed in the pockets of his jeans. The laces in his trainers trailed on the ground. He slowed down to re-tie them and, when she drew level, mumbled something she failed to catch.

'Sorry? What did you say?'

He paused. His face was hidden, just a glimpse of dark hair. The man who hung about in her road? The figure in the graveyard? Running on ahead, he dashed across the road, almost into the path of a passing bus. Had he been following her? Did he know she visited the hospital every other day at more or less the same time? *The foetus is a surprisingly good size.* He could be the baby's father, frantic to know what was happening to it. If it was going to survive.

Forget about the Indian ink, and Diana's shop. Like it or not, her only hope of finding out more, was to talk to Ava again.

Ava pointed to a table well away from the door. 'People keep leaving it open and letting in cold air. What can I get you, my darling?'

'Just an orange juice, please.'

'Coming up.' Ava's broad hips swayed between the tables, with practised expertise. She would know the orange juice was an excuse, but from the look of her she was in a better mood than last time. Either that, or she had prepared herself for another visit and knew how she was going to handle it.

The table where Erin was sitting could have done with a wipe and the floor next to her chair was covered in crumbs. Close by, an old man, with a droopy moustache, was making his cup of tea last as long as possible. Erin nodded in his direction and he raised a hand in greeting.

'Chilly today.'

'Yes. Yes, it is.' The good old weather to fall back on. Like the man in the raincoat who walked up and down Claudia's road. Her road. Was he a widower? He gave the impression he was the archetypal bachelor.

'Always nice and warm in here.'

'Yes, it is.' The café smelled of stale cheese, thinly disguised with cinnamon, and Erin considered making a deal with Ava. Tell me everything you know and in return I promise to give the place a thorough spring clean. She could just imagine Ava's face.

A glass of juice was placed in front of her and, to her surprise, Ava pulled up a chair. 'So what did you think of the play?'

'Oh. Kent told you I went to see it?'

'No, but I assumed curiosity would get the better of you.'

'I talked to him afterwards but he has no idea where Ollie is. He hadn't been in touch.'

'No?' Erin had expected Ava to be disappointed, but the expression on her face was more one of relief. 'Actually, I don't think he and Ollie were that close.'

'The play was quite unusual.'

'I'll bet.' Ava's hands were clasped together, as though she had a genuine interest. 'A parody of *Hamlet*, wasn't it?'

'Only three characters and I don't think there was a magician in *Hamlet*. Although there was a ghost.'

'But not in Kent's version. Tell me, Erin, have you thought what's going to happen after the baby's born? It's unfair, all that responsibility put on you.' She studied Erin's expression, misinterpreting it. 'You've never wanted children? Me neither.'

Erin picked up her drink. 'You mentioned that Hoshi

helped paint the walls in Claudia's loft.'

'When she knew you were coming to live there.'

'Did Claudia pay him?'

Ava laughed. 'Oh, you're thinking she paid him in other ways. I know I complained Claudia could be tactless, but only because she was so spontaneous.'

'Impulsive.'

'Yes, but that's a good trait, isn't it. Living life to the full, I was terribly fond of her.'

'When I left the hospital earlier today, a man was hanging about, waiting for me.'

'Waiting for you?' Her voice was high-pitched with incredulity. 'You're overwrought, my dear, but why wouldn't you be? Obviously, you knew your sister far better than I did, but if you want my honest opinion . . .' She broke off, checking in case a customer was waiting to be served. 'Ollie's a dear, but young for his age, much too young to be a parent. I expect he'd like to give the baby up for adoption but feels he'd be letting down your sister. I know you wanted Claudia kept on life support but—'

'If I want your honest opinion?'

'Take no notice, my darling. When tragedy befalls us, we always look for an explanation. Human nature, I suppose.'

20

As she was about to go into the house, Claudia's neighbour, Harold Lord accosted her. 'Any news?'

What did he mean? Did he think Claudia was still alive?

'Your sister and I, we used to have conversations. Had a shared interest in education. The key to social mobility.' He came very close. Too close. 'Not schools so much although they're important if you want a literate society. Higher education, universities, that's what Claudia and I used to discuss. I was in admin. I expect she told you. Not a local college, one up north. Took early retirement when student numbers escalated.'

'You knew her quite well then?' Perhaps she had felt sorry for him, except that was not like Claudia.

'She worried about the students from overseas,' he continued, 'feared they might be homesick. There was a girl from Hong Kong who was going to have to provide for her whole extended family. They'd saved up for her to come to the UK to gain a higher degree. Claudia told me her name, but I'm afraid I've forgotten.'

'Did my sister ever mention someone called Lara?'

'Lara?' He scratched his chin. 'The heroine in *Doctor Zhivago*. Russian, is she? We don't get many of those. Not that I'm up to date in such matters. Some of them have problems adjusting to our culture. There was a boy from Ceylon. No, these days it's called Sri Lanka. He kept

154

bursting into tears your sister said. Lonely, poor lad.'

'I wondered,' Erin interrupted his description of Claudia, the do-gooder, 'have you noticed a man wearing a hoodie hanging about in the road?'

'What age, young or old?'

'I've no idea. He keeps his hood up.'

Harold smacked his lips. 'Drugs. Sure to be. We've had our share of break-ins. Make sure you lock up properly. I used to say the same to your sister but she took a carefree approach. Whatever will be will be. There's a special centre for overseas students.' Warming to his subject, he moved even closer and she could smell the oil on his thinning hair. 'Claudia worked there for a time, providing advice and support, a shoulder to lean on.' He fished in the pocket of his raincoat and handed her a crumpled flyer with a picture of a redbrick house and details of the student centre.

'Thank you.' It was irritating how one of her neighbours knew more about Claudia than she did, although it was something she ought to be getting used to.

'I'm surprised she never told you,' he said, increasing her annoyance. 'Research students are often poor. Ollie used to complain he hadn't a penny.'

'Oh, you know Ollie too?'

'Haven't seen him lately. People talk, but it's always the same. Have you met Veronica at number seventeen? Terrible gossip. I take no notice. Better that way.'

Erin murmured something non-committal and, when he saw Ben approaching, Harold moved on quickly.

'I'm arranging a party for Jennie's birthday.' Ben clapped his hands and spread his fingers wide. 'But not a word to her. It's a surprise.'

'When?' A party was the last thing Erin felt like.

'Tomorrow. She doesn't like birthdays.'

155

'So how will she feel about a party?'

Ben pulled a face. 'Once everyone starts arriving, she'll love it.'

'You'll have to tell her before that so she can change.'

'Good point.' He picked at a scab on his knuckle. 'Did I tell you the joke about the life coach and—'

'The student, Ben, ex-student. Hoshi. How well do you know him?'

'Don't say you've fallen for him. Most women do. It's those eyes. Not fair. Still, if I looked like that I might get even less work. Character actors are far more employable but rarely get the kudos they deserve. In my profession, you have to put on a brave face, keep up appearances. I've always had a fear of losing my hair, and I'd like to be well over six foot instead of a miserable five foot, seven and a half, but it's the hair I worry about.'

'Hoshi?'

'I'll invite him to the party. Can't guarantee he'll turn up though. Works in a shop down at the shopping centre. Sports stuff. Expensive. Has Harold Lord been bothering you? He writes down registration numbers in case a passing van scrapes someone's parked car. Take whatever he tells you with a pinch of salt. I gather you've met Kent. He'll be coming to the party too. Writes his own plays so he can keep his hand in. Took rather a fancy to poor old Ollie. I imagine he bats for both sides. No, not Ollie, I didn't mean Ollie.'

'You liked Claudia, didn't you?'

'Liked her? Yes, of course. What have people been saying? Not that Harold Lord?'

'He told me she took an interest in overseas students. Befriended them. Only not long ago this girl came to the door, demanding to see her and—'

'As if you didn't have enough to put up with.' But he

was looking away from her and she suspected he might know who Lara was. Not that he had any intention of telling her.

Maeve was straightening things on Erin's shelves, two rulers and a pen with flexible nib, a bottle of black ink and a pile of scrap paper.

'You've got a lot of stuff.'

'I need it for the illustrations. Come and sit down, I want to talk to you about colours.'

'Why did you leave London?'

'I split up with my boyfriend.'

'What was he called?'

'Declan.'

'Were you sad?'

'A bit. Not anymore.' Erin drew up a chair next to Maeve's. 'Right, reddish colours are warm and bluish ones are cold. Warm colours advance, come forward.'

'And cool ones go back. Little children draw big yellow suns with lines sticking out but the sun never looks like that. And animals like dogs are a funny shape when they're lying down, not just sausages on legs. Dad takes me swimming on Saturdays.'

'I expect you're a good swimmer, aren't you? So you have a busy weekend. Art class in the morning and swimming in the afternoon.'

'It's so Mum can work in the shop. Have you been to it? Oh, look!' Miss Havisham had strolled through the door, tail in the air. Maeve picked her up and hugged her. 'Who does she belong to?'

'I still haven't discovered, but a cat must have lived in this house once because of the cat flap in the kitchen.'

'Mum was pleased you came to our house. Dad thinks she suffers from nerves but I think it's Dad who's the

157

nervous one, only he's better at hiding what he's feeling.'

'That's very perceptive of you, Maeve.'

She laughed, pressing her face against the cat's soft fur. 'Miss Havisham smells of mint. Is there some in the garden?'

'I don't think so, but I expect she visits most of the gardens in this road.'

'I don't think Claudia liked me.'

'What? Why do you say that? Of course she did. You only met her a few times.'

'Is Ollie dead?'

'No!' But how could she sound so sure?

'Where is he? Nobody knows, do they? A man came to our house in a van with that dresser you saw in our kitchen. An actor with a funny name. Kent, I think he's called Kent.'

So he had another string to his bow – palming people off with sub-standard antiques. 'What made you think about that?'

'I'm not going to be an actor.' Maeve tossed back her fringe. 'But I might write plays. No, I know, I could write a story, like your one about guinea pigs, and do my own illustrations.'

'Good idea. Now, let's get back to colours.'

'Can I draw my own picture? With a pencil. It won't need colours.'

'Right you are.' Erin was thinking about the money in Claudia's desk and wondering if it had anything to do with Kent's antique business. Cash in hand, a way of avoiding tax? But Kent could have kept the money himself. With a jolt, it occurred to her Claudia could have been blackmailing someone. Surely not. Would she really have sunk that low? If she needed the cash badly enough . . .

158

Miss Havisham was pretending she was too large to squeeze through the door and, as Erin opened it, she heard the post fall on the mat. 'Just going downstairs a moment. Maeve?'

No reply. She was too absorbed with her drawing. It was the first time she had asked to draw something out of her head. Was she starting to feel frustrated with the objects Erin gave her, the fruit and vegetables, and last time a pair of shoes?

All junk mail, apart from a reminder to renew car insurance that she would add to the folder she was keeping – to be dealt with at a later date. When? In her head, "a later date" meant after the baby was born. It was like the deadline for her illustrations. No, it was far more important than that. The illustrations had to be completed, but the rest of her life was on hold.

When she returned to the loft, Maeve was sitting with her arms folded.

'Finished already? Let's see.'

The drawing was babyish, as though Maeve had deliberately reverted to an earlier time. Two crudely-drawn people, a man and woman faced each other, heads in profile, mouths wide open, and next to them stood a large gravestone with RIP carved into it – she had managed to make the letters look three-dimensional – and a single name: MAEVE.

'Is it an illustration? For a story you've written?'

She shook her head.

'Who are the people? Anyone in particular?'

'I heard them.' Her voice was muffled by the fingers she had stuffed in her mouth.

'Who? Who did you hear?'

No reply. She was crying. 'Oh, Maeve, what is it, what's the matter?'

'They thought I was asleep. I go to bed much earlier than most of my friends. I heard them arguing. Dad said it was time I knew the truth and Mum said if he told me . . . And Dad said if they didn't—'

'Told you what?'

'I'm going to die. It's because I'm clumsy and I can't do Maths or climb trees. I read in one of Mum's magazines, it's called a life-limiting disease.'

'Oh, Maeve, I'm certain that's not what they were talking about. Of course you're not going to die.' Erin knelt beside her. 'I expect they were discussing which school you'll be going to.'

'Boarding school, you mean. I don't want to go to boarding school. Promise you won't tell Dad I told you? No, please, I wouldn't have said if—'

'If *you* promise you'll talk to him yourself.'

'You don't think I'm going to die?'

'No, I don't. Talk to your Dad on your way home. I'm sure it was nothing. Schools, it'll be schools. Have they ever mentioned boarding? I thought you were going to that school on the hill.'

'Are you sure?'

'Positive.' But perhaps Maeve was right and it was something to do with her health. The reason Jon kept starting to tell her something, then changed his mind?

'Erin?'

'Now what?'

'I love you.'

'Oh, Maeve, I love you too.'

160

21

Jennie was wearing a shapeless blue dress and her hair was still damp from the shower.

'Happy birthday.' Erin handed her a small parcel. 'It's the thought that counts.'

'I hate birthdays.'

'Me too, but people won't let you get away with it.'

Laughter was coming from the living room and Erin guessed Ben was relating one of his anecdotes about a film company, or the BBC, or perhaps it was his audition for the slimming drink. Erin had had actor friends in London and knew the amount of rejection they had to bear. And how they often dealt with it by turning painful experiences into funny stories.

'Come through.' Jennie tore the paper off the scarf Erin had bought her. 'Oh, thanks.' She actually sounded as though she meant it. 'Lovely colours.' She kissed Erin's cheek. 'Thank you.'

'Need any help in the kitchen?'

'Ben's done everything. Wouldn't let me move a muscle.'

The room was full of strangers, and the music – a female singer with a deep, throaty voice – was too loud for comfortable conversation. Erin joined the laughing group, moving away when Ben started on a story she had heard before. Plenty of people but no sign of Hoshi. Would he turn up later? She was rather banking on it.

161

Jon was on her mind too. Her description of Maeve's drawing had shocked him, but only because he felt guilty she had overheard him and Diana arguing. *Yes, you're right, it's about her going to a private school. Diana wants to tell her but it's not fixed yet, not what I want although Diana usually gets her own way.* Erin was relieved, poor Maeve would be too, although something about Jon's manner had made her uneasy, as though he had jumped at her suggestion of what the argument could have been about. Obviously, Maeve had not spoken to him herself.

Ben called to her over his shoulder. 'If you can't act, wear a big hat!' And he and the girl he had been talking to, both roared with laughter and wine splashed out of the drinks he was carrying. 'Red or white, Erin, or there's some other stuff in the kitchen. Kent's coming. He was flattered you went to see his play. Told me how much you'd enjoyed it! Was it any good? No, don't tell me, incomprehensible and far too long. Anyway, he's not here yet. Always turns up late so he can make an entrance.'

Erin picked up one of the hideous clay bowls Jennie had made when she attended a pottery class. 'I keep seeing this man, Ben, watching Claudia's house.'

'Watching the house?' He studied her face as though it was the first time he had looked at her properly. 'Why would someone do that? Come to the kitchen and tell me about it.'

'Not much to tell.' Ben handed her an over full glass. 'He has his hood pulled up so I've never seen his face.'

'Just getting some refills,' Ben called, but Jennie was deep in conversation with a middle-aged actor Erin recognised from a television series a few years' back

'Now.' Ben perched on the edge of the kitchen table. 'You think he's a friend of Ollie's?'

'Look, was there something Claudia was involved in? I know so little about her life before I came to live here. Ollie moved in quite soon and after that they were in each other's pockets. Only – don't mention this to anyone else, but one of the doctors remarked on what a good size the baby is. And did I think Claudia could have got her dates wrong.'

'So you're thinking . . . Did Ollie know? No? Would Claudia really have done that to him?'

'You won't repeat any of this. Well, obviously you can tell Jennie. I wondered . . . Ava said Hoshi painted Claudia's loft.'

'And you're thinking he could be the father.' For once, he was being serious. 'It's going to be easy enough to tell. Either it'll have Claudia and Ollie's fair colouring or . . .'

Jennie appeared and he broke off, asking if Kent had turned up.

'Far too early.' Jennie eyed them suspiciously. 'What were you two talking about?'

'Actors, and what idiots they are.' Ben moved to fill her glass but she put her hand over it.

'White wine gives me a stomach ache.'

'So what's in that glass?'

'Soda water.'

The three of them stood in a slightly uneasy silence until someone in the other room called Jennie's name and she drifted away.

'Has she said anything to you?' Ben had waited until she was out of earshot. 'There's definitely something worrying her.'

'Perhaps it's about the student lets.'

'Is that what she told you?'

'No.'

He gave a long, slow sigh. 'She's not normally the

secretive type, but recently I don't know where I am with her. In a world of her own. As I said before, I don't think she's well, but when I suggested a visit to the doctor she bit my head off.'

'Yesterday I thought she might like to come to the hospital with me but—'

'She doesn't like hospitals. The smell. I guess she's a bit of a hypochondriac, but aren't we all? To get back to Ollie, I suppose it's possible Claudia told Jennie something and she's protecting him.'

'Protecting him?' It was only her second glass of wine but she felt light-headed and had to put a hand on the table to steady herself. 'Surely, she'd have told you.'

He shrugged, examining one of his fingers as if he thought he might have picked up a splinter. 'I know some of the protestors were probably drunk, or high, but would they have loosened a scaffolding pole? And why was Claudia standing under it?'

'She'd crossed the road. I thought she might have recognised someone.'

'One of the protesters? Is that likely? You mean she could have known one of them?'

'That's all I can think of.'

'I suppose it's possible. Come on, we'd better join the rest. Pick Hoshi's brain if he turns up, but he may stay well clear.'

'Why?'

'I doubt if he's the partying type. Actually, I don't know him that well. He came round once or twice—'

'When he and Claudia . . . Before Ollie came on the scene?'

He nodded, vaguely, clearly relieved when we heard Kent's booming voice and the two of them could return to the other room.

To Erin's surprise, Kent was accompanied by Ava. He was holding forth about the good old days when every town had a repertory theatre and actors learned their trade, instead of trying to break straight into television. 'Without an iota of experience.' He spotted Erin and Ben and, without bothering to excuse himself to his audience, made a bee line in their direction and gave each of them a kiss on both cheeks.

'All right, Kent?' Ben asked.

'Aw right? I see you've acquired the local vernacular. Never mind, a party for Jennie was one of your better ideas, and finding Erin here is the icing on the cake.'

'I'm living in Claudia's loft.'

'Did Erin tell you, Ben, she came to see my play? Why didn't you, you traitor? Good audience, very appreciative. I'll be putting on a new one in the spring. Still under wraps, state secret.' He turned to Erin. 'We all miss your sister so much. Tell me if I'm intruding, but is the baby unaffected?'

'You're intruding.' Jennie took hold of Ben's arm and dragged him away, calling over her shoulder. 'Don't let Kent bully you, Erin.'

'Bully you?' Kent looked genuinely hurt, if any of his expressions were genuine. 'I was commiserating as I'm sure Erin understood perfectly well. The photograph you mentioned, my dear, the one taken in a bar. I remember your sister's exact words. Cosy up, you two, or I won't fit both of you in.'

'You and Ollie.'

'Me and Ollie? I hope you're not implying . . .' He roared with laughter, throwing back his head so it was impossible not to notice how his teeth were too good to be true. 'Your sister was crazy about the boy. Attraction of opposites, I imagine. Such a vibrant person. I adored her.'

Ben was calling her name and, when she turned her head, Erin saw he was standing next to a stunningly good looking young man.

'This is Hoshi,' Ben said unnecessarily, 'Hoshi, this is Claudia's sister, Erin.'

He held out a hand, with a damp palm, but avoided her eyes. 'I'm sorry about . . . about what happened.'

'Thank you.' It was right, the way people described him. He was not just good looking, his oval face with its almond shaped eyes, was beautiful. A few strands of jet black hair flopped over one eye, and his full lips could have belonged to a woman, although there was nothing effeminate about him.

'It was a terrible thing.' His voice was cool, formal, and she wondered if he and Claudia had fallen out badly. Over Ollie?

'I'll leave you two to talk,' Ben said. 'Just check Jennie's OK.'

Hoshi was shifting his weight from one foot to the other. Why was he so jumpy? Embarrassment, not knowing what to say? But it was more than that. His eye darted about the room as though he was desperate to escape.

'I hear you decorated Claudia's loft,' Erin said, 'did you choose the colour?'

'The colour?' He licked his lips. 'No, Claudia did.'

'But you did all the work.'

He forced a smile.

'I don't suppose you have any idea where Ollie might be?'

'Ollie?' He was breathing hard. 'No, I'm sorry.'

Why was he so nervous? No, it was more than that. He was afraid.

'Anyway, you painted the loft very well,' she said,

'and in any other circumstances I would enjoy staying there, using it as a studio. A cat comes to the house. My pupil's named it Miss Havisham. Because of its black and white . . . I expect you saw it. There's a cat flap in the kitchen.' She had hoped talk of the cat might put him at his ease but he was edging away.

'Did you and Ollie meet at the university?'

But already he was on his way to the far end of the room, although when he saw Ava he did a sharp turn and pretended to be inspecting another of Jennie's efforts in clay.

So far, Ava had not spoken to Erin, or even acknowledged her existence. Seeing her long, black skirt, and a scarlet top, made of some flimsy, see-through material, reminded Erin of how she had once consulted a fortune teller at a festival in a London park. *You've been having a difficult time but things are going to change for the better.* That was what they always said, although, on that particular occasion, the woman had turned over tarot cards and told her to be careful "who she allowed into my heart". Well, she had been right about that.

Her unwanted visits to the café made her hold back from approaching Ava. Kent had re-joined her, and Erin suspected they were talking about her. *Claudia's sister's a pain in the arse. Keeps asking questions. Won't leave things alone. I'd stay well clear if I was you.* Kent glanced in her direction, confirming what she was thinking. Were they complaining about her or was Kent telling Ava where Ollie was hiding out? Or were they exchanging opinions about "the accident"?

Now Ava was staring at Hoshi, and Erin could see she was annoyed with him. While he was working in the café, they must have become friends, but perhaps he had let her down, leaving, without working out his notice, when he

167

found a job in the clothes shop. Perhaps it was the first time they had met since he failed to turn up for work. So many people who claimed to be friends but were turning out to be nothing of the sort. And all of them involved with Claudia in some way. And none of them prepared to talk openly about her.

Jennie was sitting on a chair by the window, sipping her soda water. After the trouble Ben had gone to, she could at least try to look as if she was enjoying herself, although Erin had some sympathy. Surprise parties were a pain.

Oblivious of his wife, Ben was demonstrating how to have a sword fight without injuring your opponent.

'Look at him.' It was Kent, who must have crept up while she was watching Jennie. 'They teach that kind of stuff at drama school, make it look like a dance. Characterisation – that's what acting's about. Getting inside the character's head. Your poor sister understood the human mind and it tended to take her down some dangerous paths.'

What was he telling her? That Claudia had interfered in people's lives and paid the price? 'Dangerous paths?'

'A turn of phrase. Bad choice of words. What I meant, she drew people to her, took an interest in them and—'

'And then lost interest.'

'What makes you say that?' His mouth was only a few inches from her ear. 'Take my advice, my dear, and let her die in peace.'

22

The way he looked at the woman, Stella should have known it was not his wife. The belief that people got married and stayed in love with their partner was half-witted. Human beings were not like swans, mated for life. They craved new experiences, new lovers.

Because of the resident parking permits, she had been forced to leave her car quite a distance from the house. Then, hour upon hour of hanging about, with no comings and goings at the house, nothing. Where was he? The second day, the woman had come out, returning later, looking tired and depressed. Was her lover playing games, messing her about?

Where did he live? She needed a better plan. But her only hope was to carry on, watching the woman's house, and hopefully he would come back and, when he left, she could follow him home. But that would mean her car had to be close by. Alternatively, she could wait outside his university department again. Same problem where to leave the car and if he cycled it was possible he followed a route with short cuts, open to cyclists but not to cars.

Detective work was a nightmare and if she hung about much longer, a nosey neighbour would start keeping tabs on her. Wearing a hoodie was a necessary precaution, but walking up and down with your hood pulled up made it look like you were up to no good.

One afternoon, the woman had visited another house

farther down the road. Later she had returned home, and much later, according to Stella's records it was twenty to four, all her waiting had paid off and he had turned up in a car, this time with a child. It was wrapped up warm, impossible to see if it was a boy or a girl, but Stella had assumed he would have to come back for it.

And she had been right.

Just before six, he had returned and she had been ready, standing fifty yards away, head down, pretending to be checking her phone. When he turned in her direction, she was afraid he had recognised her, but he was only guiding the child into the passenger seat.

Progress at last. It was not where the child lived so it must be coming there for a particular reason. To be looked after between the end of the school day and when he finished work? No, that made no sense or he would have brought it every day. All the same, Stella had made a decision to give up her morning vigils, but come to the road each afternoon at four and sit in her car, facing in the direction of the way he drove off.

The next few days had been a frustrating waste of time but then he had delivered the child again. Except, he had come back sooner than the previous time so she had almost missed them. The woman had come out too, and the child had hopped about impatiently until he unlocked his car. A short distance away, a delivery van was blocking the road so he had been obliged to take a turning to the right, and for several minutes she had lost sight of him, sweating with relief when she spotted his car in the distance at the bottom of the hill. As she approached the junction, the lights had changed. If it had been up to her, she would have risked going through red, but the car in front had been driven by an old bloke, who had pulled up when the lights turned amber, and by the time Stella turned the corner he had disappeared.

Hours more waiting around, but at last it had paid off. Two days ago, the child had been dropped off as usual and he had returned two hours later. This time no fucking van had blocked the road. The child had been bouncing up and down and the man had turned his head, probably to tell it to sit still, then glanced in his driving mirror so Stella had been sure he must have seen her.

At the bottom of the hill, he had turned left as usual, continuing up the long straight road, then indicated left again and slowed down, pulling up outside a thirties style house, with ugly pebble-dash, painted an unattractive shade of mustard yellow.

The windows were rectangular with metal frames, and two wheelie bins, one black, one green, had been left next to a dilapidated porch. As she recalled he had never cared much about his surroundings, but what about his wife? As she watched from a safe distance, he had been greeted by a dark-haired woman, very different from the one at the other house. The child had squeezed past the two of them and disappeared, and the adults had paused for a moment, before the man walked back towards the road, but only to close the garden gate and Stella had driven off without looking back.

Today she had taken a risk, stopping on the opposite side of the road, a little farther up the hill from his house. No sign of any of them so far, but since it was Saturday they would have a different routine. How long should she wait? They might stay inside all day. Another hour and she would leave, go for drive, perhaps to Bath, returning later to check if it was possible to approach the house from behind, where she might be able to see the garden, and the windows at the back.

Did she really want go all the way to Bath? She

decided to return to the basement and see if the washing machine had finished its programme or, like last time, it had stopped halfway through and she had been obliged to give it a kick. It was a disgrace the landlady was allowed to let out the place. Cheap, she would give her that, but barely fit for human occupation. Buying to let was a profitable business. Profitable if you were not too fussy about the well-being of your tenants.

Just about to switch on the engine, she paused as someone came out of the house. The woman. Dropping a bag of rubbish in one of the bins, she looked all about her, as if she knew someone was watching her. How could she? She might have been checking parked cars, ones that were not normally left in the road. Next time Stella came she would leave her car somewhere else. She was getting careless, taking risks, but the waiting was dragging her down, and the previous evening an attack of migraine had knocked her out for several hours.

23

February, Erin's least favourite month, although just now all that mattered was that the baby had reached twenty-nine weeks. In her mind, thirty meant she would be all right, healthy, with well-developed lungs.

Don't think about it. She needed company, someone to take her mind off her worries, but when she rang the bell, Jennie answered, still in her pyjamas and, since it was almost midday, she thought Ben must be right about her being unwell.

'Oh, you poor thing, is there anything you need?'

'Come in.' Jennie held a tissue to her nose.

At first, Erin hung back, unwilling to pick up germs that would mean she had to stay away from the hospital. On the other hand, if it was flu, Jennie would have been infectious at the party. 'I could do some shopping for you.'

'Actually, there is something. Ben's in London or I wouldn't ask.' Jennie led her into the kitchen, walking so slowly and unsteadily Erin thought she must have a temperature. 'I promised the tenant in the basement flat I'd deliver a new microwave. The old one burned out . . . The previous tenants.'

'When is she likely to be in?'

Jennie held a tissue to her nose. 'If nobody answers I expect it would be all right to leave it outside in its box, provided it's not visible from the street. There's a small

173

area with a bay tree.'

'You haven't told me where the house is.'

'Oh, no, sorry, I'll write down the directions. You can't miss it. It's next to a day nursery called Happy . . . Happy something.' She found a ballpoint pen that was running out of ink, and began scribbling down the names of roads on the back of an old envelope.

'Happy Days?' Erin waited for her to show her where the box was. 'In here, is it? The microwave.'

'Oh, sorry, no, it's in the living room. I'm afraid it's quite heavy. Do you know how to get to Gloucester Road?'

'Yes, I think so.'

'You go through Horfield then turn off to the right.' She handed her the envelope. 'It's quite easy to find.'

Jennie's living room was the same as Claudia's, except Claudia had liked bright colours and Jennie's was painted white, with white curtains and a single white rug. The large sofa was also white, and, since the party, a wood-burning stove had been installed.

'We haven't lit it yet.' Jennie had followed Erin's gaze. 'Ben thought it would make the room feel cosier, but I'm worried about the smoke.'

'It'll go up the chimney, won't it?' So whatever was on Jennie's mind, it was not a lack of money.

'Yes, I suppose so.' Her voice was flat, but she was starting to look better. Was she ill or was there another reason she wanted to avoid going round to the student house? Perhaps she and her tenant had fallen out.

'What's she called, this tenant? Oh, yes, you said. Stella, isn't it? Tall, well-dressed. Was she the one who complained about the microwave?'

Jennie's fingers pressed on her cheekbones. 'To tell you the truth, I've been worrying in case the university sent her there. As a mole. Isn't that what they call them? To check up, make sure the flats are up to standard.'

'Surely not.' If the all-white room was hers, she would have brightened it up with some cushions. 'They wouldn't actually move someone in.'

'There might have been complaints from neighbours. Noise late at night. She could be from the council.'

Erin was looking at a picture on the wall, a reproduction of a Bridget Riley, with black and white stripes that made her eyes hurt.

'I know it's a bit much to ask.' Jennie bent to pick up the microwave, then gave up and asked Erin if she minded.

'You ought to be in bed.'

'If you get a chance, could you try to find out who she is?'

'Stella? Are you sure she's not a student? A visiting lecturer maybe. The undergraduates have only just returned, haven't they? Anyway, if I discover anything, I'll let you know.'

As she drove past a park, Erin could see snowdrops and purple crocuses, although the crocuses were not up to the ones in Diana's garden. Some of the ones in the park had been flattened, probably by children or dogs, and she caught a glimpse of a dog the size of a bear, and a man who could be practising Tai Chi. It was a cold, clear day and the expanse of grass was inviting. She could have done with a walk, or even a run.

The microwave was on the passenger seat and she was driving slowly in case it slid off. Up the famous Gloucester Road, that claimed to have more independent shops than any other street in the British Isles, all the while looking out for an old redbrick building that had been built as swimming baths at the time of the First World War, but was now converted into flats. Like the ones close to the centre where Claudia . . . Don't think about it. Concentrate on Jennie's instructions. They were not brilliant but she passed what appeared to be the building Jennie meant, and pulled up at the lights. Another quarter of a mile or so, then the second road on the right after a pedestrian crossing. Then look out for the "Happy Days" nursery. Checking the microwave was secure, she realised she was hoping Stella would be in. Idle curiosity, or so she could do a spot of detective work and report back to Jennie?

The pedestrian crossing came so soon she would have missed it were it not for a group of women with buggies who had stepped out into the road in a convoy. Another hundred yards and, to her relief, she recognised the name of one of the roads Jennie had written down and, indicating right, waited for a break in the on-coming traffic.

Two hundred yards, another turn to the right, and there it was. A day nursery, but called "Red Shoes" – nothing to do with "Happy". Jennie must have been thinking about *Happy Feet*, the film about penguins. *The Red Shoes* was a rather unpleasant story. Shoes that kept on dancing even when the wearer's feet were chopped off. It was one of Claudia's favourites.

When she pulled up outside the student house, two women wearing headscarves were coming through the front door. Overseas students, perhaps? Erin recalled her conversation with Harold Lord, and Lara who had come to the door, asking for "Clowda".

When she arrived in Bristol it had been the long summer holiday, but all through the autumn nothing had been said about befriending students. Had that been where

Claudia went when Erin assumed she was at her stall in the market? Why not say so? Why not tell her about it? Perhaps she was embarrassed that she had volunteered to do something helpful. It went against her self-image, or the one she presented to Erin.

No parking restrictions, so Erin left her car and said good morning to the two students, smiling to herself when the taller one of them replied with a strong Midlands accent, making her feel mildly ashamed for jumping to the conclusion they were from abroad.

The other one asked if she was the landlady.

'No. I'm delivering something to the tenant in the basement.'

'Oh.' They looked at each other.

'You know her?'

They shook their heads. 'I asked her the way to the Student Union,' the taller one said, 'but she didn't know.'

Carrying the microwave down the dangerously uneven steps, Erin lowered it to the ground, next to a bay tree that looked way past saving, and knocked on the basement door. No response so she knocked louder.

'Who is it?' The voice was deep and husky.

'Mrs Markham asked me to bring your new microwave.'

A long pause followed, as though the person inside was in a dilemma whether or not to come to the door, then it opened and a tall, elegant woman with bright red hair stood, checking her phone. She was sucking a sweet and Erin noticed her nails were expertly manicured, and her bracelet looked like it was solid gold.

'Mrs Markham is one of my neighbours,' Erin explained. 'She's not well so she asked me to . . .'

The woman was staring at her. 'You'd better bring it inside.' Now she was checking her phone again. Clearly

177

someone used to giving orders. So why was she renting this dingy basement?

Erin put the box down on the grubby carpet, and turned to leave.

The woman was standing between her and the door. 'You don't look like a landlady.'

'What do they look like? I haven't been in the city long. It's just a temporary arrangement.'

'Like me.' The woman's face broke into a broad grin. 'I'm Stella. Found this dump through an agency.'

'Erin.'

'Nice name.' She inspected the cardboard box. 'Cheap thing, is it? Still, I won't be here much longer and I don't expect whoever moves in will know the difference. If you're not a landlady, what are you?'

'Why?'

'Just wondered.'

'Actually, I'm an artist, an illustrator. Mostly children's books.'

Stella's eyebrows twitched and Erin suspected she thought an illustrator was not a proper artist. She was wrong.

'Lucky you. I love children's books, especially the old ones I inherited from my mother. *Orlando*, *The Marmalade Cat*, and the Babar books, of course. Have you read them?'

'*Babar the King*.'

'And *Babar at Home*.' They're translated from the French. What's your book about?'

'A pet shop.'

'Do you get many commissions? I imagine it's a fairly precarious way to make a living.'

'I get by.'

'In that case you must be good at your job.' Stella

178

picked up the microwave as if it was a box of feathers, and Erin turned to leave, but once again she was stopped with a question. Perhaps this Stella was as much in need of company as she was. 'You're lucky to have work you love . . . I'm assuming you love it?'

'What do *you* do?' She was so out of place in the basement flat, Erin was becoming increasingly curious.

'This and that.' She gave a short laugh, as though Erin had asked something surprising. 'Marketing, PR . . . Thank you for bringing the microwave. The last time I saw Mrs Markham she didn't look in the best of health. Worn out, poor woman, keeping tabs on all her tenants.'

On her way home, Erin remembered how Jennie had wanted her to check if her tenant was a "spy", from the university, or possibly from Inland Revenue. Highly unlikely. Whoever she was, she just needed somewhere to stay for a short period. Except, surely she could have afforded a hotel, one of those cut price places. By the look of her, there was no shortage of cash.

When she drove passed Ava's Place, Ava was standing on the pavement, talking to Kent. He was frowning and the two of them gave the impression they were having a serious conversation rather than a friendly chat. Kent had his hands in the pockets of his cord trousers, but Ava's arms were waving about, and Erin had never seen her looking so agitated.

The traffic was moving slowly and, when it speeded up again, Erin stalled the engine and was subjected to loud hooting from the taxi behind her. Had Kent and Ava been talking about Claudia or Ollie? Why would they be? Other people's lives had moved on. They had more important things to think about. All the same, she would dearly love to have heard what they were saying.

* * *

179

After an evening at the hospital, she drove up her road in the dark, searching for a parking space, and caught sight of Jon. Had he been to the house, looking for her, or was he on the way there? More to the point, had Maeve plucked up the courage to ask if they were planning to send her away to school?

'Thought I'd missed you.' He joined her as she was folding back the wing mirrors. 'Just wanted a quick word about Maeve.'

'Maeve, or the classes? You'd better come in.'

'Any news?'

'No.'

Up in the loft, she switched on a heater and started telling him about Ben and Jennie's party, and her conversation with Kent.

'He sold us a Welsh dresser. Swindled us. It had been repaired.'

'Yes, Diana told me.'

'Oh.' He started to cough. 'Yes. She was pleased you called round.'

'I'd gone out for a walk. Realised I was near your road. You didn't mind?'

'No, of course not.'

Erin was watching him carefully. 'Did Maeve talk to you about her drawing?'

'I thought it best not to mention it.'

'Why?' Erin gave a sigh of disgust.

'We may send her to a private school but nothing's been decided yet. I'll ask her what she thinks.'

'Jon?'

He spun round. 'What?'

'If you know something about Claudia, I'd far rather you told me. The man who's been hanging about . . . I thought it might be Hoshi but now I've met him—'

'When? When did you—'

'At Jennie's party. It was her birthday. Actually I thought you might be there. Anyway, being so secretive is having a bad effect on Maeve. Yes, I know she's *your* daughter, but I was the one she drew the picture for. It was disturbing. Well, it alarmed me.'

'I expect it was an illustration for a story. She likes writing stories. I keep them in a folder.'

'It wasn't. I asked her.' She disliked the way he made out what a liberal-minded father he was, while Diana was the "bad cop". Declan had played the same game, relating events that put him in a good light and making his "estranged" wife sound like a nightmare.

'Did she do any more drawings like that?'

'Isn't one enough? Is that why you came round here? Talk to her. I may not have any children but I know it's a mistake to keep things from them. They always imagine something far worse than it actually is.'

He nodded, but said nothing, and with a dull thud in the pit of her stomach, it occurred to her that poor Maeve might be right when she thought her "syndrome" meant her life expectancy was shorter than normal.

24

Painting the glossy, black feathers of a mynah bird was tricky. Hints of purple, blue and green. Beautiful birds, so it was no wonder that in their native home of India they were considered sacred. And their ability to talk was legendary.

When they were children, Erin and Claudia had been fond of the mynah bird that lived in the local pet shop. He was not for sale, but sat on a perch and imitated the jingly bell when someone opened the shop door. Then one day he disappeared and the owner of the pet shop said he was ill. Erin had cried, but Claudia was more practical. *What's wrong with him?* And the pet shop people explained how someone had fed him fruit that was bad for mynah birds. Apples, bananas, pears and melons were good, but not avocados or rhubarb. *Someone gave him rhubarb?* Claudia's horrified voice was imprinted on Erin's memory.

Later, to everyone's relief, the bird got better, but when the door opened, instead of imitating the bell, it now recited the phrase it had heard repeatedly while it was recovering. *Ah, poor thing, poor thing.*

Erin felt like a poor thing. Not that she was ill, but she slept badly, and worried continually – about the baby, about Ollie, and about the pressure on her to finish he illustrations. Even though, surprisingly, the illustrations were turning out rather well.

She ought to call round and ask Jennie if she was feeling any better. On the other hand, it might mean she dragged her out of bed. Go or stay? Her eyes were tired from painting tiny brush strokes. She needed a change of scene.

Ben answered the door, looking almost as rough as Jennie had done on her previous visit.

'Oh dear, have you got it now?'

'Sorry?' He rubbed his eyes with the back of his hand. 'Jennie's out. No, come in. Actually, I was going to call round. Thought I saw Ollie.'

'Where?' Erin stepped inside the over-heated house. 'Are you sure?'

'Shopping centre. Ran after him but he must have gone into a shop. It was near that place that does piercings and tattoos.'

Erin started to leave but he caught hold of her arm. 'No, he won't be there now. Anyway, it probably wasn't him. Have you got a minute?' He guided her into Jennie's office, lifted the lid on her laptop, and started tapping the keyboard with his two index fingers. 'Something's wrong.'

Wrong in what way? If she had gone out she must be feeling better. Ben liked to moan about his lack of work, and the lot of the poor actor, but it was the first time he had shown such undisguised anxiety.

'I've been struggling with it ever since she went out, but I can't find anything apart from her accounts for the student house. There's a woman living in the basement flat.'

'Yes, I've met her. Jennie asked me to deliver a microwave.'

'She seems to think there's some mystery about the woman. It's all part of the crazy way her mind's been working.'

183

'Where is she?'

'Search me.'

'She didn't say?' Erin had visions of her walking in on them, and had no wish to be caught red-handed, checking her laptop. 'Have you asked what's bothering her?'

'She denies there is anything. Is it possible to check which websites someone's visited? Either she's ill or she's having an affair. She's always accusing me of seeing someone else but it could be her guilty conscience.'

Erin leaned over and clicked "history", but Jennie had wiped it clean.

Ben sighed. 'You would tell me if she'd said something. She agonises about her health, laps up all that stuff on the news, what you should and shouldn't eat, takes no notice when I point out how it changes from week to week.'

'If she talks to me I'll do what I can, but she must have friends she knows far better than me.'

'And pass on anything she tells you.'

'That I can't promise.' Erin wanted to leave but Ben was glued to Jennie's chair. 'Listen, are you sure you saw Ollie?'

He chewed his knuckle. 'Thought I did.'

'Come on, let's get out of here. If Jennie comes back, this certainly won't improve her mood.'

He switched off the laptop and Erin gave him her number and watched to make sure he put it in his phone. 'In case you see Ollie again. Any work coming up?'

'Small part in a radio play.'

'What about the slimming ad?'

'They decided I was too old. Too old, I ask you, imagine how that made me feel? Thank you, Mr Whatever Your Name Is, we'll let you know. A couple of years ago

I was offered a part in a panto. Thought it was a monkey but it turned out to be a flunky! A servant. Apparently they used to call them flunkies.' His expression changed. 'I'm worried, Erin, no, not about the lack of work. When it comes to the crunch, all that really matters is your health. I mean, Jennie's. It could be depression. Does she strike you as being depressed? Oh, sorry, you've enough on your mind without involving yourself in our problems.'

'I'll see what I can do.'

'Thanks.' As she let herself out of the house, he had returned to chewing his knuckle.

Saying he thought he had seen Ollie could well have been a way of luring her into the house. Even so, she felt compelled to go down to the shopping centre and check. Heavy rain was forecast but so far had not materialised. Just as well since she had left the house without an umbrella. The last time it poured – the time she had been to talk to Ava – she had arrived home with water down the back of her neck and squelching shoes.

As she passed the baby goods shop, she visualized herself putting the baby's feet into the tiny shoes, talking to her, explaining about her real mother even though she was far too young to understand. Thinking about the future was becoming a way of keeping going. But it had to stop. Instead of picturing herself as a mother, she ought to be preparing for the worst. When a baby died, or was stillborn, people were given prints of its hands and feet, something to keep, put in a frame. She had never understood it before. Now she did. The piercing and tattoo shop was closed. Not that Ollie would be there. He was not the type to have a tattoo although Erin had a vague memory of Claudia suggesting he have her name on his thigh. *Only joking, Ol.* Had he minded her jokes? He had loved her, and love tends to overlook minor irritations. Where *was* he? He could be miles away and have no intention of coming back – ever. But he would need a job and, if he applied to a different university, they would ask for a reference. If that happened, would Jon tell her, or would he keep it to himself?

Speak of the devil. As she turned away from the pictures of tattoos, she spotted Jon, standing outside a shop, and hurried over to ask if he had seen Ollie. But before she could speak, he was joined by Diana, and an excited Maeve.

'Erin!' Maeve ran towards her, swinging a bag. 'Look.' She pulled out a pair of black trainers with red flashes. 'Mum wanted me to have lace-ups but I prefer Velcro.'

'Very smart.'

'My feet have grown a whole size.'

'Calm down, Maeve.' Diana was smiling and had linked arms with Jon. Her dark hair gleamed as glossy as the mynah bird's feathers. 'Hello, Erin.'

'Ben thought he saw Ollie, but I doubt it *was* him.'

'How are you? The baby . . . Do they think . . . ?'

'Gestation has reached twenty-nine and a half weeks. Twenty-nine and three-quarters actually. Every day is important.'

'I'm sure.' Diana let go of Jon and gave her a brief, unexpected hug. 'Such a worry for you, but they work miracles with premature babies these days.'

Maeve was playing hopscotch on the paving stones. 'Ollie's gone missing,' she said, 'like on TV. A man disappeared and his body was washed up on the beach.'

'Maeve!' Diana pulled her away from her game.

'I didn't mean Ollie was dead. You knew that, didn't you, Erin? I think he's staying with a friend.' Maeve handed her new shoes to her mother. 'He has a lot of friends, doesn't he, Dad? I'm going to university. Oh no, I forgot, I'm going to Art College. If you want to go to Art College you have to have a portfolio with all your drawings and paintings.'

Diana gave Erin an apologetic smile. 'Erin knows what a portfolio is, darling.'

'Can I make one, Erin? No, I'm not good enough yet. I know, I could keep all my drawings and paintings and it would show if I was getting any better at it.'

'Good idea.' At the mention of Maeve's drawings, Erin had expected Diana to flinch, but her face had remained impassive. That meant they had not spoken to her about the picture of a gravestone with MAEVE. RIP. In fact, Erin suspected Jon hadn't even told Diana about it.

First thing on Monday morning, Erin's editor phoned to inquire how the illustrations were progressing.

'No pressure.' Sara's voice was edgy with expectation.

'I'll send you the pen and ink drawings.'

'If you could.' Erin had told her just enough of what was going on to make it hard for her to complain too vigorously. 'How's your sister?'

So she had forgotten. Or failed to take in what Erin had said. 'She's not going to get better. It's a question of keeping her on life support until her baby can be born.'

The silence that followed was gratifying and she hoped Sara was feeling as guilty as hell. 'I'm sorry, I hadn't realised.' But if Erin thought she was going to tell her not to worry about the illustrations, she was out of luck.

'I'll get back to you by the end of the week,' Erin said.

'If you could.' And she rang off.

The painting she was working on was of Mrs Moffatt,

187

who owned the pet shop. She had brought her little friend, possibly her granddaughter, to choose one of the guinea pigs for her birthday present. The double-page illustration showed the little girl crouching down to pick up the smallest one, whose nose was peeping out of its house.

Erin thought about Ollie, hiding away somewhere, terrified of responsibility and grief- stricken about Claudia. Was he grief stricken? With Ollie, it was so hard to tell. Had something happened before the accident, something she knew nothing about? Did Hoshi know what it was? Ava, Erin was beginning to suspect, knew nothing and simply enjoyed being enigmatic.

Miss Havisham was winding herself round Erin's ankles. She had bought her some dry cat food but it was clear the cat preferred meat, and she had greeted the pellets with noisy wails. 'Go away, you ungrateful creature.' More loud wails were interrupted by the doorbell. Jehovah's Witnesses? Mormons? But it could be Jennie so she would have to check.

It was Jon.

'Can I come up?

'All right, but I'm working flat out.'

He followed her up the two flights of stairs, past Claudia and Ollie's bedroom, with its firmly closed door, and on to her garret in the attic – because that was how it was starting to feel.

'I should have told you before.'

'Should have told me what?'

'You don't know what . . . God, you've no idea how much I wanted to but . . . It's so hard to know where to begin.' Returning to her easel, she started painting Mrs Moffatt's frizzy hair. Jon was still standing by the door, moving his weight from one foot to the other. Did he want to make a quick getaway? It was going to be something about Claudia, something he should have told her weeks ago.

'It's about Maeve.'

'Go on.'

'When she was born . . . I was worried, I could tell there was something wrong. No one said very much but . . . They took her away and . . .'

'Get to the point.' She sounded callous but she was determined that this time he was going to tell her the truth.

'Oh, God.' He sighed, and she turned away, pretending to be concentrating on her painting. 'The doctor asked to see us and I thought she must have brain-damage.'

'But she didn't. Diana told me. I'm no expert, but I'd say her intelligence is above average.'

A spotlight she had fixed up the previous week illuminated the beads of sweat on Jon's forehead, and when he spoke, his voice was so quiet she had to strain to hear. 'I thought you might have guessed. No, how could you? When we met you down at the shopping centre . . . Oh, God, there's no way to break it gently. Diana is my sister.'

'What?'

'No, let me explain.'

Her phone rang and she snatched it up, the familiar voice made her paintbrush drop from her hand. 'What's happened?' Her heart was beating so loudly she could barely take in what Andrea was saying. 'Yes, yes of course. Yes, straight away.' She pushed past Jon. 'It's the baby.'

'What's happened? I'll drive you there.'

'No.'

'I could come with you.'

'Come with me? You're just about the last person in the world I would want to.'

25

When she found the Scottish doctor by Claudia's bedside, she felt weak with relief. Andrea was there too and they were making preparations.

'We're taking Claudia down to theatre,' the doctor explained, 'it's a very quick procedure.'

'What happened?'

'The placenta. We were worried it was starting to fail. I believe your sister carried an organ donor card.'

'Yes.' He knew she did, but had to check, and she knew what was coming next.

'As soon as the baby's delivered we'd like to—'

'You'll switch off her life support, I know.' They needed Claudia's organs but were afraid of upsetting her. 'I understand.'

Andrea put a hand on her arm. 'We thought you'd like to say goodbye.'

'But the baby . . .'

'A short time will make no difference. We'll leave you on your own with her.'

For the first time since the accident, she held Claudia's hand. She knew she couldn't hear anything, even so she promised to take care of her baby, and love her, and keep her safe, and try to make sure she was happy. It was the end, she would never see Claudia again, but just now that was too difficult to take in. Later, like everything else that had happened, she would go over it in her head, again and again until it lost some of its power to hurt. She kissed Claudia's warm forehead, turning away, too distraught to cry. 'Goodbye. Your baby's going to be born now. I love you and I'll love your baby, I promise I will.'

Andrea accompanied her to the waiting room and told her to try not worry, she would be back shortly.

'How long will it take?'

'Make yourself some coffee.'

The room was packed, but a quick glance told her no one was particularly concerned about their relative, they were just waiting to be allowed into a ward. A woman with swollen legs offered to move up so Erin could sit next to her, but she shook her head and started pacing the floor, like all the expectant fathers she had seen in the movies. Crossing to the window, she stared out at the brick wall opposite and at a couple of scruffy pigeons, then retraced her steps for fear she was getting on people's nerves. Amazing how conventional good manners still applied even at the most stressful of times.

When she reached the woman who'd offered her a seat, she sat down, explaining that her sister was having a baby. The woman murmured something about a cup of tea, but she shook her head, attempting to return her smile. Time dragged. She checked her watch endlessly – it was two minutes ahead of the clock on the wall – and pressed her nails into her palms, trying to get a grip on herself. If the baby died . . . If there was something wrong with her . . .

Twenty minutes. Was that a good sign or a bad one? Wheeling Claudia to the operating theatre would have taken several minutes. The caesarean section would . . . No, there would have been checks first. What kind of checks? A scalpel would slice into her abdomen and the baby would be lifted out, snatched up by a nurse and wrapped in a towel. If she cried . . . If not, they would give her oxygen – if they thought she had a chance.

The book she had bought described tests to make sure the baby's heart and breathing were satisfactory, that it moved or lay limply in the nurse's arms, that its skin colour was pink or bluish, and it had a reflex response. According to the book, most babies scored between seven and ten. What happened if the score was only three or four? But Claudia's baby was premature and would be taken to special care the minute she was born.

Thirty-five minutes. The baby was dead but no one wanted to tell her. Andrea had offered but the doctor had insisted it was his job only just now there was an emergency and . . . A male nurse put his head round the door and she started towards him, but he was looking for someone else. 'Mrs Gladwell?' he asked, but there was no one of that name in the room.

After he left, she spooned instant coffee into a cracked mug, telling herself that would make it more likely she would be sent for. Stupid, ridiculous, but when all else failed what was left but superstition? Sugar. She hated sugar in her coffee but in times of stress . . . No, that was for shock. No sugar. No coffee. She tipped the granules into the sink and ran the hot tap. If she washed up, cleared all the rubbish off the draining board . . . She searched for some washing-up liquid, but there was none.

'Erin?' It was Andrea, standing in the doorway, and she was smiling.

'Is she all right?' They hurried down the corridor together. 'Please tell me. You are allowed to, aren't you?'

'A beautiful little girl.' Andrea stopped walking and gave her a huge hug. 'Come and meet her.'

The Special Care Baby Unit was in another part of the building and, as they walked through the maze of corridors, Andrea told her everything she knew. The baby weighed nearly three and a half pounds, a good weight considering, and had been put in an incubator so her temperature could be controlled and oxygen supply adjusted, according to her needs. The birth itself had been straightforward and the doctor was pleased with her general condition although, obviously, it was early days yet.

Erin was finding it difficult to breathe. All those hours she had spent, visualising this moment, but now it had come it had no reality. Claudia's baby. Her baby. How dare Ollie have stayed away when he must know his baby could be born at any time? His baby? She hoped he would never come back. The baby was going to be all right, she knew she was, and when she was strong enough she would take her home and buy her everything she needed.

'In here, Erin, you know the drill with hand-washing. She's tiny, and in an incubator, but don't be alarmed. Ready?'

She was lying on her tummy with her head turned to one side, wearing a nappy and a vest and a doll-size knitted hat. The small amount of hair that was visible was so light, and her eyes so round, there was not the faintest possibility Hoshi was her father.

'She's lovely, isn't she?' Andrea said.

'As far as you can tell, is there anything wrong with her?'

'She has all her fingers and toes.

'Do you know how long she'll be in an incubator?'

Andrea turned to the special care nurse. 'This is Erin, the baby's aunt. She's going to be the one who comes to visit.'

The nurse nodded and smiled. 'She's likely to be here in the unit for four or five weeks. Maybe a little longer, until she puts on weight. She needs to be kept warm and the incubator's high humidity helps to prevent her skin drying out and cracking. Premature babied are unable to regulate their temperature well. She's not strong enough to suck so she'll be fed through a tube. Slowly to prevent infection.'

'That's something that could happen?'

'Steroids were given to accelerate lung maturity, and she'll be monitored carefully.'

'What happens if she stops breathing?' Too many questions. But she needed to know everything.

'If her breathing deviates from normal an alarm goes off. Alarms often go off though so there's no immediate cause for worry.'

Erin opened her mouth but Andrea pre-empted another question. 'Have you thought about a name? No rush. When you go home you can think about it.'

'Phoebe. It was Claudia's middle name. I've only got one.'

'Me too. Phoebe – that's a beautiful name. Her birth will need to be registered. I'll give you the address of where to go.'

'I know where it is.'

'Of course you do. I'm sorry. When you had to register your sister's death.'

'It was only an interim certificate. I'll need to get another one.' *Once a diagnosis of brain death has been made, the individual is pronounced legally dead. The time of death is not the time when the ventilator is removed.* Erin had looked it up and, in spite of finding it so difficult to accept that Claudia had died, the words had stayed in her head.

Small snuffling sounds were coming from the incubator. Erin longed to hold her, but of course that was impossible.

194

'You can touch her if you like.' The special care nurse pointed to a hole in the side of the incubator, and Erin placed one of her fingers on the palm of the outstretched hand and the baby's fingers curled round it.

'Visit whenever you like, but don't feel you have to come in every day. We'll take good care of her.'

'And you'll let me know if . . .'

'Of course. We have your mobile and your home number.'

'Thank you.' She hesitated, half reluctant to leave, half wanting to go into the open air and clear her head, and to tell Ben and Jennie. But not Jon. 'I'll see you again soon, and thank you, thank you so much, all of you.'

Ben was delighted, but Jennie's response was muted and Erin decided Ben was right about her being depressed.

'What does she look like?' He had used the occasion as an excuse to open a bottle of wine. 'How much does she weigh? Only twenty-eight weeks, isn't it?'

'Twenty-nine and three-quarters. She's tiny and has hardly any hair, but she's definitely not Hoshi's.'

Jennie let out a shriek. 'Is that what you thought?'

'Only because the doctors said the baby was larger than they would have expected. She's lovely, perfect. She's in an incubator but I was allowed to touch her. I expect you could come and see her in a day or two, if you'd like to.'

Ben grinned. As usual, the house was too hot, and he was wearing a T-shirt. 'Certainly would.'

'If you weren't allowed into the room, they'd definitely let you look at her through the window. Jennie?'

'I'd love to, but I think I'd better wait until I'm germ-free.'

So, in spite of Erin's relief the baby had been born, Jennie was not prepared to set aside her dislike of hospitals.

'If there's anything we can do.' Ben patted the sofa, inviting Erin to sit beside him.

'Yes, anything,' Jennie added, without much enthusiasm, 'and I'm so glad she's been delivered safely. Have you given her a name?'

'Oh, yes, I forgot. Phoebe, I'm going to call her Phoebe. It was Claudia's middle name.'

'A lovely name.'

'They switched off Claudia's life support,' Erin said. 'No, it's all right, I knew how it was going to be and she would have wanted her organs . . .'

Ben took her glass and put it on the table. 'We think you've done brilliantly, don't we, Jen? It must have been awful, all that waiting and . . . I'm so sorry about Claudia.'

'Yes, so sorry,' Jennie repeated. 'It's so sad she'll never see her baby.'

Ben glanced at Jennie. 'Actually, now the baby's been born—'

'Not now, Ben.' Jennie made a move to pull herself up from her chair, changing her mind when it was clear he was not going to be put off.

'It's about Claudia, Erin. I wanted to tell you before. Before someone else did. But you had enough on your plate.'

'Erin's exhausted, Ben, she's only just returned from the hospital.'

'Yes, sorry, I'll tell you another time.'

'No, now,' Erin said.

Jennie's eyes were focussed on last Sunday's newspaper, scattered over the carpet. 'I don't think it was Claudia's idea.'

'No I agree.' Ben looked as though he had been given an escape route. 'Kent's. It must have been Kent's. They were friends. You probably know that. Kent sees himself as something of an expert on English literature. Used to teach part-time at a tuition college. That play you saw. Most of his plays are adaptations, modern day versions.'

Jennie sighed. 'Get on with it then, Ben'

'He and Claudia . . . I think it must have been just before you came here that they had to stop.'

'Had to stop what?'

'The two of them had this scam going. Post-grad students who had to write dissertations, some of them from overseas and not fluent in English, some who just couldn't be bothered, or weren't up to it.'

'Claudia wrote their dissertations?' Erin thought about the list of names in her desk, and the roll of twenty-pound notes. 'Are you sure? She was never much good at that kind of thing.'

'No. Kent wrote them. At least, I think the students wrote them and Kent improved them. I'm not too sure. Claudia acted as middleman. She helped at a centre for overseas students, befriending them and helping them settle in.'

'Yes, Harold told me. She and Kent shared the spoils.' At any other time, she would have been horrified, but what did it matter? Nothing mattered now, only Phoebe.

'Sixty-forty,' Ben was saying, 'that's what Claudia told me. Rather steep I thought, since Kent did most of the work.'

'But Claudia had the contacts,' Jennie said.

'Sounds profitable. Why did they stop?'

'Someone told Jon.'

So all this time he had known what Claudia had done but never said a word.

Jennie guessed what she was thinking. 'I don't expect

he wanted to upset you. Criticising your sister, I mean.'

'He should have reported them to the university. Why didn't he?'

Ben was looking relieved that the secret he had kept to himself was out at last. Jennie had known about it too but chosen to keep quiet. Erin should have been annoyed with them, but all she could think was if she told him about Jon and Diana, brother and sister, Claudia's crime would fade into obscurity.

'I think Jon issued an ultimatum,' Ben said. 'Stop the scam now, or else.'

So the phone calls, Lara who had come to the door, the man with a hoodie who had been watching the house, none of them had anything to do with the accident. All they wanted was their dissertations, or their money back.

26

Someone had written an obscenity in the dust on the passenger door. Stella rubbed off the illiterate letters, pausing a moment to listen to barking dogs in a nearby park. She liked dogs because they were friendlier than cats but she could never have one, she was away from home too much. Home. Thinking about her flat in Chiswick made her even more determined to leave the basement, with its depressing décor and smell of damp. But not yet, not until she had achieved the purpose of her self-imposed imprisonment. She thought about Erin who had delivered the microwave. And liked Babar the elephant. Always a good sign.

The previous evening, one of the female students from upstairs had knocked on her door and asked if she had a bottle opener.

'No idea. I expect so. They usually have one on the end of corkscrews. Come in, I'll check what's in the drawer. What are you studying?'

'Politics.'

'Is it interesting?'

The girl shrugged. 'It's all right.'

Stella gave a snort. 'You don't realise how lucky you are. What are you planning to do when you finish?'

She shrugged again and Stella wanted to take her by the shoulders and give her a good shake. Some people had to struggle to make a life for themselves. Others had it handed to them on a plate. 'Here you are.' She handed her a rusty bottle opener. 'Keep it. I don't want it back.'

'We're having a party at the weekend.'

'Are you now? With any luck I'll be gone by then. Actually, it's the people next door that make all the noise. Drilling, hammering, filling up that skip that takes up two parking spaces, yelling at their kids.'

'At least, it's too cold for a barbecue.'

'True.' Stella managed a smile. 'Have a good party.'

Two more days. She would allow herself two more days. But if the days passed, without success, she knew she would have to stay longer.

Why now? Why not last year or the year before? But it had become an obsession, a madness, something that was interfering with the rest of her life.

The weather had turned colder and, leaving her car at the bottom of the hill, she wound her scarf round the lower part of her face, and looked about for a place to hide. Until today, a scarf would have been unnecessary so it was fortunate the temperature had dropped. A good omen, some would say, along with a whole lot of rubbish about coincidences and phases of the moon. Stella despised irrational people, although recently her own rationality had started to go down the pan. *If the next car that passes is red . . . If it takes less than thirty paces to reach that tree . . .* Too many days had been wasted, catching glimpses that only lasted a few seconds, hearing voices, moving closer then retreating for fear of being spotted.

So far, so good. His car was squeezed in between a brand-new people carrier and a motor bike, spattered in mud. The people carrier had a sticker on the back window that made Stella curl her lip. "Little Princess on board". God help us. Some people were gross. An elderly man, a few yards ahead of her, kept slowing down to let his dog cock its leg against a tree. Marking out its territory, and people were the same, flaunting their gentrified properties and manicured gardens. Money was good, but only for providing new opportunities, new challenges. Money gave you choices.

A shiver ran though her body. She needed to find a better position, one where the front garden was clearly visible. Could she will them to come out? Could she, hell? A black transit van had been parked a short distance away and should provide enough cover. Looking up, she saw the sky had become dark, menacing. It might snow, or was it too cold? Feeling in her pocket, she found the remains of a bar of dark chocolate and broke off two squares, pushing them between her cold lips, and biting hard. Her nerves were on edge, and she focussed on an Asian woman with a double buggy, who was struggling up the opposite side of the road. One of the flats above the basement housed Asian students, but she had never spoken them. Like her, they preferred to keep themselves to themselves.

Now what? She could have killed for a cigarette. Before she left the basement, she had studied a map of the whole area and been surprised how close to the coast she was. Once, years ago, she had stayed in a B&B with Auntie Linda, who was not actually her real aunt. The sea had been far out, where the sand started to change into mud, and she had ridden on a donkey called Daisy – that plodded along with its head down – and eaten fish and chips, and candy floss.

With her brain fully occupied, estimating the distance from the city to the coast, she almost missed the child that had appeared in the front garden. In spite of the cold, she had no coat, and she was coming out onto the street, calling someone's name. Someone that turned out to be a cat, sitting on a low wall. Now she was stroking it, talking to it, then she held out her hand, testing for non-existent drops of rain.

She was small for her age. Not pretty, but with a pleasant intelligent face and hair that had been cut very short and was more or less the same colour as the cat.

Stepping out from behind the van, Stella asked if the cat belonged to her.

'My mum won't let me have one.'

'That's a shame. What about a guinea pig?'

'My friend's got one. It's called Sanders.'

'Great name.' Stella was keeping half an eye on the house, listening for sounds, voices, someone calling the child's name. Taking her phone from her pocket, she asked if the cat was Siamese.

'No, Burmese. They're very friendly and they like you stroking them. He's called Rex. He never scratches.'

'He's beautiful.'

'Some cats pretend to be friendly, then they bite your hand. Have you got one?'

'A cat? No. I live in a flat and cats like a garden. What's *your* name?'

'Maeve. Is Rex in the photo you took?'

Stella held it out for her to see.

'Oh, it's got me too. I'm having a phone for my birthday. Most of my friends have had one for ages but Mum said I had to wait till I was eleven.'

'When will that be?' As if the date was not imprinted on her mind.

'Next month. Which house do you live in? I think I saw you before. There've been quite a lot of new people in the road.' Maeve stopped stroking the cat, and pointed. 'I live in that yellow one. Mum likes it, but Dad doesn't.

He says white would be better.'

The woman was coming through the front door. She spotted Maeve and shouted to her. 'What on earth are you doing? You'll freeze. How many times have I told you—'

'That's my mum. I have to go.'

'Bye, Maeve.' Stella held up the phone for her to have a last look, and started walking, half running, calling over her shoulder. 'Have a good birthday.'

'Maeve!' The woman's voice was high-pitched with anger. 'Come back here at once. I'm tired of telling you . . .'

'I was talking to Rex.' Her voice faded as Stella slammed her car door, started the engine, and moved off, glancing in the driving mirror but seeing nothing. Her eyes were too blurred with tears.

27

Since Phoebe's arrival, Erin had not spoken to Jon, and would be happy if she never saw him again. Except for Maeve, of course – it would unfair to make her suffer – but he could drop her off on the doorstep. Any problems Maeve might have, must be the result of being the child of an incestuous relationship. No wonder she thought they talked about her behind her back. What did it say on her birth certificate? Sooner or later they would have to tell her the truth.

Jon's repeated phone calls were getting on her nerves. As soon as she heard his voice, she rang off, and texts begging her to let him explain were deleted. One of the reasons she was out now was in case he came round again and she had to endure five minutes of him ringing the bell and banging on the door. What was there to explain? How he and Diana had been separated as children and only met up again as adults? Somewhere she remembered reading that this produced strong physical attraction. Maybe it did, but to have a child together was unforgiveable.

It was late afternoon and she was standing outside the police station, where steps led up to uninviting glass doors. The building was a mixture of stained concrete and grey brickwork, more like a high security prison than a place where the general public could seek advice or provide important information. What could she tell them? She was not there to talk about Claudia and Kent's scam since she was fairly certain it had nothing to do with Ollie. Neither did it explain why a length of scaffolding had destroyed Claudia's brain. Paying money for a dissertation that was never received was hardly grounds for murder.

Two officers were coming through the main door, one male, one female, the female one considerably younger than Erin's companion at the mortuary. She wanted to ask if they had a colleague called DS Smith. Her presence on that day had created a bond. Not that DS Smith would have found it traumatic, or did you never become totally immune to tragedy?

At the time of Claudia's accident, the police had made investigations, but by now they seemed to have lost interest. Ollie had committed no offence, unless deserting your unborn baby was a crime. Did a part of him want to be found? As a child, Erin had been tricked by Claudia into going to the end of the garden after dark and, when Claudia made owl noises and chased her, she had been so afraid she had stood still and begged to be caught, just to get it over with. Her little sister, but she had always had the upper hand.

'Erin?'

She spun round, as though she had committed a crime, and came face to face with Hoshi.

'Are you going to tell the police?' His dark eyes were full of fear.

'Sorry?'

'Ben said you know about the dissertations. When Ollie found out, he went mad.'

'How did he find out? Who told him?'

He stared into the distance. 'People knew about it.'

'Ava, was it?'

He shrugged, and she thought – it was you, you told

him. To punish Claudia for dumping you?

'The baby.' He swallowed hard. 'Is it all right?'

'Oh, Ben told you that too.'

'What's going to happen to it?'

'Her. She's a girl. Listen, if Ollie's still in Bristol he needs to know.'

'He hasn't done anything. He wasn't like that. I mean, he isn't . . .'

A shiver of fear made her reach out to him to steady herself. 'You think he's dead. Please, Hoshi . . . If you know anything.' But he was walking away and it would be useless to run after him.

The nurse on duty told her the baby was doing as well as expected. *As well as expected?* Seeing the panic in Erin eyes, she back-tracked a little, but it was no good. Phoebe was not yet out of danger. Her birth, and Andrea's optimism, had given a false impression.

Pulling up a chair, she sat by the incubator, watching her tiny chest rise and fall, alarmed when it stopped for a couple of seconds, relieved when it moved again.

'Premature babies can hear when you talk to them.' The nurse was sorting clothes in a cupboard. 'They get used to the tone and rhythm of a particular voice.'

In a whisper, then more loudly, Erin started to tell her about her mother then changed her mind and began describing Maeve's art classes in the loft, and Miss Havisham who was named after the character in *Great Expectations*. The nurse was listening, but what did it matter? She must be used to spending time with desperately anxious people. It was a special place, cut off from the rest of the world, a place where tiny babies struggled to survive. Some did, some failed to pull through. Everyone did their best, but they were unable to work miracles.

'You're lovely,' she whispered, and Phoebe's lips parted a fraction and Erin could see the tip of her tongue.

Another nurse appeared, who lived up to the stereotype of fat and jolly. 'Dear little soul, isn't she?'

Erin nodded. All the nurses in the unit were wonderful and, in her eyes, could do no wrong. 'Does she need anything? I could buy her some clothes if you can buy them that small.'

'No need, love, not yet. Some days we keep them without clothes, apart from a nappy, so we can spot any changes of skin colour or condition. Next time you come, I expect she'll be wearing one of these.' The other nurse held up two sleeping suits, so small they would have fitted a doll. 'And you should be able to hold her,' she added.

'I'd like that.' But she looked so fragile, and Erin was not sure she could trust herself not to cry, and if her nose ran she would have to scrub up all over again. 'I worry about her all the time but you probably have babies who are even more premature.'

'You concentrate on your little one,' the fat nurse said, treating her as though she was Phoebe's mother. Perhaps she thought she was. But probably not. More than likely they all knew what had happened and talked about it during their coffee breaks. *Poor little mite, mother's dead and father's done a bunk.*

'Touching them and talking to them helps their weight gain,' The other nurse had closed the cupboard and was on her way out of the cubicle. 'Makes them feel loved, that's what I say. The doctors might have different explanations.'

* * *

207

First thing the following morning, Jennie put in an appearance. 'Are you going to the hospital?'

'Yes. Why?'

'I'm so sorry about Claudia.'

'Thanks.' Erin had no wish to talk about it. Neither was she going to tell her about Jon and Diana, and poor Maeve. 'Come in, I'm not going until later. Coffee? No, you don't drink it, do you? Tea?'

Jennie looked unwilling to climb the stairs so Erin suggested they sit in Claudia's kitchen.

'Is that the one you use?'

'No, but it doesn't matter. It's silly really, the way I stay in the loft, but it would feel wrong if—'

'I understand.' Jennie was wearing grey jogging bottoms and a baggy sweatshirt, but she looked better, not so pale.

'I usually feed Miss Havisham in here. The cat from down the road. She comes through the cat flap. Scruffy creature but Maeve's fond of it. She chose the name.'

Jennie gave a token smile. She had no interest in the cat. 'Are you busy?'

'No more than usual. My editor's been on at me about the illustrations, but I need a break.' Perhaps Jennie was going to tell her what was wrong. If so, she owed it to Ben to listen. Besides, she and Jennie were friends, although lately it had occurred to Erin she might have said something to offend her. Something about the basement flat? As far as she could remember, Jennie had asked what she thought and she had been particularly tactful, saying nothing about the peeling paint and rickety iron steps, or the mysterious Stella, who worked in PR and liked Babar books.

It was cold in Claudia's kitchen but Jennie seemed not to have noticed. She was searching for something in her pocket. Had her conscience got the better of her and she was going to admit she had known all along where Ollie was hiding out? She held a piece of paper behind her back and a string of possibilities floated through Erin's head. She thought Ben was having an affair. *She* was having an affair. Ben had no acting work and the student house needed a new roof?

'I wanted to tell you before.' Her voice shook. So did her hands.

'I wish you had,' Erin said.

'You don't know what I'm going to say.'

'Something else Claudia did? Something illegal?'

Jennie held out the slip of paper, except it wasn't paper, it was a photograph.

'What is it?' Erin gave a gasp. 'Are you . . . Is it . . . ?'

She nodded.

'That's wonderful. It is wonderful, isn't it? Yes, of course it is.'

'I only told Ben last night. I know you wanted me to help you find Ollie, but I've had three miscarriages and I was so afraid I'd have another. Ben said he'd come to terms with not having a family, but it wasn't true, he was just being kind. Only it's almost twenty-one weeks now and the doctor says I can relax except I know I won't be able to. Only the miscarriages were much earlier than this. I know what you thought of me.'

'Oh, Jennie.' Erin sat down opposite her, coffee and tea forgotten. 'I'm so sorry. No, don't look like that, the doctor's right. I'm sure everything will be fine this time. Twenty-one weeks, that's getting on for five months. How come nobody's noticed? Surely Ben . . .'

'I didn't want to disappoint him all over again.' She lifted her sweatshirt to show Erin the bump. 'I slept in another bed. I know. He thought I'd gone off him.'

All Erin could think was how she had kept going on about Claudia's baby, and its chances of survival, and all the time Jennie had been frantic with worry. 'I'm so sorry. If I'd known.'

'I meant to wait a bit longer before I told Ben but I thought he'd guess. My first pregnancy lasted eleven weeks and by then they have eyelids and ear lobes. It seems wrong to be happy when you're so worried about Phoebe.'

'No, of course you must be happy. I'm happy for you too.' All those weeks she had thought Jennie a self-absorbed hypochondriac. No wonder she had asked her to take the microwave to the basement flat. No wonder she had been reluctant to accompany her to the hospital. Now, all being well, she would carry the baby to term, whereas Phoebe was in an incubator, and still not out of danger.

'I thought if anyone knew I would be more likely to miscarry. I know. You must think me stupidly superstitious.'

'Actually Jennie, I don't think that at all. In fact, I'd probably have done exactly the same myself.'

28

When she reached the unit, a nurse Erin recognised by sight saw her coming through the swing doors.

'Oh, you got the message all right?'

'No.' She should have checked her phone. How had she missed it? 'What's happened?

'Baby developed an infection and tests showed it was more virulent than we thought. I'll take you to her.'

'She's been moved?' Erin's heart began to thump.

'Only to a different cubicle.'

Why? How was it different from the other cubicle? Was it for very sick babies? Did it have more equipment? 'Has she been given antibiotics?'

'The doctor will be here soon.'

Because of Phoebe, or because it was time for his normal round?

She was lying on her tummy, with just a nappy and her knitted hat, and her arms and legs out to one side, her legs bent at the knees. Her hands were almost translucent, her skin so thin Erin could see the veins, and she looked smaller, thinner, but how could she be? Premature babies sometimes lost weight. Putting on weight was a good sign. Losing it meant . . .

'Babies as small as Phoebe have hardly any fat.' The nurse was talking as though it was Erin's first visit. 'And she's fed through a tube because her reflex to suck has not yet developed. There's a lot to take in all at once. You can sit with her, stay as long as you like.'

Sit with her? As long as you like? Everything the nurse said was laden with doom. 'How long does it take for the antibiotics to work?'

'The doctor will be here quite soon.'

'Is she in danger?'

'Talk to the doctor, he'll be able to explain.'

The nurse left and Erin pulled up a chair and began talking to Phoebe, not like the last time, more like when she had talked to Claudia. No, that was wrong. Phoebe was alive. She was going to be all right. She had to be. Where was the doctor? Had anyone bothered to tell him she was here? If she had been Phoebe's mother, they would have taken more trouble to keep in touch. No, that was unfair. But she needed someone to blame – for Claudia's death, for Phoebe's precarious hold on life, for Jon lying to her, for Jennie being so happy.

A sudden movement caught her eye. Phoebe had stiffened then gone limp. Erin knew this was because her nervous system was not fully developed, but it still frightened her. Surely a nurse ought to be with her all the time. They said she could recognise voices. Did that mean there was nothing wrong with her hearing, or were they talking about babies in general? In the book, it said they could recognise their mother by her smell, but Phoebe had no mother, just a series of nurses and doctors.

'How do you do?' The man who had come through the door was short and stocky, with thick, dark hair and bushy eyebrows.

Erin started to stand up but he gestured to her to stay where she was. 'My name is Doctor Samood and you, I believe, are Phoebe's aunt and guardian.'

'Her mother's dead and her father's gone missing.'

'Leaving you holding the baby. As I'm sure you are

aware, with premature babies we take each day as it comes. Infections are not uncommon and the baby may be doing well one day and quite sick the next.'

'How ill is she? When will you know if she's going to get better?'

'We have your telephone number and I believe you live quite nearby. Phoebe is a pretty name.'

'Can I ask you something?'

'Of course.'

'Is she going to die? Please tell me the truth. Will the antibiotics work?'

'By tomorrow we will know more.' He bent towards the incubator. 'Such a sad thing – your sister – but you are here which is a blessing.'

After he left, she told Phoebe how beautiful she was, and how she was going to get better because people loved her. An alarm went off and Erin sprang up, leaving the cubicle just as a nurse she had not met before arrived.

'Nothing to worry about.' She adjusted a pad on Phoebe's tiny chest. 'You must be Erin. I heard you talking to her. Voice, touch, another human being's presence, it all helps.'

During the day, nurses came and went, and a different doctor made checks. Erin's research had covered infections but she struggled to remember what she had read. Breast feeding was important for premature babies because the live cells provided protection. Claudia had been going to breast feed. If she was alive, she could have expressed the milk. In the past, Erin had thought that sounded horrible, like milking a cow. Now she would have given anything for Phoebe to have the advantage of breast milk, except she could be having it already, provided by a mother, who had too much for her own baby.

'How is she?' She kept asking, finally giving up when a nurse told her there was unlikely to be any change for several hours.

Phoebe looked different, less alert, less active, or was she imagining it? How had she developed the infection? Everyone was so careful. Was it *her* fault? Three days ago, she had touched her hand, but only after she had washed her own hands meticulously. Once, she thought she stopped breathing and ran out of the cubicle to fetch a nurse, but it was a false alarm. Time passed painfully slowly and she had no means of knowing if the antibiotics were helping or not. If Phoebe died, she would have lost everything, first Claudia, then her baby. How did anyone ever get over the loss of a baby? If a baby was going to die, it was given to the mother so she could say goodbye, wrapped in a shawl with only its tiny face showing.

If Phoebe died that would mean Ollie had never seen her. Would he be relieved? Would her death justify his wish for her and her mother to die in peace? What a coward he was, disappearing and not even phoning. Even if someone else was the father, he could at least have talked to her, told her what had happened. In fact, if he knew he was not the father, he could have asked for a DNA test that would let him off the hook. Off the hook – how typical of a man. But not all men would have behaved as badly as Ollie had done. He was so immature, she wondered what Claudia had seen in him.

Aware that she was digging her nails into the palms of her hand, she made a supreme effort to breathe slowly and relax. Anger with Ollie was not going to help. He had opted out and no longer had any rights. Phoebe was *her* child.

One of the nurses appeared, with the offer of a cup of tea.

'No, thank you.' It was a long time since she had eaten anything, or had a drink, and her mouth was dry, but accepting a cup of tea was like joining the normal world and she had no wish to join it, not until she knew. A doctor looked in, but left, having carried out fewer checks than she expected. Was that a good sign, or because it was hopeless? Phoebe gave a small shudder, then relaxed again and resumed breathing more evenly. One of the nurses suggested Erin go home and return in the morning, but she shook her head. She was exhausted but there was no way she was going to fall asleep.

She did, of course, but not for long, waking with a jolt to check if Phoebe was still breathing. She ached all over, but she was glad. If Phoebe had to suffer, she wanted to suffer with her. It was dark outside, and would not be light for ages. It was only three in the morning. Phoebe's head moved and she yawned. It *was* a yawn. Erin was sure it was. And that was a good sign. It must be. She longed to pick her up. If she held her she would know if the antibiotics were working. Phoebe would open her eyes and she would be able to tell.

She must have dozed on and off because next time she checked her watch, it was five-forty, and six felt like the home straight towards a time when Dr Samood would come back on duty. Was that right? When did one shift end and another begin? Groggy with fatigue, she reluctantly accepted the cup of tea a nurse put down on a small table next to her. Had the table been there before? She had no memory of it. Footsteps approached and she held her breath, but they moved on and the sound was replaced by the noise of a trolley. How long was it since one of the nurses had checked? Surely they ought to come more often.

Phoebe stretched out the fingers of one hand and

moved her left leg, the one with her name band round her ankle. Was she in pain? She had no idea where she was. Or what was happening to her. Or who her mother was or . . . More footsteps, and Dr Samood's head came round the door.

'Good morning. Oh, you poor thing, look at you. Have you been here all night?'

As he studied the charts, Erin held her breath. The expression on his face told her nothing. Was Phoebe worse? Was there no hope? He inspected her, holding her head steady and listening to her heart, or was it her lungs, then turning to Erin with a smile. 'She's responding well.'

'Is she? Are you sure?'

'Yes, she's a beautiful little thing. All babies are beautiful but some especially so. Time for you to go home, I think, and get some well-earned rest.'

29

February, the twentieth and a few spring flowers had come up in Claudia's garden. Weeds too, but what did that matter? Nothing mattered now, except Phoebe. And Ollie, of course, but he was an adult and should be acting more responsibly. Not true. She worried about him, wanted him to know about Phoebe, wanted to talk to him, wanted him to be safe.

At the preliminary inquest, the coroner ruled that Claudia's funeral could go ahead. A quiet, low-key affair. Ben and Jennie came to the crematorium. Also, Ava and Kent, but obviously not Jon. Erin knew she should have tried to contact Claudia's friends – the people at the indoor market, or anyone else who might like to have come – but because of the long gap since the accident, it had felt too difficult. And too upsetting. In spite of the anguish it caused her, Erin hoped several of Claudia's organs had been used for successful transplants. She could have asked the hospital, but had decided it was better not to think about it. What happened? Did they remove the organs then sew up the body? Had they taken her eyes? Knowing was always better than not knowing but, in this case, that might not be true?

Ava and Kent had brought expensive white lilies – and Ben and Jennie had chosen roses. Erin's contribution was a large bunch of the primulas that had survived Claudia's lack of gardening. Would the gesture, that Erin found comforting, have appealed to her sister or would she have made a remark about saving money? *Only joking, Erin.*

Claudia had been the only person who could remember their parents, the good times they had all shared, and the not so good. Birthdays, Christmases, starting school, having chicken pox. Claudia had been born when Erin was still a baby, and the two of them had shared a bedroom during their early years, whispering to each other after the light was turned off, playing games with zoo and farm animals, and separate dolls houses – their father had been diplomatic enough to make two. Now she was alone.

After the short service, they had lunch in a pub in Totterdown. Going back to Claudia's house had felt wrong – the pub had been Jennie's idea and no one had raised objections – and Ava and Ben competed to tell anecdotes, and Erin and Jennie pretended to find them funny. Nothing was said about Jennie's pregnancy and Erin certainly had no intention of mentioning it, except to Ben who she had congratulated earlier, while reassuring him she was sure it was going to be all right this time, and agreeing it was no wonder poor Jennie had been behaving oddly. Neither did she mention how ill Phoebe had been. They would have asked if she was better and Erin would have said she was "as well as could be expected" and they would have looked relieved and changed the subject. Because Phoebe was not that important to them. And it was perfectly possible she would pick up another infection. And if she did, Erin would sit with her again, all day and all night, keeping watch.

Walking up her road, the following day, Erin's heart sank as she saw Harold Lord approaching. He was wearing a deerstalker hat and carrying his usual bag of shopping, and it was clear he was hoping for a chat.

'A little warmer today.' He opened the bag to show her

the vegetables he had bought. 'To make a casserole,' he explained. 'Keeps me going for several days.' He cleared his throat. 'I was hoping I'd see you. You wanted to know if I'd seen any suspicious characters hanging about. Think I may be able to help. Not an immigrant. Didn't look like one. But not English, could have been of Mexican origin. I have Icelandic ancestors although you wouldn't know from my appearance. If I see him again, I'll put a note through your door, shall I?'

'You saw his face?'

'Not exactly. Wearing one of those hooded jackets, zipped right up to the chin. But you get an impression, don't you?'

'Yes.' He knew nothing, just wanted an excuse to chat. Out of the corner of her eye, she could see Jon standing outside Claudia's house, and rage rose up in her. She could walk away, or drive off in her car, but it was no good, sooner or later she would have listen to his squalid explanation.

Harold had seen him and was moving on, reluctantly. 'Could have been Turkish,' he called over his shoulder, 'or possibly Albanian.'

Jon hurried towards her. 'The baby?'

'She had an infection.'

'A girl? I thought it was a boy. But she's better? She's all right? I know you don't want to speak to me, but it's not what you think.'

As she put her key in the lock, she remembered how she had intended to have a mortise one fitted. Tomorrow she would ask Jennie and Ben if they knew the number of a locksmith, get it fixed, without fail.

'Five minutes.' She jerked her head to indicate Jon could go on ahead, and he gave a long, slow sigh and started up the stairs.

Once in the loft, she crossed to her easel and began studying the rabbit painting, tracing her finger round the shape of their paws. Some were eating, one was scratching its ear, and another was lying on its side, asleep.

Jon closed the door. 'Ollie ought to be here. He ought to know.'

'As far as I'm concerned, he's lost all rights to her.' Not true. How could it be if he was the biological father? *If* he was the father. And if not, who was it? Did Hoshi know? Did anyone know?

Jon was telling her something but she had not been listening. 'Go on then,' she said, 'but whatever it is won't make any difference. I'm only talking to you because of Maeve.'

'I don't know where to start.'

At the beginning, she felt like shouting, but there was no way she was going to help him out. People found silence difficult to bear. Preferred to fill the air with meaningless small talk rather than endure the tension silence produced.

'Diana,' he said. 'She's not Maeve's mother.'

'What do you mean, not her mother? Maeve thinks she is. Oh, she's adopted but you haven't told her. No wonder she thinks you're keeping something from her. What happened? You kept putting off telling her and then it never seemed like the right time and—'

'She's not adopted.'

'All right then, she had a surrogate mother. How did you manage that? I thought they made meticulous investigations. They'd have found out—'

'Maeve's my daughter but Diana's not her mother.'

'So who is? And why haven't you told her?' Erin sat on the bed and leaned against the wall, hugging her knees.

'All this past week I've been imagining . . . Why didn't you tell me before?'

'You thought it was something about Claudia.'

'I didn't know. How could I? You kept talking in riddles.'

'If the hospital hadn't phoned . . . Phoebe's all right? I'm so glad. I checked with Ben.'

'Hang on, I can hear Miss Havisham. I'll have to go down and feed her.'

He made a move to accompany her, but she shook her head. She needed time on her own, time to absorb what he had told her, time to adjust. She had been unfair, but it was his own fault. He could have explained weeks ago. Why had he left it so long? But she knew the answer to that? Because if he told *her* he would have to tell Maeve.

'Claudia,' he called after her.

'They switched off her life support.'

'I'm sorry.'

Down in Claudia's kitchen, she scraped meat from a tin and added it to the remains of the dry biscuits in the cat's bowl. It had greeted her ecstatically. Cupboard love, but who cared? She wished it was one of those soppy cats that sit on your lap and purr. So Jon and Diana had looked after Maeve since she was a baby, letting her think Diana was her mother. Where was her real mother? Married to someone else? No, that made no sense. She had gone ahead with the pregnancy and Jon had stood by her. Perhaps she had other children. Perhaps she was a drug addict, or an alcoholic and Jon had used this against her.

When she returned to the loft, he was still standing where she had left him. 'I had an affair.' He moved a pile of clothes off a chair and sat down. 'The pregnancy was a shock, a mistake, but we decided to keep the baby. Then, when it turned out Maeve was less than perfect . . . No,

221

don't look like that. I'm only telling you how her mother reacted. She didn't stay around long enough to discover how mild her symptoms are.'

'So where does Diana come in?'

'She offered to help and at the time it felt like the obvious answer. She'd been working as a housekeeper, for a man with two boys, but they were going away to school so she wasn't needed any more.'

'Go on.'

'We should have told Maeve.' He was sitting up straight, staring at the window. 'I wanted to, but Diana's always been afraid . . . She thinks of Maeve as her own child and every time I said she ought to be told the truth . . . We didn't have a very happy childhood.'

'Oh, that one. No, I'm sorry, go on.'

'After our mother died, we had to go and live with our grandfather. He did his best, but he didn't like it if we made a noise. And he forced Diana to eat food she disliked.'

'What about your father?'

'He'd left when I was five and Diana was only three. Married again and moved to New Zealand. I don't even know if he's still alive. Our grandfather died when I was fourteen.'

Miss Havisham strolled through the door and jumped onto the plan chest.

'Get off.' Erin was thinking about Phoebe and how determined she was no one would lie to her. The truth – she would be told everything, all her questions answered, nothing glossed over.

Jon stood up and started walking backwards and forwards. 'I'm going to tell her next week.'

'Good. There's something else you didn't tell me about. Claudia and Kent's scam.'

'Oh, you know about it.'

'Ben told me.'

'I threatened to report them to the university. I should have done. If anyone found out, I'd be in serious trouble.'

'Why didn't you?'

'I don't think Kent had written very many.'

'You know that, do you? As far as I can tell, he wrote quite a number. Or, even if he didn't write them from scratch, he improved on what the students had produced. That's what Ben and Jennie said.'

'I suppose I felt sorry for the students. They come over here with limited English and—'

'Yes, but Claudia and Kent were making money out of them. The man who phoned, and the woman who came to the door, and the man I've seen hanging about in the road . . . I expect they want their money back.'

Jon picked up the cat. 'You know what Claudia was like. When I said I wouldn't report her as long as she and Kent stopped immediately . . . She reacted just as I expected her to. Flung her arms round my neck—'

'—and kissed you. I can just imagine. A reward for getting her own way. What was Maeve's real mother called?'

He sighed. 'Does it matter?'

'It will to Maeve.' But a new possibility had occurred to her. Supposing Jon was another of her sister's beautiful young men. Not that he was as young as Ollie and Hoshi, but Claudia appeared to have collected a string of lovers, hapless victims, caught in her web. 'I'm sorry I didn't give you the chance to explain.'

'You had the baby to think about.'

'Even so.'

He should have relaxed now he had told her the truth, but he was still pacing up and down, with the cat struggling to break free. 'I feel what happened to Claudia was my fault.'

'You dropped a scaffolding pole on her head?'

'She was short of money, desperate.'

'So what were you supposed to do? Not your problem. Anyway, I have to go and see Phoebe.'

'Erin?' He moved towards her. 'I just . . . I'm so sorry I didn't tell you before.'

She opened her mouth to say, yes, she was sorry too. But everything had changed and, against her better judgement, when he gave her a hug she responded as though the two of them had been set free, as though all the taboos on their relationship had disappeared. Not true, of course, but the tension between them had melted and, for the first time for weeks, she felt like something approaching her old self.

30

Ava kept phoning to ask how Phoebe was getting on.

'I'll keep in touch,' Erin said, 'let you know if there's a problem.' Would she? Ava had loved Claudia and been devastated by the accident. At the funeral, in spite of her smart clothes, or perhaps because of them, she had looked quite haggard, as though the tragedy had aged her.

'I expect you're too busy to come round.'

'To the café?' This was a surprise. 'I spend a lot of time at the hospital. And I have to finish my illustrations. When I have a moment, I'll drop by and show you a photo.'

'Of Phoebe? That would be wonderful. When can you come?'

'Tomorrow?' Ava, eager to see her? That was a change-about. Now she was asking if there was any news of Ollie.

'No.' Erin was tired of people asking. Why did they think he would have been in touch with her? Wherever he was, he would be blaming her for insisting Claudia was kept on life support. Wherever he was? If he was still alive.

Ava asked if she was eating properly. Funny the way people thought food was a measure of mental wellbeing. Perhaps it was. Perhaps if she ate better she would feel less tired. 'I'm fine, apart from worrying about Phoebe.'

'But they're pleased with her? And she was quite a good weight considering.'

Considering? But Ava meant since she was premature.

'Oh, by the way, have you seen Hoshi recently? I expect, since he used to work in the café, he comes to see you quite often.' Not what she actually believed but it might prompt Ava to give her some information.

'Not since Jennie and Ben's party.' Ava sounded tight-lipped. 'People who work here . . . I'm always on the lookout for a pensioner. They're more reliable.'

Someone was knocking on the front door. It was Ben, standing on the doorstep with a rueful expression. 'The stuff I told you about Claudia and Kent's scam, Erin. Jennie's annoyed with me, she thinks I shouldn't have told you.'

'Well, tell her I'm very glad you did. In fact, I wish you'd told me sooner. And if there's anything else about Claudia's life . . .'

She was offering him the chance to let her in on any other secret he might have been keeping. But he failed to take the bait. Either he knew nothing, or she had been right about him and Claudia, but confessing an affair was a step too far. Was he Claudia's type? Was anyone *not* Claudia's type? Erin would give everything she owned – well, almost anything – to know who Phoebe's father was, but it was possible Claudia herself had been uncertain.

'Don't give it another thought, Ben. The scam business. To be honest, all I care about at the moment is Phoebe.'

Ben was humming, tunelessly, under his breath. 'Yes, of course. Anyway, come round whenever you like, we're always pleased to see you.'

'Thanks.'

'You're all right?'

'Will be when Phoebe's out of danger. Incidentally, did Ava know about the scam?'

'Shouldn't think so. She and Kent are friends but I doubt he'd have told her.'

'But she may know where Ollie is.'

'What makes you think that?'

She shrugged. 'Perhaps because I'm always the last to know what's going on.'

Miss Havisham had caught a thrush. One of its wings was missing, but the rest of it lay on the floor, just inside the cat flap. Erin found a brush and pan, flicked in the remains of the feathered body and transported it to the wheelie bin at the front, bumping into Jon and Maeve as she opened the front door,

'What's that?' Maeve never missed a trick. 'Has Miss Havisham been sick?'

'No, she caught a bird.'

'Can I see?'

'No.'

'Please.'

'Stop it, Maeve.' Jon hurried her through the door and Erin heard her clumping up the first set of stairs, then the uncarpeted ones that produced an even louder noise.

'I'll be back about six,' Jon avoided Erin's eyes. 'If that's all right?'

'Fine.' So Maeve still knew nothing about her real mother. When were they going to tell her?

'She had a snack in the car, so don't fall for it if she says she's hungry. I have to be in London on Thursday but I'll be back on Friday evening if you need me.'

'OK.' She was thinking about the relationship that produced Maeve. Had he loved Maeve's mother? Had

227

she loved *him*? If she ran out on their baby, how could she have done? Had she been in touch since? Did she know about Diana?

When she reached the loft, Maeve was buttoning up an old shirt Erin kept for her.

'Would you like to see a picture of Phoebe?'

'Is that her name? Oh yes.' Maeve waited impatiently while Erin found the photos on her phone. 'Oh, look, she's so small, but she's not all funny looking. Poor Claudia, she'll never see her. And poor baby, she'll never see her real mother. Is Claudia dead?'

'Yes.' Erin almost added, but not suffering any more, although when someone died it was the people left behind who suffered, and the fact that she and Claudia had never been close seemed to have made her death harder to bear.

Maeve was inspecting Erin's painting of Mrs Moffatt and the little girl. 'Is it her birthday?'

'I don't know, it doesn't say. Yes, I expect so.'

'Is Mrs Moffatt her grandmother?'

'It doesn't say that either.'

'I hope she chooses the frightened little guinea pig. I haven't got any grandparents. They're all dead.'

Erin found a sheet of paper and some poster paints. 'No drawing today. I want you to make use of what we talked about, the effect of one colour on another.'

'Just do a pattern?'

'A picture if you like. The seaside? Sand, water and sky.'

Maeve frowned. 'I'll paint the beach in Ollie's photograph, only his is black and white and it looks very gloomy. You know Jennie? Is she your friend?'

'Yes, yes she is, why do you ask?'

'She invited Mum and Dad but they couldn't find a babysitter. Anyway, they don't like parties. I'm not very good at patterns, Erin, and I can't do mirror images in Maths. Dad wants me to have a tutor. It's because he's clever and I'm stupid. Why do people talk behind your back? It makes you think you must have done something bad.'

'I'm sure there's nothing like that. They could have been discussing money, anything, nothing about you.' What was she doing? Maeve was worried, hoping she would reassure her. Erin returned to the safer subject of Jennie. 'Jennie has a house she lets out to students.'

'Ollie might be living there.'

'I don't think so.'

'He's got a degree in Maths. I'm the only one in my class that can't turn fractions into decimals. Or decimals into fractions. Sometimes I get it right. Then I forget and . . . Tell Dad.' Her face was scarlet. 'He'll listen to you. Yes, he will. Why are you looking like that?' She stood up, noisily. 'I thought if I told you, you'd say you'd—'

'Calm down.'

'Why should I? That's what everyone says.'

'All right, I'll talk to your dad.' She would, but not about Maths.

'Promise?'

'I promise.'

'Oh, thank you, Erin. And you'll ask him why they keep whispering. I hate it when people whisper.' She bumped against the plan chest, knocking over a glass jar and as Erin watched, frozen with horror, water ran over Mrs Moffatt and the little girl, and she knew she would have to start the painting all over again.

31

After several visits to the hospital, combined with frantic work on the illustrations, Erin returned to the Special Care Baby Unit the next morning, only to be told Phoebe had not had a very good night.

'Her heart rate dropped,' the nurse explained, 'but it's back to normal now.'

'Why would that happen?' The infection had cleared up. Now there was another problem. 'And why has she got a mask over eyes?'

'Nothing to worry about. She was a little jaundiced so she's having phototherapy.'

'A compound called bilirubin builds up. I read about it. Lots of babies have it, don't they, not just premature ones?'

'It's quite common, yes.' The nurse had her back turned, searching in the cupboard where they kept the tiny clothes. 'A present arrived.' She handed Erin a toy cat with a long, fluffy tail.

'Did it say who it was from?'

The nurse shook her head. 'But it must have been someone who knows her name. When the phototherapy's finished, I'll prop it up where she can see it. Tomorrow she'll be having a brain scan. Don't look so worried, all premature babies have them.'

'In case there's any bleeding? You'll let me know? No, it's all right, I'll come in. What time would be best?'

For the staff, the test was routine. For Erin, it meant another interrupted night, falling asleep then waking with a start, dozing, listening to the radio, and finally dropping off again when it was almost time to get up. And now she had another worry. The soft toy must be from Ollie. Anyone else would have attached a card. Someone had told him about Phoebe and he was putting in a claim. Who had told him? Someone who knew where he was staying but had chosen not to say. Her hands, that she had washed so carefully, were sticky with sweat.

'Are you sure there was no card with the toy?' She wiped her hands on her jeans, making a mental note not to touch Phoebe until she had washed them again. 'Did it come through the post or was it left at reception?'

'Not sure.' The nurse was adjusting Phoebe's knitted hat 'People usually buy a teddy bear, but I like cats, don't you?'

'Except when they catch mice and birds.'

As she approached the shop where Hoshi worked, a guy with a shaved head, was locking up.

'Hoshi?' Erin said. 'I need to talk to him.'

'That makes two of us. Didn't turn up today.'

'I know which road he lives in, but not the number of the house.'

'Can't help you, I'm afraid.' He fingered his double chin. 'Not allowed to give out addresses of employees.'

'It's important. A relative of his is in hospital.' She stared at him, willing him to make an exception. 'She's dying.'

He looked away, unable to deal with bad news.

'I've been asked to get in touch with him but—'

'You don't know the house number.' His eyes moved from side to side. He suspected she was lying. But she might be telling the truth. 'Hang on.' He unlocked the door again and disappeared into the back of the shop, returning a few moments later with a piece of card in his hand. 'If you find him, tell him if he wants to keep his job—'

'Yes, yes, I will. Thanks. Thank you very much.'

The house, with its patches of crumbling stonework and a front garden full of weeds, could have been a student let. A tiled path led up to a front door, with peeling paint and a row of bells with names next to them, written in ink on yellowing cards. It was getting dark and, since there was no street light nearby, they were difficult to read, but in any case, as far as she was concerned, Hoshi was just Hoshi. He had no second name.

Erin chose the bottom bell, hoping it was for a flat or room on the ground floor and would cause the least disturbance, and after a short pause the door was answered by a girl, dressed in Scooby-Doo pyjamas and holding a slice of toast and jam.

'I'm sorry to disturb you, but I'm looking for Hoshi.'

'Not here.'

'But you know him? He lives here?'

The girl shrugged.

'Any idea where he might have gone?' A large, brown and white dog had appeared, wagging its tail. The girl grabbed its collar and started to close the door. Erin put her foot in it.

'I'm sorry to be a nuisance, but it's important. Someone's ill. A relative. If you can think of anywhere he might be, a club, a friend's house . . .'

The girl's face was expressionless. 'The Chinese guy, is it?'

'Japanese.'

'Whatever.' With her free hand, she gave Erin a push, and the door closed in her face.

It was a one-way street and she had left her car some distance away. Retracing her route, she realised she should have taken the trouble to memorise the names of the roads. Each one looked like the one before, big old semi-detached houses with narrow gaps between them that led to an alleyway behind. She thought her car was three streets away but there was no sign of it and when someone stepped out of the shadows, she was not sure if she screamed out loud, or the scream was inside her head.

'Hoshi! I've been looking for you.'

'Graham said you'd been to the shop.'

'He phoned? Look, the part about a relative in hospital—'

'Is the baby ill?'

'No. No, I think she's all right.' Erin was too superstitious to give a definite answer. 'I just needed your address.'

He was dressed all in black. Black trousers, black hoodie, black woollen gloves. His voice was cold and she should have been afraid, but there was something about the way he was clasping and unclasping his gloved hands. He was the frightened one. He made a sound in his throat and when he spoke it was so muffled she had to ask him to repeat what he had said.

'Ollie.' He lurched towards her and she took a step back. 'I . . . I think he may be . . . The wind's so cold. He only took a few clothes and it's always cold by the sea.'

'The sea? You know where he is. He's staying near the coast? Why didn't you tell me before? Come on then.' She started walking, willing him to accompany her. 'When was the last time you were in touch with him?'

'His phone's switched off. He may not be there any longer.'

'You can explain on the way.' She had spotted her car. 'Has he got any money?'

'I don't know.'

'He's been there ever since he disappeared? That was weeks ago. Why didn't you say? He could be in a bad way. He could be ill.'

They stared at each other but neither of them spoke. Then Hoshi gave a choking sob. 'I should have gone there but . . . Supposing something's happened, what if he's dead?'

32

Erin drove and Hoshi gave directions. 'We cross the suspension bridge. It'll be the quickest way. Then we have to get onto the motorway, the M5.'

'Sure you know where we're going.'

'I can check on my phone. Last time we went on the train. Took our bikes.'

'You and Ollie?'

He nodded.

'Did you go with him this time?

'He wouldn't let me. I wanted him to stay in Bristol. He could have stayed with me, slept on the floor, but . . .'

'Can you find a pound?' She pointed to the glove compartment. 'For the bridge.'

He pulled off his gloves and unzipped his hoodie. Underneath he was wearing a white T-shirt with something written on the front in curly black letters. He was breathing hard. 'He may not be there.'

'I know. You said.'

'A bungalow. It's being done up. It belongs to someone at the university but he's in California. On sabbatical. Last April. We saw it last April. When we walked on Brean Down.'

'With this person from the university.'

'No. We met him in a café. Ollie knew him. Sort of. James – he's called James. He said he was doing up the bungalow as a holiday let. Everything will be turned off now, electricity, water. Ollie knew but he didn't care. He just wanted to escape.'

Ahead of them, she could see the lights on the bridge. 'Money, Hoshi.'

'Oh. Yes.' He opened the glove compartment and, along with Erin's box of loose change, a jumble of other stuff fell out; painkillers, maps, and an old photo of her and Declan on a day out at Southend. Who had taken it? A stranger, must have been. *Do me a favour, mate? Come on then, Erin, big grin.*

Hoshi handed her a pound, and began returning the rest of the things. 'Ollie thinks . . .' His head was turned away and she was afraid he might be crying.

'Ollie thinks?'

'It was my fault.'

'What was? Come on, Hoshi, you need to tell me everything.'

'The day before it happened . . .' He sat up straight and stared through the dusty windscreen. 'He and Claudia had an argument. A bad one. He thought you heard them. He thinks you think he killed her.'

'That's crazy.' But where *had* Ollie been that afternoon? Claudia had mentioned something about a meltdown and how she was going to cook him a special meal to make up for it. Ollie, a meltdown? Erin had thought it so unlikely that Claudia must be exaggerating as usual.

Hoshi had read her thoughts. 'He was walking in Leigh Woods.'

'That's what he told you?'

'I wanted to go with him but he wouldn't let me. He was so angry.' He swung round to face her. 'Ollie never got angry. I'd never seen him like that before.'

It had started to rain, a fine drizzle that meant the wipers squeaked, but if she turned them off the screen soon became obscured. Driving in the dark, in the rain, to a place she knew nothing about, with a man she barely knew. As they crossed over, she glanced down at the trickle of river, moving between slabs of thick mud, and illuminated by the lights on the bridge.

'Where are you from, Hoshi?'

'Manchester.'

'Really?' What had she been expecting? Tokyo? Yokohama? 'What did you come to Bristol to study?'

'Physics. My father's an engineer.'

'But you dropped out of your course and found a job in a clothes shop? No, before that you worked at Ava's Place.'

'I want to be a fashion designer.' He was fiddling with his phone. 'You have to go to Art College. I've been saving up. The shop and other jobs as well. That's why I agreed to paint Claudia's loft. But when I'd finished it she got mad with me.'

'Why?

He hesitated. 'If Ollie's still there—'

'Why did Claudia get mad at you?'

'She wanted me to stay.'

'Stay? Oh, you mean . . .' Erin gave a short, bitter laugh. 'You mean stay the night. But you turned her down. Did she pay you for the decorating you'd done?'

He shook his head. 'It was my fault. I was the one who introduced them. We were at a club and Claudia came in with some friends. I thought she'd cut me dead but she sat down with us and started talking to Ollie.'

The headlights reflected what could be the eyes of a cat. Or a fox. If you saw an animal on the road, you were supposed to brake, not swerve. Erin swerved, and the car went perilously close to the hedge, and Hoshi caught his breath.

'When he moved in with her I thought . . . But they were so happy together and she wanted them to have a baby. I didn't know.'

'What didn't you know?' But she had guessed what was coming next. 'She was pregnant already. So who's the baby's father?'

'I don't know.'

'Oh, come on Hoshi, if Ollie said something I need to know.'

The rain had stopped. She switched off the wipers and rubbed at the misted up windscreen with the side of her hand.

'Ava knows,' he said. 'I overheard her when I was working at the café. She was in the storeroom, talking on her phone.'

'Who to?' But she was asking too many questions when she ought to be encouraging him to tell her at his own pace.

'I don't know.' He pushed a lock of hair behind his ear. 'Ollie would never have hurt her. If you knew him—'

'If you want the truth, Hoshi, I thought you might be the baby's father. No, don't worry, I know you're not. Is that everything then?'

'I don't think he'll still be at the bungalow.'

'But he could be so we have to check. If he's not, where else might he be?'

A car was overtaking them on a bend. Erin swore under her breath, but the stupid show off had got away with it.

'Fucking idiot,' Hoshi said, and they both laughed, nervous laughter but it dissipated some the tension between them.

'He cycled there,' he said.

'All the way from Bristol? So he can't have taken

much with him. I checked his clothes but it was impossible to tell, although I think he may have taken Claudia's phone. Why would he do that?'

She was thinking about the rolls of banknotes in Claudia's desk. Perhaps there had been more. Perhaps Ollie had helped himself and who could blame him? The day after the accident, when she thought he was going to the university, he must have talked to Hoshi. But not about whether the baby should be given a chance to be born. He had made up his mind about that as soon as he knew Claudia was not going to recover.

They had reached a roundabout and she took the first exit onto the motorway, going west towards Devon and Cornwall. She was thinking about Claudia's attempt to seduce Hoshi, luring him into the loft on the pretext of wanting him to paint the walls then . . . Had it been like that, or was it a spur of the moment thing? What did it matter? But it mattered that Claudia had felt rejected, humiliated, and lost no time in adding Ollie to her collection. When they reached the bungalow what would they find? If the owner was in America that meant no one else would have been near the place. Were there other houses close by? Or caravans. But even if there were they were probably unoccupied during the winter and no one would have noticed Ollie camping out in the derelict bungalow.

For the rest of their time on the motorway, neither of them spoke. A truck in front kept slowing down, then speeding up. Traffic was heavier in the opposite direction and the oncoming lights dazzled. At the best of times, motorways had a hypnotic effect, and distances were harder to judge. Erin was aware it was only adrenalin keeping her from falling asleep.

After her visit to the mortuary, she had convinced

239

herself Ollie was still alive. But the fact that the poor boy who had hanged himself, had not been Ollie meant nothing. If Ollie was dead, it would be her fault. For overruling his wish to let Claudia and the baby die in peace. Except, if he knew he was not the baby's father, it was not his decision to make.

'Next exit,' Hoshi said, 'in half a mile.'

'Sure you know where we're going?'

'I'm just checking.'

'What does it say on your T-shirt?'

'Sorry? Oh. The perfect square lacks corners.'

'What does it mean?'

'I don't know. It's a Taoist saying.'

She glanced at him. He was so startlingly good-looking he ought to be a model. But that was not what he wanted. He wanted to be a designer.

'You're a Taoist?'

'No.'

After they left the motorway, one roundabout led to another. Then another. Third exit. Second exit. Second exit. First. She should have bought a sat nav . . . But once, when she borrowed one from a friend, it had instructed her to turn up a cul-de-sac in the centre of Guildford and the disembodied voiced had ordered her to – *make a u-turn. make a u-turn.*

Another roundabout, and she was certain they must be lost.

'Carry on.' Hoshi opened his window and leaned forward. 'No, slow down, we've gone too far. Turn when you can. From here to the end there are only caravans. The bungalow – it's back from the beach. It's all my fault. I shouldn't have told him. He didn't believe me, thought Ava had got it wrong, but when he asked her—'

'Asked Claudia?'

'The day before the accident. When you heard them shouting.'

'Actually, I didn't. I expect they were in the kitchen, with the door shut, and I was up in the loft.'

'Claudia lied. At first she did. Then she said . . . She thought it didn't matter. She said it made no difference, it was just a baby. I suppose she knew he was going to find out.'

'He might not have done.' *Are you sure your sister got her dates right. Obviously, the larger the foetus and the better developed . . . .* She thought she could smell the sea. Was this where Ollie had taken the photo, the one Claudia had hung in the loft? 'When you came here in the spring did Ollie bring his camera? There's a photograph in the loft.'

'No, I took that. Ollie was teaching me. Later we saw this bird of prey. On top of Brean Down. A falcon. I think it was a falcon. There are falcons in Leigh Woods but they're difficult to see. And goats. No, I mean the goats are on Brean Down.' He broke off. 'Oh, Yes, I know where we are. Next on the left.'

'Sure?'

'Certain. Look! Over by those trees.'

'If he is there, how would he have got in?'

'Pull up behind that skip.'

'Wait! We need to plan what we're going to . . .' But, even before the car had come to a standstill, he had jumped out and started running.

Erin stayed where she was. If Ollie *was* there he was less likely to run off if only Hoshi had come. She could see him peering through the windows at the front. Then he moved out of sight and she climbed slowly out of the car and opened the boot, searching among rugs and maps and a pair of boots, until she found the flashlight she kept for emergencies. It was months, years, since she had used it but, miraculously, it still worked, lighting up the branches of the trees and the white walls of the bungalow.

Hoshi reappeared. 'He's not here. He could have left weeks ago. I should have come before. I wanted to, but his phone was switched off and I thought—'

'Where else could he be? Think!' The flashlight flickered and she was afraid it was going to go out. Something moved in the trees, but it was only a bird. Now she was close up to the building she could see moss growing on the roof tiles, and ivy sprawled over a lean-to shed alongside it. Pulling open the rickety shed door she shone the flashlight inside. 'No bike. That means he must have left. Or never been here in the first place. 'Is there a window at back?

Hoshi picked up a stone.

'No, hang on. There's no point breaking the glass if he's not here. The police checked with his mother but she hadn't seen him for months.'

'She's not well. Her nerves, Ollie said.'

'And his father died. How much has he told—' Erin broke off in mid-sentence. A sound, close to the shed, had made her swing round and the searchlight had picked up the dark shape of a man, dressed in filthy jeans and a thick roll neck sweater. His hair hung over his eyes and his rough beard made him look like a tramp. But there was no doubt who it was.

'No, wait!' She stepped forward and grabbed hold of his arm. 'We only wanted to make sure you were all right.'

'I had to tell her where you were.' Hoshi had moved closer, blocking Ollie's escape although he was making no attempt to break free. 'I was afraid you might have—'

'Topped myself?' Ollie pushed his hair out of his eyes.

'The baby's been born,' Erin said. 'I know it's not yours.'

'Is Claudia dead?'

She nodded.

'Was there a funeral?'

'Yes.' She took out her phone to show him a picture of Phoebe, then thought better of it. 'Hoshi told me what happened. I'm so sorry.'

He closed his eyes and, for a brief moment, she recalled the face of the poor dead boy at the mortuary. Ollie's face was similar – small features, fair hair – but the boy in the mortuary had looked peaceful. Ollie looked done in. 'How's Maeve?' he said.

'Maeve?' The fact that he had asked about her gave Erin hope. 'She's fine. She misses you, worries about you. Remember how the two of you used to play with Miss Havisham?'

Somewhere close by, a dog had started to bark. A woman shouted and the barking stopped for a few seconds, then started again. Hoshi shouted above the noise. 'Come back with us, Ol, please. You can sleep in my bed, I don't care.'

'We'll collect your stuff,' Erin said. 'How did you get in?'

'There's a spare key in the shed, it opens the door at the back. I locked it at night in case . . .'

'The neighbours. Didn't anyone—'

'I said I was doing repairs. I found some tools.' He turned and they followed him round the back of the bungalow and into a large empty room, empty apart for a pile of what looked like old curtains, and some fast food containers. And a bike with a flat tyre. And a hammer and a rusty saw.

Ollie muttered something she had to ask him to repeat.

'She didn't give a toss.'

'Who? You mean Claudia. I'm so sorry. If you'd told me. No, it's all right. Even so, I have to ask you. Who *is* the baby's father?'

'She wouldn't tell me. I don't think she knew.' He stared into the darkness. 'When Hoshi told me, I didn't believe it. And Claudia said it wasn't true. But then I saw her face. She thought I wouldn't mind, said it didn't matter, it was just a baby. I lost my temper. I was shouting. You must have heard. I said I'd kill her. They think it was me. The police think—'

'No, Ollie, it was an accident. I'm certain it was. I thought they might bring a case against the scaffolders, but it would never have stuck because no one saw what happened and most of the protesters had run off before the police arrived.'

But in the silence that followed, Erin knew what the two of them were thinking. Since there were no witnesses, how could she be so sure it was accident?

33

Time to leave. Stella stuffed her clothes into two zip-up bags and stared round the wretched basement, wondering how she had endured it for so long. Did she feel better – or worse? But it was something she had needed to do and regret was pointless.

Checking the bathroom, with its dripping tap, she moved on to the kitchen, the bedroom, the living room. Nothing in any of the cupboards. Nothing under the bed or down the sides of the battered sofa, no incriminating slips of paper, receipts, addresses. If the landlady came nosing about, it would be as though no one had been living in the place. She would leave the city without trace and it was unlikely she would ever return. Her stomach churned, but she had prepared herself. She could handle it. When tears threatened, she blinked them away and got a grip on herself.

As she was zipping up the second bag, she heard a sound. The postman? At this time of day, after lunch? Since no one knew where she was staying it would be another load of junk mail, flyers advertising pizza, and Thai takeaways. Who would move in after she left? If the landlady had a conscience, she would have the whole place ripped out and refurbished, but most likely she would let it to a couple of students, unconcerned about the state it was in. Maybe the illustrator woman needed somewhere to live. She had an air of desperation – it took one to spot one – and it was possible the basement could be turned into a studio if she was one of those artists that preferred artificial light.

Paid up to the end of the month, it felt like a waste to be leaving. She could stay one more day, drive up the road one more time . . . But she was unlikely to see anyone at this time of day. Back in London, she would slot into her old routine and concentrate on building up the business, and it would be a relief to sleep in a decent bed, and cook in a well-equipped kitchen. The anguish she felt was deserved and there was something clean, clear-cut, about it, a punishment that fitted a crime.

One last look round. The place was cleaner and tidier than when she moved in. The new microwave contrasted with the old appliances – a greasy cooker and a fridge, covered in rust marks. Returning to her immaculate flat would be a pleasure. It had to be. Put her bags in the car. Lock the door to the flat. Key in an envelope, posted to the landlady, who would be glad her tenant had left early since it meant she could re-let to some other poor mug.

People often underestimate the sense of smell. It must be coming from outside in the road. Road menders, heating up tar? But long before she reached the hallway, she knew it was inside. Smoke filled her eyes and, as she attempted to wave it away, she spotted the burning rag that had been pushed through the letterbox and had set fire to the straw mat. She stuck out a foot – but she was only wearing socks and had to run back to the bedroom and search about for her shoes – and by the time she found them the fire had spread to the greasy carpet. Stamping it out, she kicked the charred remains through the open door, ran up the iron steps, just in time to see a figure with the hood of his jacket pulled up. He was standing at the end of the road, waiting, watching the house, hoping for flames, but as soon as he saw her he shot round the corner.

Did he have a car? If he had, she would lose him. Who was he? A local tearaway, an arsonist who loved seeing fire engines? Anger spurred her on and she caught up with him as he was attempting to start his car. As the engine fired, she wrenched open the door and switched off the ignition. He struggled to break free, but she was too strong for him.

'What the fuck did you think you were doing? She dragged back his hood, determined he was not going to get away with it.

'You!' The shock was like a bucket of icy water in her face. 'What did you think I was going to do? I'm leaving, going back to London. How did you know where I was living? You followed my car, is that what you did? No, I'm not going to let go of you, not until you tell me. The house could have burned down. Someone might have been killed. Is that what you wanted? You're insane. What were you afraid of? It's not me you should fear, it's that artist woman.'

34

When she pushed open the door to Ava's Place, Ava made a beeline for her. 'Come through.' She nodded in the direction of the girl with a nose ring. 'She can cope for five minutes. Did you bring the photos of Phoebe?'

Erin followed her into a room filled with boxes, some empty, some half-full. 'Stock', Ava explained unnecessarily, 'one of these days I'll have a proper clear out. Let's have a look.'

Erin showed her the pictures. Phoebe, awake, Phoebe fast asleep. And one a nurse had taken of Erin holding Phoebe in her arms.

'Oh, look at her.' Ava took the phone from Erin's hand and studied each picture. 'She's lovely, such a pretty little thing.'

'Who's her father?'

'Her father?'

'Ollie's been camping out in a derelict bungalow. Hoshi told me where he was. We've brought him back to Bristol.'

'To Claudia's house?'

'No.'

Ava locked her fingers, a signal that meant she was going to try and fob her off with lies. 'Is he all right?'

'Phoebe's father, Ava. Hoshi heard you talking about it on the phone. No, not the details or he'd have told me. Why didn't you?'

'I thought the baby might die.'

Erin erupted with anger. 'And the problem would go away. How could you? Hoshi told Ollie the truth – how Claudia had been pregnant when he moved in with her – and now he thinks he'll be accused of killing her. He thinks I heard them having a blazing row.'

'But you didn't?' Ava sat down heavily on a box of canned tomatoes. 'She wanted a child. God only knows why, but you know your sister. Once she'd got a bee in her bonnet . . .'

'She got pregnant deliberately?'

Ava nodded.

'And then regretted it?'

'Heavens, no, she was ecstatic. Boasted how it had worked first go. Made me feel a bit queasy, but the two of them . . . She was fond of him.'

'Who?'

'I thought you'd have worked it out.'

'How?'

'It was Kent.'

'What! I thought he was gay.'

'Ambidextrous. And in any case he'd have done anything for Claudia. And she'd read somewhere that older men pass on better genes, produce brighter kids. All nonsense, in fact I think I've heard the opposite's the case, but once your sister got something into her head there was no reasoning with her. "Impregnating a dear friend" – that was how Kent described it.'

'You tried to talk her out of it?'

'Hardly. The deed was done long before I found out. He's dying, Erin. Kent. Inoperable brain tumour. Won't be with us for more than another month or two. He only told me a few days ago. I was devastated. That play you saw was his final performance.'

'I'm sorry.' Was that what he and Ava had been talking about when she saw them together, outside the café? *I'm dying, Ava. The baby. I know Claudia wanted me to have nothing to do with it, but after she was killed . . .*

Ava let out a long, weary sigh. 'When I told you about the play I was hoping he might confide. I said you deserved to know. And so did poor Ollie. Your sister was so—'

'I know. Single-minded, stopped at nothing to get what she wanted.'

'You said it, my darling. But she had her good points. She was such good company, so amusing, so lively. What will happen to the poor little mite?'

'Oh, you don't have to worry about that.'

'You'll bring her up as your own?'

All these weeks, she had believed Ava was Claudia's biggest fan when, in reality, she had thought her selfish, ruthless, indifferent to how much she hurt people.

'She told Ollie it made no difference who the father was. It was just a baby.'

'Poor boy. He was besotted with her.' Ava held out an arm for Erin to pull her up. 'Better go and see who's waiting to be served. Old nose ring's not that reliable on her own.'

'If you'd told me before . . .' But her anger had evaporated. The news about Kent had been a shock, but now she felt only relief.

'Was it Hoshi who told Ollie about the baby?' A flicker of doubt crossed her face. 'No, it doesn't matter.'

'Yes, it does. You think Ollie—'

'But he couldn't. He wouldn't.' She glanced at the storeroom door. 'He's such a sweet boy.'

Erin gave her a cold stare, 'You'd better get back to your customers. I only came here because I needed to know who the father is. Please don't talk to anyone else—'

'What do you think I am. First, you accuse me of keeping it to myself. Now you're saying I can't keep my mouth shut. Oh, I'm sorry, my darling, but it's over now and the two of us mustn't fall out. Can I tell Kent you know? I won't if you don't want me to. He was worried he might be left holding the baby, so to speak, but now he's so ill there's no question of him taking any responsibility. And it's not as though he's got any money. He rents where he lives, gets by with odd bits of coaching. No, don't look like that, she's your sister's baby, your baby. There won't be a problem, will there? They will let you keep her?'

In an attempt to relax, Erin was having a bath, trying out some of Claudia's array of bath oils – rainforest flowers, cocoa butter, chamomile. Claudia had liked company when she had a bath. *Come and sit with me, Erin, bring us a couple of glasses of white wine.* Once she had asked Ollie to join her in the water. Erin smiled to herself at the memory of the expression on his face. There was not much else to smile about.

Later, she would call round at Jennie and Ben's. Would she tell them about Kent? Not yet, not until she had convinced herself Ollie had been in Leigh Woods when the accident happened. Leigh Woods was on the opposite side of the river. She had never been there herself, but you could see it from the suspension bridge, a nature reserve, known for its rare trees and various species of orchids. Would anyone go there after dark?

On an impulse, she decided to talk to Jennie and Ben. If Jon had been around she would have talked to him, asked his advice. What would he have said? That Ollie had probably walked in the woods earlier in the afternoon, and was on his way home at the time of the accident. Jennie and Ben were less likely to let him off the hook, and she needed to work out what she was going to say to Ollie. What questions she was going to ask him.

Any resentment she had felt towards Jennie, had disappeared the instant she understood why she had been unwilling to help. In the same circumstances, she would have kept quiet herself in case the pregnancy ended in a miscarriage. She admired people who were so open they told their friends everything, even things that showed them in a less than good light. Admired them, but would never be one of them. Maeve might be, or would she grow out of her ability to express her feelings so freely? Jon was wary, self-contained. Maybe Maeve's birth mother had been an extravert. She would never know.

Lying back, in the blissfully hot water, she closed her eyes and thought about a time when Phoebe was strong enough to leave the unit, when she could buy her a cot, and a car seat, and plenty of clothes. What with? She was running short of cash and tempted to use some of the money from Claudia's desk. At least part of it was probably owed to overseas students, who had failed to receive their dissertations, but they were unlikely to claim it.

Using Claudia's Snoopy mug, she poured warm water over her hair, feeling it trickle down her back. Phoebe was not yet out of danger, but every day she grew stronger, more resilient, and she was putting on weight. Somehow, Erin had got it into her head, if she finished the illustrations by the end of the month, Phoebe would be out of the incubator, and out of danger. Then she could relax and it would simply be a question of waiting until she reached a weight where she was allowed home. Could she really relax? Only if she was certain Claudia's death had been accidental. But in all likelihood she would never know.

Outside the warmth of the water, the bathroom felt chilly. A draught came through from the top of the sash window, that refused to close. Downstairs, Miss Havisham was mewing loudly. Then she heard her padding up the stairs, pausing on the landing, wondering whether to carry on up to the loft, or were the sounds she could hear coming from somewhere else. Putting in an appearance and demanding food, was a daily event now. Erin could have blocked off the cat flap, but knew she never would. In spite of the occasional dead bird or mouse, she had grown attached to the cat.

Something soft touched the back of her neck and her head jerked up, knocking against the side of the bath. Water ran down her face, and she reached out for a towel, but it was too far away, and when she tried to stand up she was held down, and through streaming eyes, she saw a figure towering above her.

'What are you doing?' Diana's hand was on her shoulder. Breathe deeply. Try to stay calm. 'How did you get in?'

'Oh, Jon's always had a key.' Her voice was light, almost lilting. 'He used to help Claudia with her computer. Well, that's what he said he was doing.' The steam from the bath was making her cough but the hand never lost its grip. 'The baby is Jon's.'

'The baby? No, it isn't. I know who the father is—'

'I saw them.'

'Who? When?'

'They were kissing.'

'Oh, that. I know the time you must be thinking about, but she was only kissing him because he agreed not to tell the university about the dissertations. Jon told you, he

253

must have done, Claudia and Kent – they had this scam . .
. Claudia kissed everyone, she was that kind of . . .' Erin
tried to climb out of the bath but Diana pushed her back
and she lost her balance and her head went under the
water before she emerged, spluttering and coughing.

'You'll take Maeve.'

'Maeve? What are you talking about?' The two of
them were more or less the same height, but Diana was
standing, and she was sitting in tepid, soapy water.

'You and Jon,' she said. 'When he couldn't have your
sister . . .'

'No, no, you've got it all wrong. Let me get dressed
and we can talk properly.'

'He came here by himself. When Maeve was at
school.'

'To give me money for the classes.' Not entirely true,
but a thought had come to her. The man with the hoodie.
'You've been watching the house?' Why was Diana's
other hand behind her back? What was she holding?

'I saw the two of you at the shops.'

'When? The shops? You couldn't have done. I've
never been to the shops with . . .' But that was not what
she meant.

'People like her don't deserve to have children. They
don't deserve to live.'

The building site. The scaffolding. 'It was you.'

Diana's left arm swung out from behind her back and
the corpse of a rat fell into the water with a splash. Erin let
out an involuntary scream as it bumped against her.
Bedraggled, and with blood on its neck, it floated for a
moment then sank.

'Maeve's mine.' Diana's voice was a snarl.

'Yes, of course she is. Tell me what you want and we
can—'

'Stella said you're the one I should fear.'

'Stella?' The dead rat was wedged between her legs.

'Maeve's birth mother. Birth mothers, that's what they call them. Mothers who don't want their children.' Both her hands were on Erin's head, pushing her under the water and holding her down until the breath left her lungs and she squirmed and struggled, finally breaking free and sliding over the side of the bath. Scrambling to her feet, she stumbled, half ran, along the passage, and on down the stairs, hanging onto the rail, slipping, scraping her knees and jumping up again.

Diana was coming after her, getting closer. Reaching out a dripping hand, Erin wrenched open the front door and fell through it, into the path of a tall, smartly dressed woman. Stella.

'No!' She tried to squeeze past, but Stella caught hold of her, spinning her round and pinning her naked body against the wall. 'Don't run. I'm not going to hurt you. Where is Diana? Is she here?'

As Erin sank to the ground, Stella took off her jacket and crouched down, wrapping it round her, and the two of them watched as Diana raced across the road, almost getting hit by a passing motor bike, and jumped into her car and drove off, turning left at the top of the road without bothering to check if anything was coming in the other direction.

35

They sat on Erin's bed. Erin was wearing her pyjamas and a thick sweater, and holding a mug of tea.

'How did you know?' The shock was starting to wear off but she still spoke through chattering teeth.

Stella stood up to study a drawing. The little girl, holding the smallest guinea pig. 'She put a burning rag through the letterbox of the basement. I thought it was some kid who enjoyed seeing places go up in flames. If I hadn't been there, smelled the smoke . . .'

'Why?'

'Mm?'

'Why did she do it?'

'It was only when I was leaving, to return to London, that it struck me I'd inadvertently dropped you in it. I've seen the way Jon looks at you.'

'You watched the house? Why?'

'I had to find out where Jon lived. To make sure Maeve was all right. All these years.... I had no right, but it had started to prey on my mind. The regret, and if I'm honest the curiosity. A few days ago Diana saw me talking to her.' She turned away from the drawing. What's it called? The book you're illustrating.'

'The . . .' For a moment she had forgotten. 'The Littlest Guinea pig.'

Stella nodded. 'I'll look out for it in the shops. I'm Maeve's mother.'

'Her mother? You mean her birth mother?' She was so unlike the woman Erin had imagined, the one Jon had been in love with, the one who had given up on her own child. 'They haven't told her. She thinks . . . How did Diana know where you were staying?'

'Must have followed me. At first, I thought you were Jon's wife. Later, I realised he lived somewhere else, but brought Maeve to your house. And sometimes he came by himself.'

'She has art lessons. Does Jon know you're in the city? I don't think Diana meant to harm me. I think she came to the house to talk. I thought she had a knife but it was only a dead rat.'

'A dead rat? She's off her head.' Stella checked her watch. 'Does Maeve walk home from school on her own?'

'Yes. Yes, I think so. Oh God, what time is it?'

'Ten past three.'

'She comes out at half past. Or it could be earlier.'

'Come on then, hurry up and get some clothes on. We'll go in my car. You're in no fit state to drive.'

The car heater was turned up high but Erin still shivered with cold. What had Diana planned to do? She had killed Claudia so what difference would one more person make? What was she doing now? Had she gone straight home or was she driving round Bristol? Or waiting for Maeve to come out of school so she could bundle her into the car – and drive up north, or into Wales? You read about parents – although it was usually fathers – who killed their children rather than lose them. Surely Diana . . . But if she was in her right mind, she would never have admitted she dropped the scaffolding pole on Claudia.

Normally it would have taken ten minutes to reach the

257

house, but the road ahead was blocked by scaffolders, unloading poles. Stella shouted at the men and one of them held up a hand, spreading out four fingers to indicate when they would be gone. Reversing so fast Erin was sure they would scrape a parked car, Stella yelled at her to take an alternative route.

'Next on the right, then left, then down to the bottom of the hill.' Erin's head was fuzzy and she was finding it difficult to focus. 'Then left again and keep straight on. She'd never hurt Maeve. She's her whole life. She thinks of her as her own child and as far as Maeve's concerned, Diana is her biological mother.'

'She's never been told?' The car swerved to the right and Erin remembered the fox, or had it been a cat, that she had only just missed when she and Hoshi were on their way to Brean.

'She came to help,' she said. 'When Maeve was a baby. And stayed on. They've put off telling her. Jon wanted to but Diana wouldn't let him. Yes, I know, he should have insisted, but—'

'What's she like? Not Diana, Maeve?'

'Great. Perfect. Apart from being a little clumsy and not very good at Maths. Oh, and she suffers from allergies but I'm not sure what.'

If Jon had told Maeve the truth, none of this would be happening. But, even though she was an expert at concealing it, he knew now how unstable Diana was and had felt compelled to protect his little sister. Something he had done for most of his life.

Stella was asking if she had been to the house.

'Only once. Maeve's lovely, so bright and so affectionate.'

She was being cruel, rubbing it in, but how could this woman have abandoned her? If she had stayed, made a life with Jon, Diana would have been a shadowy figure in the background, Auntie Diana.

'Left here!' But she had told her too late and there was a screech of brakes and hooting from the car behind them. Stella took the next turning on the right, made a U-turn, and waited, muttering under her breath, for the oncoming traffic to pass. What time was it? Nearly twenty past. Was Maeve on her way home?

'Next on the right.'

'I know where we are.' Stella swung round the corner. 'There's Diana's car. Further up on the other side of the road.'

'Perhaps we'd better go straight to the school.'

'You know where it is?'

'I think so.' They should have followed Diana as soon as she drove off, but how could they when Erin was naked and freezing cold. Even so, they had wasted time, talking when they should have been thinking about Maeve's safety. 'I hope they come out at three-thirty. It's not far from here so—'

'Check the house first.' Stella made it sound like an order, switching off the engine but staying put. 'Don't worry, I'll be watching like a hawk.' She took a packet of mints from the glove compartment. 'Don't smoke, do you?'

'No.'

Standing in the porch, Erin felt her strength returning. No response when she banged on the door so she looked through a downstairs window. Nothing. Had Maeve come home already? Or never gone to school in the first place? No, Diana would never have left her on her own. Stella's head was moving, as if in time to the beat of music, then she opened the car window and shouted.

'She's coming down the road.'

For a split second, Erin thought she meant Diana, but it was Maeve, and running back towards the car, she saw Stella step out and block Maeve's way. She was guarding her, but that was not the way Maeve saw it.

'What are you doing? Who are you? Oh, it's you.'

Erin caught up with them. 'It's all right, Maeve, this is Stella.'

'She took a photo of me and Rex. What's happened? Why are you . . . ?'

'We need to talk to your Mum. Have you got a key?'

'Why? Is someone—'

'Key!'

She lifted a string over her head. 'Is it Dad?' The puzzled look had been replaced by one of fear. 'He's gone to London. Has there been a train crash? Is he dead? Please tell me.'

'No, nothing like that. I promise. We just want to talk to your Mum. I'll explain everything, but first we have to make sure your Mum's—'

'She wasn't feeling well. She had a headache. But she ate some of her breakfast, muesli with soya milk.' She glanced at Stella. 'Is she a friend of yours?'

'I'll wait here,' Stella said, 'in case she comes back.'

Inside the house, Maeve raced from room to room.

'I'll try upstairs,' Erin said, but Maeve pushed past her and ran on ahead. Doors were flung open and her heavy footsteps echoed through the house. 'She's not here,' she shouted. 'Where is she? She never goes out when it's time for me to come home.'

Erin was in a utility room. A washing machine. Dryer. Large chest freezer. Her hand shook as she opened the lid but it was empty, apart from some bags of peas and a tub of strawberry ice cream.

'I know,' Maeve shouted, 'she must be in the garden.'

Erin was the first to reach the back door and one glance told her the garden was deserted. A bird flew up from a branch of the beech tree. Next door, someone was singing *The Phantom of the Opera*, and she thought she heard the sound of a rake. Maeve had reached the fence at the end and was looking at an adjoining garden. Then she turned to check behind a shed.

'Perhaps she's gone to the shops,' Erin called. 'Is there one near here? Where's the nearest one? She could have—'

'No!' Maeve let out a piercing shriek. 'Quick! She's in the greenhouse. She's hurt.'

'Don't go in.' Erin grabbed Maeve but she broke free, dragging open the door and kneeling beside her mother. 'Mum? Did you hurt yourself? What's wrong with you? Mum!'

Diana was jerking up and down, clutching her throat. Her skirt had ridden up, exposing the white skin of her thighs, and her parted lips looked dry and stiff. 'It's all right. What happened?' Erin turned to Maeve. 'Has she ever had a fit before? Does she suffer from epilepsy?'

'No. Never. What's wrong with her?' Maeve opened a cupboard, full of gardening tools and old clothes. Folding a hoodie into a pillow, she tried to ease it under her mother's head, but Diana rolled away. 'She's got rabies. I think she's got rabies. She must have been bitten by a mad dog.'

The greenhouse was airless and the smell of herbs was suffocating. 'Does she take any tablets?'

'No, not even for headaches. Can you sit up, Mum? If we make her sit up. Please, Erin.' Tears streamed down Maeve's face. 'What's wrong with her? If Dad was here . . . He's in London. I don't know when he'll be back. We could lift her, she's not very heavy. If we

261

carried her into the house . . .'

Stella was standing in the doorway. She had a faint smile on her face, and was still holding the packet of mints. 'Leave her where she is,' she said. 'There's an ambulance on its way.'

EPILOGUE

It's the first of April and Erin is in Claudia's kitchen, preparing Phoebe's bottle. Claudia's kitchen – she will have to stop calling it that, although it's unlikely she will stay in the house. She has started paying instalments on the mortgage and quite soon, she and Ollie will need to discuss what to do about it. But not yet.

Maeve will be coming round soon. Poor girl – the last few weeks have been awful for her – but she loves Phoebe and, now she's been allowed to come home, helping with her seems to be a comfort. There's no antidote for monkshood, the herb in Diana's greenhouse, that has purple flowers in the winter. And by the time she reached hospital she had ingested the poison and it was too late. Why did she grow it? How could she possibly have known what was going to happen? Had she always dreaded that Stella would return, or Jon would find a partner, and she would lose Maeve? But she knew what she had done, killing Claudia, then creating a new threat in her mind, first Stella, then Erin, as the person who was going to steal her daughter and her brother.

Stella did the right thing, attempting to induce vomiting with a tablespoon of salt in a cup of warm water, but it was too late. Diana had died of heart failure.

Maeve knows everything. How Stella left after she was born, and Diana came to help. *I miss her, Erin. I know she wasn't my real mother but I thought she was because nobody said.* Being Maeve, she is able to talk about it and ask endless questions. Will she want to see Stella again? She says not, although it's possible she may change her mind when she's older. Stella returned to London the day after Diana died, without saying goodbye to Maeve, just a brief word to Erin, ringing her bell to make sure everyone was all right.

Of the two of them – Maeve and Jon – Jon seems to have taken Diana's death the hardest, probably because he blames himself. The day Diana saw Stella standing in the road, and recognised her from an old photograph Jon had hidden away, he returned home to find her hysterical. He thought he had convinced her Stella had no right to Maeve, but she must have watched out for her and followed her back to the basement flat. Later, she saw her talking to Maeve and the cat, and, losing all judgement, made the plan to set fire to the house. Was that what happened? They will never know for sure.

It was Kent who sent the toy cat to the hospital. Erin had visited him in hospital a few days before he died and his confirmation that he was Phoebe's father had left her with mixed feelings. She could have arranged a DNA test. Hair from Claudia's comb. Another plucked from Kent's white mane. But there was no need. *Impregnating a dear friend.* How could the two of them be so cold-blooded? One day, Phoebe would want to know about her father and she would tell her the truth, but not the sordid details of her conception.

Ollie is still staying with Hoshi, but he comes round to Claudia's house quite often, and they have discussed the money in Claudia's desk and decided it should be spent on stuff for Phoebe. She asked him about Claudia's phone, and it turned out she had thrown it away, after it fell in the bath. Erin often thinks about the girl who knocked on the door and asked for "Clowda". Had she paid money and never received a dissertation or was she someone Claudia had helped? After all, Claudia could be generous and kind, and that is how Erin wants to remember her.

Phoebe is gaining weight all the time and looks a little like her mother, or does Erin imagine it? Under pressure, Jon admitted he feared Diana might have killed Claudia. He knew she had followed him and seen Claudia fling her arms round his neck and kiss him. If he had told Diana about the dissertations . . . But she would have insisted he inform the university, and of course she would have been right. As it was, Claudia used her seductive charms to swear him to secrecy. Sealing her fate with a kiss.

That fateful Saturday afternoon, Diana had been working in the health food shop and must have caught sight of her and Claudia, followed them, and decided to join the protesters. Should Erin tell the police? What good would it do? And how would Maeve feel? So no police. And no recriminations. Claudia's death will remain a tragic accident.

The illustrations have been despatched to Sara, who appeared satisfied but said nothing about how long it had taken Erin to complete them. She has more work for her and Erin is not going to complain, although fitting it in round looking after Phoebe will not be easy. Obviously, Maeve will continue with her art classes, and Erin guesses the two of them will take it turns to pick up Phoebe when she cries. Jennie has offered to help, says it will be good practice, and later, after her baby is born, they will walk round the park together, with their buggies.

Inevitably, a social worker was brought in, but he agreed to Erin fostering Phoebe for the time being, and said there would be no objection to adoption. The tiny shoes, with an engine on one foot and a carriage on the other, are still far too big and Erin is going to keep them in mint condition, so Phoebe can see them when she was older and she can tell her how she and her mother bought them for her. On that fateful day . . .

She can hear Maeve outside the front door, and hurries to let her in.

'Can I give Phoebe her bottle? Dad's parking the car. There weren't any spaces near your house. Actually, he won't be back for a bit. He had some shopping to do. He's going to buy a lemon drizzle cake.'

The noise has woken Phoebe and she is making whimpering sounds, preparing to cry. Erin lifts her out of her Moses basket and holds her tight. 'Not time for her bottle yet, but if you sit on the sofa, Maeve, I'll hand her to you. Can you hold her for a few minutes while I write a letter?'

'A letter? Why not an email, or a text?'

'I don't know the email address. I don't even know her second name. I'm going to send it to the hospital and hope it reaches her.'

Maeve holds Phoebe, propped up so she could see what was going on, 'What's her name – the person you're writing to?'

'Andrea.'

'Is she a doctor?'

'No, a nurse.'

'Was she there when Phoebe was born?'

Erin nods. 'And before that.'

Miss Havisham has put in an appearance but Maeve ignores her, addressing her next words to the baby. 'Yesterday, I had this brilliant idea, Phoebe. I thought either you and Erin can come to live in my house, or me and Dad can move in here with you and Erin.' She looks up, grinning. 'Then we'd be a proper family!'

266